HER SPI

William and Georgina Forsythe were twins—and as different as twins could be.

William was slow, steady, and properly devoted to the demands and duties of being a gentleman. Georgina was quick, mercurial, and ready to flout every rule society could devise to keep a young lady in her boring place.

Needless to say, their guardian, the Earl of Settle, was completely delighted with William and thoroughly dismayed with Georgina.

He had to learn, just as William had, that the only way to handle Georgina was to let her do exactly what she wanted, because no amount of disapproval, danger, and possible heartbreak could stop Georgina from enjoying life. A quality of character, the earl finally had to admit, that charmed even as it irritated—and made Georgina a most irresistible nuisance. . . .

The
Impetuous Twin

by
Irene Saunders

A SIGNET BOOK

NEW AMERICAN LIBRARY

SIGNET TRADEMARK REG. U.S. PAT. OFF. AND FOREIGN COUNTRIES
REGISTERED TRADEMARK—MARCA REGISTRADA
HECHO EN CHICAGO, U.S.A.

SIGNET, SIGNET CLASSIC, MENTOR, ONYX, PLUME, MERIDIAN
and NAL BOOKS are published by NAL PENGUIN INC.,
1633 Broadway, New York, New York 10019

First Printing, April, 1987

1 2 3 4 5 6 7 8 9

PRINTED IN THE UNITED STATES OF AMERICA

1

"Come on, William," Georgina called, glancing over her shoulder, "I'll race you to the old barn. Last one there's a duffer!"

The wind whipped William's protest from his lips as Georgina flicked Starlight lightly on the neck and urged her to a faster pace. Now several lengths behind, William strove to catch her.

The rhythmic thud of horses' hooves on the dry, uneven turf sent a rabbit scurrying to his burrow, and a flock of starlings scouring the stubble took hasty flight.

A long stone wall lay ahead, and just beyond it, a deep ditch. Georgina whipped Starlight forward, and horse and rider sailed gracefully over the wall, clearing the ditch with inches to spare.

Her triumphant laugh rang out, and she looked over her shoulder just in time to see William approach the wall, then, at the last minute, balk at the jump, turn, and gallop alongside until he reached a gate. He dismounted, walked his horse through, then closed the gate behind them.

Once she knew he was all right, Georgina headed for the shade of the barn and waited for her twin brother to join her.

"All right, I'm a d-duffer, I know," he told her good-naturedly. "You d-don't have to rub it in."

"But you did it once. I can't for the life of me understand it, for when I do something once, it's always much easier to do it after that," she protested.

"We're just d-different, that's all," he said with a wry smile, looking at her long chestnut hair and gray-green eyes.

One would have never guessed they were twins, for he had inherited the Forsythes' lustrous black hair and silver-gray eyes, while her unusual coloring came directly from her mother.

"Shall we go inside and see if there have been any squatters in the barn?" Georgina suggested, preparing to dismount.

William shook his head. "We'd best start b-back. If we're not home b-before dark, Grandmama will s-send out a s-search party for us," he told her.

"For you, you mean," she said, making a comical face. "If I stayed out all night she'd just say 'Good riddance' and pray that I'd drowned at the very least."

Skirting the barn, they broke into a gallop once more until they reached the home woods, then headed for the stables, where the elderly groom, a relic of better times, waited to take their horses.

Holding hands, they ran swiftly indoors through the back of the house, and up to their bedchambers, unconsciously avoiding the stern-faced, straight-backed dowager who was waiting for them in the main hall.

Georgina washed her face and hands, then took off the patched breeches and worn shirt that had once been William's. Looking in the mirror as she combed her hair, she thought of how saddened her mother would have been to see her only daughter so poorly attired. She still remembered her mother's beautiful face and lovely creamy complexion, so different from her own sun-bronzed one. Could it really be seven years since her mother had died? She and William had been just thirteen years old when the accident occurred. Returning one afternoon from a drive in the curricle, their mama and papa were actually on the estate when a gunshot close by frightened the horses and they bolted, throwing the twins' handsome, dashing father onto the road. His neck was broken in the fall, and their mother, badly injured when her gown caught on the seat and she was dragged by the frightened team, survived him by only two days.

Before she died she took her young daughter's hands in hers and told her earnestly that she must look after William for them now. "Your brother is very special. He's not quicksilver like you. He'll need your help, for it takes him a long time to learn,'' she had said, and, young though she was, Georgina had understood.

As she slipped into an old, faded gingham gown made over, years ago, from one of her grandmother's, Georgina noticed how tight it had become due to the curves which, to her dismay, were changing her thin, boyish figure. Smoothing the creases from her skirts, she strode from the chamber and ran lightly down the stairs and into the dining room, where William was seating the dowager. Not waiting for her brother's assistance, Georgina took her usual place.

The room had the shabby-genteel appearance of the rest of the house. The tapestry chairs and the Axminster carpet were all but threadbare, and though there were still crystal, china, and silver on the large mahogany table, its beauty was dimmed by lack of proper care. Only six candles burned in the huge chandelier, and the hearth would not see a fire until winter set in.

Grandmama was sitting ramrod straight in a gown of black, the only color she had worn since the death of her son. Her white hair was covered, as usual, with a black lace cap, and her mouth was set in a thin line as her icy gaze passed completely over Georgina and she slowly inclined her head, indicating to the ancient butler he should start serving.

The meal was eaten in silence save for the click of knives and forks connecting with china plates, and at its conclusion they retired to the drawing room. When tea was poured and the three were alone, the dowager, still carefully ignoring Georgina, addressed her grandson.

''While you were careering around the countryside, I received a reply to the letter I told you I had written.'' She paused for emphasis. ''It was fortunate that your guardian, Lord Meredith, happened to be in the country at the time my letter was delivered. He regrets he is unable to present you in London, as he is serving with his regiment and not at liberty to spend any length of time in the city.''

Georgina's inaudible sigh of relief was short-lived.

''Although not exactly in the way I had in mind, he has offered to help you, however, by buying your colors for you in his own regiment. You will, in all probability, see action, as he writes that the regiment is setting out for Portugal very shortly to join the British expeditionary force there, under the command of Viscount Wellington. It would seem that he and Lord Meredith have been friends for a number of years.''

William's silver-gray eyes shone with excitement. He would far rather become an officer in a crack regiment than spend a Season in London.

But Georgina could not share his joy. She had followed the progress of the wars in the Peninsula with unusual interest for a female, and knew that a new French commander, a Marshal Massena, had begun another offensive against Portugal. This was the action in which William would most likely become involved, and she could not like it.

''Listen to me when I'm speaking to you, missy!''

Georgina looked up and realized her grandmother was, for once, addressing her. ''I beg your pardon, ma'am,'' she murmured, too surprised to resent the dowager's tone.

''What I said was, it's time you did something around here for your keep. When William leaves, I'm going to have Cook teach you how to bake bread, roast a joint of meat and such, in the mornings, and in the afternoons Mrs. Cooper can teach you how to mend some of the linens that are wearing out. Give you something to do,'' the old lady snorted, a malicious gleam in her watery old eyes.

Georgina stiffened, lifted her head proudly, and regarded her grandmother with keen distaste. ''I would remind you, ma'am, that I am the daughter of this house and not your servant,'' she said, her eyes changing to a frosty gray-blue. ''When we become so impoverished that you bake bread and mend linens, then I will do so, but not until then.''

Lady Forsythe flushed with rage. ''How dare you speak to me like that, you insolent chit. Go to your bedchamber at once and don't dare show your ugly face again until you have improved your manners.''

Giving her grandmother a look of contempt, Georgina remained seated. ''I'm afraid you'll have to look at my ugly face a little longer, unless you decide to leave the room yourself, dear Grandmama,'' she said calmly. ''You are not my appointed guardian and, in fact, have less right to be here than I. You may not like me, ma'am, any more than I like you, but I'll not permit you to turn me into a servant.''

The dowager was on her feet, appealing to her grandson. ''William, are you going to allow your sister to speak to me like that?'' she asked, unwittingly acknowledging him as the rightful head of the family. ''You tell her she has to mind me, grandson.''

He shook his head slowly, visibly upset at the sudden conflict. ''Georgie's r-right, Grandmama,'' he finally said.

He smiled gently, trying to placate the old lady, then rose and put an arm around her, but she shrugged it off. ''I might have known you'd take her side, like your father always did,'' she muttered angrily, and stormed from the room.

There was a silence after she left, until they heard a door slam on the floor above, then Georgina's poise left her and she dropped her head in her hands.

William came and sat beside her on the couch, putting a comforting arm around her. She raised her head and looked at him bleakly. ''Whatever will I do when you're gone?''

''I w-wish I could t-take you with me,'' he said slowly.

Breakfast was always one of the best meals of the day for the twins, for their grandmother broke her fast in her bed-chamber and they were able to relax and enjoy themselves. The dining room looked even more drab by day than it did in dim candlelight, as the twins sat down to an early breakfast together, but they were used to it and no longer noticed. Servants were in and out of the room more than usual, hoping to hear something further about last night's row between Georgina and her grandmother.

''I suppose Grandmama w-won't t-talk to you at all n-now,'' William remarked when they were finally alone for a moment.

She shrugged and said casually, ''It's so close to her usual manner, I'll scarce know the difference. But I had to say something. This time she went too far.''

He nodded, glad he'd not been more involved. ''If you l-looked l-less like our mama, Georgie, she m-might feel more kindly toward you. But you're t-too t-tall, and you

9

d-don't even walk like a girl." There was a pause and then he said, "Mama was t-tall and had hair l-like yours, I remember."

Georgina had been waiting until they could be alone and uninterrupted, before telling William of the plan she'd devised in the hours she'd lain awake thinking of his imminent departure. She was getting impatient. "Aren't you through breakfast yet? Must you have that second cup of tea?"

"N-not if there's something m-more important." He reached over to cover her hand with his own reassuringly.

He was so very handsome and nice at the same time, Georgina was very proud he was her brother. His silver-gray eyes were always kind and understanding, and his gentle temperament, which made him slow to anger as well as slow to learn, was just the opposite of her own. She was the impetuous twin, the one who would fly into rages and come up with mad schemes. She wondered what he'd think about her latest.

They left the dining room, and the butler's keen ears, and hurried up to the old nursery, now a seldom-used sitting room. As soon as the door was closed Georgina swung around to face William, her eyes dancing with excitement.

"Before I fell asleep last night I had a monstrously good idea," she told him. "You remember you said you wished you could take me with you?"

He was confused. "I d-don't remember, but I d-do wish I could t-take you."

She looked triumphant. "Well, I've found a way," she declared. "I'll cut off my hair and flatten myself out." She looked with embarrassment at where her small breasts made her shirt stick out a little. "You've said I walk like a boy and behave like one."

He smiled at her fondly. "He'll not b-buy colors for you, Georgie," he remarked, his smile turning to a lazy grin at the thought.

"Don't be such a widgeon, William. I mean to go as your servant, to take care of your uniforms, clean your boots, and look after you," she pronounced eagerly.

He reached over and gave her a sympathetic hug, then slowly shook his head. "It w-won't f-fadge," he said.

She looked disappointed, but still persisted. "At least we could give it a try. Think what a fine jest it would be to go to London together when Lord Meredith sends for you. If I went with you and no one suspected I was a girl, you'd feel better about it and perhaps—"

"Grandmama w-wouldn't allow it," he objected.

"Silly, she wouldn't know. I don't propose to leave dressed as your servant! I'll write to Mrs. Johnson and ask her to invite me to Oxford for a few months. Grandmama will jump at the chance to get rid of me, for she desires my company even less than I wish hers."

Mrs. Johnson was their old housekeeper, who had helped bring them up as children, and who was very fond of them both, but especially of Georgina.

Georgina continued. "I'll leave servants' clothes in the hut in the south woods where we used to camp out. We'll go there first and I'll cut my hair and disguise myself. I don't know where I'll get boots to fit me, though, for the stable-boys have quite enormous feet."

He felt bewildered, not knowing what to say. "L-let me think about it, Georgie. Don't r-rush me."

Georgina smiled. She knew he'd ponder it for a day or so, but she also knew he was going to agree to take her as far as London, if only to stop her badgering him. After that she'd think of some way to get to Portugal with him.

She meant to keep her long-ago promise to her mama, that she would look after him, at least until he married and had a loving wife.

William left the nursery then, as he'd offered to help the groom this morning, but Georgina stayed on, idly looking out of the windows that faced onto the now overgrown and unkempt kitchen gardens.

To her surprise, she saw her grandmother, up and about at a remarkably early hour, walking toward the old potting shed, holding a piece of paper in her hand. Her furtive manner as she looked around before entering the shed made Georgina most curious, and she continued to watch, wondering what the old lady was about. In just a few minutes she saw the door to the shed opening again and she watched intently.

It was not her grandmother who emerged, however, but Smithers, their former gamekeeper, a man she had never liked since she was a little girl. He was pushing a white piece of paper, remarkably similar to the one that had been carried by her grandmother, into the inside pocket of his extremely well-cut jacket.

He turned and made an exaggerated bow to someone still in the shed, and even from this distance Georgina could tell that he was behaving in a most unseemly manner. Then he sauntered slowly away.

When he was out of sight, the shed door opened once more and her grandmother emerged. She again looked carefully around before stepping into the garden, then hurrying toward the house. As she drew nearer, Georgina could see the worried expression on her face. She was no longer carrying anything in her hand.

It was a mystery, and Georgina vowed to talk to William about it as soon as the opportunity arose.

Lord Matthew Meredith, eighth Earl of Settle, was seated at the handsome desk his father had commissioned when he became the seventh earl many years ago. The massive chair had been made at the same time, to fit the huge proportions he'd acquired while he waited to come into the title, but he'd left the rest of the book room unchanged, for he was no great reader, preferring a game of cards, a day's shooting, or hunting to hounds when in the country.

The present earl was not without vices, but their form differed slightly from those of his father. He had added considerably to the collection of books that lined the walls, and had had the furnishings restored, but he could not imagine the room without his father's desk and chair.

He looked up from the letter he was writing, then walked slowly over to a cabinet, opened one of the doors, and took out a heavy metal box. Unlocking it, he leafed through several bundles of papers until he found the one he was looking for. Then he put away the box, returned to the desk at which he'd been working, and untied the ribbon around the documents.

There were a number of letters, perhaps a half-dozen, and he studied the dowager's spidery hand, starting with the first one, written some six or more years ago.

He remembered receiving that letter when he was just getting used to the idea of being guardian to a young boy he'd never seen. He could recall having met the boy's mother and father once, about five years before that, when his own father had still been alive. The only reason he remembered it at all was that to a youth just home for the holidays from Cambridge, she had seemed the loveliest creature. She had chestnut hair and laughing hazel-green eyes and was kind to everyone she met, even to an awkward young man, who instantly became infatuated with her.

He had been shocked to hear of her and her husband's death, and later, when he was informed that, as the Earl of Settle, he had been named guardian of their thirteen-year-old offspring, he realized Lord Forsythe had intended to appoint his father, the seventh earl, who had been a friend and first cousin, rather than himself.

It was a little afterward that the first letter came from the dowager Lady Forsythe, grandmother of the boy, suggesting that the youngster remain in her care in the home in which he'd always lived. It had seemed an excellent solution, and he'd intended to visit the property when he had the time. According to the lawyers, it was a trifle run-down, as there was little money left to put into it, and their yearly reports showed a slow drain but no startling changes and the tone of the grandmother's letters gave him the impression that she would bitterly resent any interference.

His involvement in the running of his own family estates, and in an arranged marriage which later proved disastrous, left him little time to spare for the Forsythe boy, particularly as he seemed to be in the very capable hands of his grandmother. She had informed him, in answer to his suggestion that the boy be sent to Eton, that he was, regrettably, an unusually slow learner and she felt a private tutor would be preferable.

He looked once more at the latest letter from Lady Forsythe, to which he had replied a few days ago. She wrote that the boy had grown to be very handsome, and he detected for the first time a touch of the eccentric in her desire for him to wed a wealthy heiress and restore the family estates. She wanted the earl to sponsor the youngster for a Season in London, but it was out of the question. He still had a commission in the army, and expected shortly to be needed overseas again, so he would not be in town to keep an eye on the boy. If he was still a slow top, he would have to be watched carefully.

The suggestion he had made was, he felt, an excellent one, given the circumstances, and could be the making of the youngster. He had proposed to buy colors for the boy in his own regiment, where he could watch over him and give him whatever guidance he needed.

He read once more the letter he had sent to the dowager, copied for his records by his secretary. It would set the wheels in motion so that before orders to leave England came through, young William would be an officer under his command. He would be very interested to find out what the son of the late and lovely Lady Forsythe was really like.

Lord Meredith, although remarkably good-looking, with classic features, black hair, and blue eyes fringed with thick dark lashes, was very much a man's man. His firm jaw and well-shaped lips could soften readily into an easy smile, and he had been known as quite a prankster at Eton and Cambridge, but the years had hardened him, and his biting wit had cut many a too-familiar fellow officer down to size. He was a born leader, and his men thought much of him, considering him a fair and just commanding officer.

Except for the women of his immediate family and a few good friends, however, he now had only one use for the female sex. Every woman he had ever desired, and many he had not, whether of aristocratic background or the serving classes, had been his for the asking, and the number of satisfactory relationships he had experienced with women since the early days of his marriage could be counted on one hand, with fingers to spare.

A notable exception was, of course, his small daughter, who could do no wrong in his eyes. Only she could disturb him when he was working in his study, could demand a good-night story before she went to sleep no matter what he was doing. And the hours he spent playing with her when he was home were the happiest he had known in many years.

He looked at the clock and his face softened. It was time to visit the nursery.

2

The dowager had unwittingly made Georgina's deception simple. When a communication came from Lord Meredith requesting that William report to him in London, she had still not spoken a word to Georgina since the night of their quarrel.

"I'm about to make your life at Broadacres a little more peaceful, dear Grandmama," Georgina had announced later that morning with a cold smile. "Mrs. Johnson has invited me to Oxford for several months, and it would be most opportune if William could escort me there on his way to London."

"You'd best let me see the letter, missy," Lady Forsythe grunted, glaring at her granddaughter.

"By all means, ma'am," Georgina mocked, as she withdrew a letter from the pocket of her gown. "It is indeed gratifying to know how much you trust me."

The dowager's eyes were failing but she would not admit to the problem, a fact Georgina had not overlooked when making her plans. Fortunately for her, William did not ask to see the letter. With no more than a glance at it and a nod, Lady Forsythe handed the letter back.

"I'll send you a note from time to time to let you know how I am, ma'am," Georgina had offered.

"You needn't waste the money, for your goings-on are of no interest to me. I shall not reply, and there's no call for you to hurry back on my account." There was no mistaking the gleam in her eye as she realized she'd be rid of her granddaughter for some time.

William had taken Georgina's arm and hurried her from the room before she could say more and ruin their plans.

Now, a week later, the dowager Lady Forsythe was sitting in the parlor savoring the prospect of having the estate and its running entirely to herself for some months. Georgina and William were departing for London within the hour, and at last Lady Forsythe would be free of the interference of that wretched "Graymore gal." In her mind, her son's wife, the former Lady Penelope Graymore, was still working through her firstborn child, Georgina, to take over Broadacres, which had always been in the Forsythe family.

Before the "Graymore gal" was born, the dowager had picked out a suitable wife for her only son, George. She was Lady Barbara, only daughter of their nearest neighbor, Baron Andover, and if the marriage had gone as she planned, Broadacres would have almost doubled in size, for the large Andover estate was not entailed.

Instead, the "Graymore gal" had come along, with her chestnut hair and green eyes, and captivated her son so that he had to have her. Two years later, Andover's daughter had wed, the baron had been killed in a hunting accident, and Lady Barbara had inherited the property.

When she saw everything working out the way she had planned, but not with her son, the dowager's hatred of the wife he had chosen increased, and when Lady Barbara's new husband died suddenly, before any heir had been born, the dowager became so completely impossible that George had the audacity to threaten to send her to the dower house to live. She had realized he meant it, and kept quiet after that.

But he was still besotted with his wife! The afternoon that the "Graymore gal" took the curricle into Knaresborough, the dowager had plans to make everything right again, but then George had gone to the stable, had a horse saddled to go and meet her, and ruined everything. By the time the dowager heard, it was too late to stop Smithers, the gamekeeper. She'd instructed him to take some guns and clean out the infestation of rabbits in the woods alongside the lane to the house, and to do it in the late afternoon, which was just about the time her daughter-in-law would come racing back, testing the pair of grays she'd just bought.

George had apparently met his wife, tied his horse to the back of the curricle, and taken over the reins to put them through their paces himself. The horses had shied at the sound of a gunshot close by, and her son had been the one thrown to the ground and killed instead of his wife, but at least she had died two days later.

Smithers had been retired now some five years. He had little need to work, for the dowager had proved more than willing to meet his demands in return for his silence, even if it did put a heavy burden on her beloved Broadacres.

Lady Forsythe's thoughts were interrupted as the butler appeared in the doorway and announced that her grandchildren were about to depart. Slowly she got to her feet and made her way to the front entrance, where the twins were waiting to say good-bye.

"Just take care and don't do anything to damage the good name of Forsythe," the dowager admonished William.

She made no move to touch him, but when he put his arms around her she allowed him to bend down and kiss her cheek. Her eyes were moist as she stepped back, but she quickly recovered and looked scornfully at her granddaughter.

"As for you, the longer you're gone, the better I'll be pleased, so don't hurry back," she said frostily.

Under other circumstances, Georgina would have made an appropriate response, but her grandmother's manner fitted so well into her own plans that for once she remained silent.

"It's a good thing Grandmama did not come outside to see us off," Georgina remarked as they trod the dewy grass toward the stables. "Now I can ride astride with my skirts pulled up until we get to the hut."

"D-did you l-leave everything in there?" William asked.

"Everything I could get. The boots are far too big, but I've stuffed the toes with paper and they'll do as long as I don't have to walk too much." She knew that William had little enough money for the journey, so she made light of it.

Once at the hut, they dismounted and William stayed outside until she had changed into the worn servant's clothes she had exchanged for an old shawl and her faded gowns. First she bound around her a piece of sheeting she had brought to conceal her breasts, then donned the shirt and breeches, the jacket, and finally the wretched boots. She practiced walking in them until she was sure she wouldn't trip, then turned her attention to her hair.

She had left a broken piece of mirror in the hut, and packed a pair of kitchen scissors, which she hoped would not be missed. After she had hacked off her lovely tresses to just below her ears, she called William inside.

"Just cut it straight in the back for me, William," she begged, despite his emphatic shake of the head. "I shall be wearing a hat, so it only has to look neat."

"I've n-never d-done anything l-like this before," he grumbled, but took the scissors, nonetheless, and made a straighter line in the back, then matched up the front where she had left one side longer than the other.

She stuck the hat on her head, then gathered up the shorn hair and the clothes to discard after they had put some distance between themselves and Broadacres, for these things would give them away should they fall into their grandmother's hands. Then, mounting once more, they began their journey south.

On their arrival a week later in London, Georgina and William went directly to the rooming house where their guardian had made a reservation and were pleased to find a clean bedchamber with a sitting room and a dressing room.

Because they were for William, Georgina gave no thought to the menial tasks she had, of necessity, to perform. In fact, she concluded that menservants had a very easy time of it, and told William this a few days after they had settled into their lodgings.

"I'm too k-kind to m-make demands," William returned with a grin. "B-by the way, I m-met our c-cousin today."

"You did?" She was excited. "What does he look like? An old army-colonel type with a white mustache and a walk like this?" She jumped up, bent over, and put a hand on her hip, then waddled around the room with the aid of an imaginary walking stick.

"You are a g-goose, Georgie. He's a c-colonel, but he's quite young. I l-liked him."

"Did he ask about me—I mean your sister, not your manservant?" Georgina was perishing with curiosity.

"N-no, he d-didn't, and I c-could hardly t-tell him you were here. Wh-when is Mrs. J-Johnson expecting you?"

Georgina looked embarrassed and her color deepened. She bit her lip and said nothing for a moment.

"Georgie, d-don't t-tell me you n-never wrote to her," William said with exasperation.

"I did write and say I might be coming for a visit if it was all right, but, you see, it wasn't. She was just leaving to go to her daughter-in-law in Wales, who is increasing, and she won't return to Oxford for several months." She gave a helpless shrug.

"You and your b-birdbrained ideas, Georgie!" he exclaimed. "Wh-what am I g-going to d-do with you?" Throwing up his hands, he asked, "Wh-why do I let you t-talk me into things?"

"You could always take me along. It's quite the thing for officers to take their menservants with them, and I've learned how to clean your uniform and keep it looking smart. There are lots of wives in the Peninsula with their husbands," she said airily, having heard of one such wife and confident there must be many like her.

"W-wives, perhaps, b-but not sisters!"

"But I'll not be going as your sister. I'll be going as your servant. My disguise has deceived everyone we've met so far, and if there's fighting, I won't be anywhere near it, and I'll—"

"You b-bet you won't," William retorted, for once very angry with her. "You'll be b-back in B-Broadacres with Grandmama."

Georgina paled. 'I'm not going back to live with her on my own, William. If you won't take me with you, I don't know yet what I'll do, but whatever it is, it won't be in Yorkshire.

You can't make me, you know.'' Her voice was almost a whisper, and her eyes had a haunted look.

''I can't, b-but I know who c-can. If I told C-Cousin Matthew, he'd have you b-back b-before you c-could turn around.'' He looked at his wits' end, unable to think fast enough to handle this kind of situation.

When a knock sounded on the door, he turned with relief to see who might be calling, only to find it was a messenger from their cousin.

''That really d-does it, Georgie,'' William told her as he closed the door on the departing messenger. ''I have orders to r-report immediately to the d-docks, as my regiment is l-leaving for Portugal r-right away.''

The decision about Georgina was out of his hands, for there was little time to do aught save pack up and take her with him.

''What arrangements did you make about the horses, William?'' It was the only question Georgina dared ask, in case he should change his mind about her.

''D-don't worry about Starlight. As she's still in the army stables, she's b-being transported with the other officers' horses and w-will be there wh-when we reach the P-Peninsula,'' he assured her.

Georgina's excitement was tempered by her extreme nervousness, and she was glad when William gave her a purse of money in case they should get separated, helped her into a hackney with their baggage, and directed the driver to take them to a certain dock.

The hackney passed through steadily worsening neighborhoods until they came to streets so squalid, and their occupants so dirty and evil-looking, that she shrank back against the seat, anxious not to be seen. The driver knew where he was bound, however, and guided his hack through the maze of docks, forested by scores of masts, until he reached the one William had indicated.

''Your fellow officers would appear to be already boarding, William. I'd best join that group over there, who appear to be the serving class, like me,'' Georgina said, feeling a thrill of excitement as their adventure was about to really begin.

"Y-yes." William's own excitement was making him more nervous. "I'll pay the hack and get aboard, b-but you'll have to take the b-baggage or it will look strange."

William hurried off, and Georgina, her hair concealed beneath a knit cap, was left standing on the dock with the two pieces of baggage. Grasping a piece firmly in each hand, she started toward the group of men wearing various types of civilian apparel who appeared to be making a move to go aboard. In her anxiety not to be left behind, she failed to see a sergeant who was wheeling a cart toward the ship and she stepped right into his path. A moment later she lay sprawled full length on the ground.

"Why don't yer look where yer going?" the sergeant yelled as he picked up a couple of pieces of luggage that had fallen from the cart.

Momentarily stunned, Georgina was trying to scramble to her feet when she felt a strong hand grasp her elbow and haul her up.

"Nothing broken, I hope?" a deep voice asked, and she turned to see an extremely handsome officer with enough gold braid to denote high rank. "My sergeant was right, though. You walked into the cart without looking."

Georgina pulled her cap more firmly on her head. "Yes, sir, I'm very sorry," she said gruffly. "It was my fault."

"That's all right, lad. Do you work for one of the officers?" he asked.

"Yes, sir," she grunted, hoping he wouldn't ask her which one. She looked anxiously at the ship, where the other servants were already boarding.

"Don't worry. She won't sail until I'm aboard. Davis, put the lad's bags on your cart and let's get moving." He smiled kindly at Georgina. "Come along, my boy. Let's not hold them up any longer."

With a firm pat on her shoulder, he started toward the waiting ship, and Georgina, completely intrigued by his looks and manners, mumbled her thanks and followed the sergeant with the cart. As soon as she was on deck, she took the two bags and watched the officer until he disappeared belowdeck; then she started to search for William.

It was with much relief, several days later, that Georgina saw land ahead and realized the voyage was finally over. William had become seasick almost as soon as they sailed, and she had spent all save the last half-hour caring for him.

William joined her on the deck as the boat drew into the dock. Saying he was much recovered, he insisted on carrying the larger of his two portmanteaus, and Georgina gratefully trailed behind him down the gangplank and into the hive of early-morning activity on the dock. There were several ships unloading soldiers at the small port just outside Lisbon and, farther away, fishing boats were making ready to depart.

Graceful girls with huge baskets of fish on their heads walked in the direction of the town, calling out in their native tongue as they walked, as though offering their wares, while older women somberly dressed in black with dark-colored shawls covering their heads and shoulders stood around in groups talking.

Georgina didn't have much time to study the sights, however, for the English regiment set off almost as soon as they disembarked. They were to meet up with a British army unit camped outside a small village that was within a day's journey of the port, then march north with them to join Wellington's forces at Torres Vedras.

William, as an officer, rode this whole way, but once they joined this other unit, Georgina had to march through the hot, dusty terrain on foot with the rest of the servants. Blisters formed on her feet from the heavy boots as she trudged mile after mile behind the army. It took just a few hours for her to realize that the charade of posing as a boy had gone on long enough, but she could think of no satisfactory way to end it.

Finally, they reached camp around nightfall. With William on duty elsewhere, Georgina had been observing a group of lively Gypsy camp followers, when she heard a child's cries coming from behind a hut. She moved swiftly, despite the clumsy boots, to investigate the other side of the hut.

A short, swarthy-faced, bearded man, wearing a black cap

pulled down over one ear in peasant fashion, and a dirty shirt that had once been red, stood menacingly over a little girl not more than five years old. As she came closer, Georgina saw him raise his right arm and bring a stick down across the child's back.

Calling "Stop that at once," she ran toward him. With an angry curse the peasant swung around and raised his stick to attack Georgina.

As she quickly stepped out of range, there was a whistling sound. The stick dropped harmlessly to the ground as the man's arm was pinned firmly to the hut by an ornate knife, the hilt of which still quivered with the impact. A slight black-haired young woman in Gypsy dress, screaming words completely unintelligible to Georgina, followed swiftly after the knife, picked up the stick, and began to beat the man's other arm, rendering him helpless to free himself.

Georgina and the little girl, whose dirty face was streaked with tears, stood watching until the peasant succeeded in dragging his arm away. Leaving the knife in the wall, he ran off as though the devil himself were after him.

The Gypsy gave Georgina a broad, suggestive wink, then crouched beside the child, her full red skirt sweeping a cloud of dust into the air. Murmuring soothingly, she produced a somewhat used kerchief and wiped away the little girl's tears, unbuttoned the back of the faded blue cotton frock, and examined her back. Apparently satisfied, she lightly touched the child's long, tangled black hair, pointed to something in the distance, and the little girl ran off.

Turning swiftly, the Gypsy retrieved her knife with a quick tug, then raised her many petticoats and slipped it back into a garter secured to the calf of her leg. Finally she turned toward the curious Georgina and gave her a bold smile and a flutter of her long black eyelashes.

"*Lección numero uno, muchacho inglés*. Never, never *interferir* with no *pistola o cuchilla!*" she smilingly scolded, her teeth white against her dusky skin.

Tossing her long black hair away from her face, she linked her arm through Georgina's, and as she did so, her hand brushed against Georgina's body. The Gypsy swung around

24

to face her, eyebrows raised knowingly above laughing black eyes. *"Sí. Muchacha inglesa!"* she said, with an expressive shrug of her shoulders. "You come with us."

With no more than a token protest, Georgina allowed herself to be drawn into the friendly band of Gypsies, and soon her feet no longer hurt and the miles seemed only half as long.

"Mi nombre es Isabella. Y su nombre?" the Gypsy girl asked, then wrinkled her nose at the masculine-sounding name and introduced her to her friends as Gina.

As Georgina's and William's tutor had given them many lessons in Latin, she could make herself understand most of the Spanish and Portuguese and quickly picked up a number of important words and phrases. Isabella could, with not too much difficulty, make herself understood in English, so with much laughter and many gestures, they conversed.

When they stopped and made camp for the night, the men made a fire and Isabella joined the other women in preparing a hearty soup. Georgina's contribution of coarse bread and fruit was gladly accepted; then the two girls moved into the shadows and sat on the rough blankets they carried to sleep in.

"Is not good." Isabella nodded vehemently when Georgina told her of her fears that her disguise would be found out. "I have idea."

She went over to the small donkey cart they all shared for carrying the heavier baggage, cooking pots and such, and came back holding an old portmanteau. Reaching inside, she produced two blouses that had once been white but countless washings had turned into a yellowy cream.

"Thees too tight," Isabella said, proudly pushing out her chest until the clearly visible rounded breasts almost escaped. She shook her head with a frown. "As *muchacho* you have beeg *problema*."

She burrowed in the depths of the bag once more, and drew out a faded green skirt with several petticoats.

"You wear thees, and when *hermano* not there, you stay with *gitanería*—safe." She threw out her arms to encompass the whole camp. Isabella thrust the garments into Georgina's hands and pushed her behind a large tree. Her meaning was very clear, and though Georgina had qualms about her brother's reaction, she knew she could not continue as a boy without detection. She peeled off the shirt and trousers and gratefully slipped into the cotton blouse and skirt.

Without a mirror she had no idea how she looked, but Isabella's reaction was instant and flattering.

"Bella, bella!" she exclaimed, so loudly that heads turned nearby and soon Georgina's newfound friends gathered around with broad smiles and nods of approval.

Once they reached Torres Vedras, William obtained a billet in an empty house with several other officers. Wellington's forces had arrived two days before and slipped through the lines to safety. The French were outside the fortification the very next day, but there they stayed, for there was no way to break through.

The other officers quickly obtained help from locals and camp followers, and Georgina helped William, but she was the only servant living there and he took much teasing from his fellow officers, who had seen her transformation from manservant to Gypsy maid and thought him not so slow as he had at first appeared.

Georgina had wanted to bring her pistols with her, but William had been adamant. Now she wished she had not obeyed him, for there had been several occasions since arriving in Portugal when she had wished she had them.

She mentioned this to Isabella one afternoon at the encampment while she watched the Gypsy girl preparing a dish of rice with spices, wild berries and leaves, and the remains of a hare that had been trapped some days before and hung to ripen.

"You want to learn how I throw knife, Gina?" Isabella asked. "Finest weapon for *muchacha! Rápido, silencioso—* and you hide it under the gown or skirt."

The usual murmur of many voices around the camp changed tone and Isabella glanced up. "Look . . ." she hissed to Georgina.

This was one of the days when Lord Meredith, with an

aide and a fellow officer, was making a periodical inspection of the camp followers to check for any obvious sickness or diseases that might spread to his men. Georgina's chestnut hair stood out against that of the swarthy, dark-haired Gypsies, and it was this that caused him to pause, then come toward the lively group, though he appeared at first not to notice her.

It was not uncommon for soldiers of any rank to come into the area, but they seldom bothered the Gypsies. When Georgina first noticed him, Meredith was half-turned away from her, looking toward the campfire, and her impression was of a man who sat his horse confidently, using a shapely, well-muscled leg to guide it rather than the reins.

Accustomed as she was to men in uniform, there was still something in the way he held his shoulders and head that made him stand out as superior.

Suddenly he swung the horse around and she got her first look at his face. It was the officer whose good looks and kindness had so intrigued her on the dock in London.

He was more than handsome, she thought as she looked at him again. He could truly be described as beautiful, like the statues she had seen in London of Greek gods, quite masculine and arrogant, but with a touch of the gentleness he'd shown her. Remote, yet with something that made her feel close, as though she knew him. Perhaps it was the touch of humor around the corners of his mouth, or perhaps a feeling about the lips that made warm shivers run suddenly down her back.

Unsmiling, he looked directly at her, then beckoned with a flick of one autocratic finger. Isabella gave her a push. "Go, *muchacha. Es un hombre importante!*" she whispered.

Georgina rose slowly to her feet, shaking out the full skirt of her Gypsy dress, then stepped around her friends, carefully controlling the shaking in her limbs, taking her time in presenting herself before him.

His eyes raked her from head to toe. "Unusual coloring for a Romany," he remarked finally. "What is your name?"

"Gina," she snapped insolently, with a toss of her head, resenting his gaze.

"Gina what?" His mouth was set in a grim line and he raised one thick black eyebrow.

When she made no answer the aide, who had dismounted, grabbed her arm. "Say 'sir' when you address Colonel Meredith," he snarled.

"Take your filthy hands off me." Georgina spat the words out, pulling her arm from out of his grasp. "I'm not one of your soldiers . . ." she started to say, then stopped as she realized the officer's name.

Her words, delivered in an obviously cultured English, had at first taken the aide aback, but he quickly recovered, and before she could defend herself, he knocked her to the ground and lifted his riding crop, ready to thrash her.

"Johnson, stop that immediately." Though his voice was not raised, Meredith's words caused the aide to drop the whip as though it were a red-hot poker, giving Georgina a chance to scramble to her feet.

She did not see her Gypsy friends standing menacingly behind her, and though her cousin did, he ignored them as he dismounted swiftly and came closer to her.

"Are you hurt, Gina?" he asked, the hard look leaving his eyes for the first time as he saw the red mark on the side of her face. He touched the bruise with gentle fingers.

"No, my lord," she said, her voice trembling a little, as his touch, though delicate, seemed to burn her skin.

"Please accept my apology," he said in a voice loud enough for all to hear. "The man was not acting on my orders and he will pay for it, I assure you." His tones were quieter as he asked, "How do you know who I am?"

"Your man," she mumbled, gesturing at the now very subdued aide.

Meredith shook his head, and a small smile twitched at the corners of his mouth. "He gave my rank, not my title," he murmured, waiting for an explanation.

Georgina shrugged helplessly. She could not tell him who she was, or William would be in trouble. Behind her she could hear Isabella and her friends laughing and conversing in Spanish as they resumed their meal.

"Where did you get these chestnut curls?" he asked, his finger twisting a strand. "Not from a Gypsy, I'll be bound."

"From my mother," she said a little breathlessly, wishing with all her heart she could tell him he was her guardian.

"You're not a Gypsy, I know. What are you doing here?" he asked.

"What everyone else does," she told him. "The Gypsies are my friends. They're very good to me."

"I noticed." He smiled, a look coming into his eyes that would never have appeared had he known their relationship. "If you should need help, come to headquarters and ask for me. Do you remember my name?"

"Lord . . . I mean, Colonel Meredith," she told him.

He nodded. "Don't forget. I mean it."

He appeared to be fascinated with that strand of hair as he turned it around and around his long, sun-bronzed finger. "I once knew a lovely lady who had hair the exact same shade," he mused, "but it was a long time ago."

The conversation had been so quiet that neither the Gypsies nor the other officers could hear, but Isabella was quite excited and wanted to know everything that had passed between them.

Georgina was reluctant to speak about it, but when Isabella said it was in the cards that they would meet him again, she told her of his offer of help.

"*Sí!* I tell you! He ask you go see him. And he never, never ask another!" Isabella was excited. "You go, not tomorrow, but next day. You wear *mi vestido blanco* and he know you *inocente.*"

Despite the anguish she felt, Georgina had to laugh at her dear friend. Then she explained sadly. "I can't, Isabella. You see, though he doesn't know it, he's my guardian."

Isabella was taken aback for a moment, but quickly recovered. "It is forbidden that English lady marry guardian?" she asked.

"Not forbidden, but most unlikely." Georgina's voice held a note of regret. "I think he was the nicest man I've ever met," she said, "and certainly the most beautiful."

She decided to tell no one else, not even William, that she had met Lord Meredith.

Isabella made good her promise. In a clearing in the woods, Georgina learned how to hold a knife concealed in her palm until the moment it was needed, how to throw at a target marked out on one of the trees, and how to use it to best advantage when her enemy was too close for it to be thrown. Her eye was good, and it was not long before her aim became true, and then deadly accurate. At that point Isabella presented her with two knives and showed her how to keep them razor sharp.

Georgina was most grateful until she suddenly realized she had no money with which to pay for them, but Isabella was firm in her refusal to let her borrow from her brother. They were a gift, she insisted.

"I steal them," she said with a shrug. "How can I take money from my good friend?"

It was now more than a month since they had left Yorkshire, and the army and its followers had settled into what was almost a peaceful routine, with only small skirmishes with the enemy, who occasionally attempted unsuccessfully to break through the fortification.

Perhaps familiarity with her chores had made her careless, for Georgina forgot to lock the back door when she left the house one day in search of food for her supper. William would not return until late, so she stayed away until it was almost dusk, unlocking the front door and walking through the dim, mosaic-tiled hall to the stone-flagged kitchen without troubling to light a candle, the noise of her heavy boots echoing through the silent house.

As she crossed the kitchen, she sensed someone there and tried unsuccessfully to reach for her knife as a rough hand grabbed her and pulled her into the scullery. She caught just a glimpse of a ruddy face and red hair before the scullery door was pulled to and she and her attacker were in total darkness.

"I've been waiting for you a long time, Gina. Where have you been all day, my pretty?" a deep voice asked, while strong hands forced her head upward. "It's downright mean of young Forsythe to keep you all to himself."

The brandy-laden breath made Georgina want to choke, and she struggled to move her head away as his lips came down, grinding savagely on hers. She kicked and wriggled in his strong grip without avail, then suddenly remembered some advice Isabella had given her. Balancing carefully on one leg, she thrust the other knee with all her might into her assailant's groin; then, as he groaned and doubled over in pain, she pulled herself free, pushed open the door, and ran for the hall and up to William's room, swiftly throwing the heavy bolt on the inside.

Within a few minutes there was the sound of boots pounding up the stairs and fists beating on the door, interspersed with curses and threats. Praying the door would hold, Georgina made no sound, and only resumed normal breathing when she finally heard footsteps going away. She was exceedingly hungry, as she had been about to prepare her first meal of the day, but hunger was preferable to a second confrontation with the officer, whom she recognized even in the half-light as a newcomer to the regiment, who had moved in a few doors away.

Later in the evening, she lit a candle and prepared herself for bed. Bruises were already visible from the rough handling, and there were particularly dark ones on her thighs and right breast.

The next morning, anticipating further trouble, she decided not to say anything to William for now, and tried to act as normally as possible while she shaved him and helped him into his uniform. As soon as he was ready, however, she found an excuse to leave the house with him, and parted company from him only when she could blend into a group of other camp followers she knew and slip away to meet her Gypsy friends.

Isabella was about to eat breakfast when she arrived, and she saw at once Georgina's hungry glances at the plate of food.

"Gina, you have thees," she insisted, putting the plate so near to Georgina that she couldn't resist. "I make another."

She was back in a few minutes with more food, only just in time, as Georgina could not have politely waited for her friend's return for one more moment.

They ate in silence, Isabella with an amused smile, and Georgina not willing to talk until she had appeased her hunger. When they were finished, Georgina looked shamefaced.

"I must apologize for my greed, and promise to bring some food for you next time, Isabella," she finally murmured, sipping the warm tea mixture her friend had placed in front of her. "You see, I didn't eat at all yesterday, and I left the house with William just now before I had a chance to have breakfast."

Isabella nodded slowly. "*Sí. Por qué?*"

"It's a long story," Georgina began, "but I'll try to shorten it a little." She told her friend everything from entering the house yesterday to the bruises on her hips and breast.

The two girls spent most of the day together, but toward the late afternoon they became aware they were being watched. He was a brute of a man, the bulge of muscles showing through his uniform, and his fiery red hair and bushy eyebrows made it impossible to mistake him. Seeing him in daylight, Georgina marveled that she had managed to elude him last night. He must be waiting for her to leave Isabella to take his revenge.

"*Hola!*" Isabella had seen one of her friends, a large, friendly Gypsy whom Georgina had met many times before. It was only a matter of minutes before he had agreed to stroll back with the two girls to William's house, and although the brutish officer followed at a distance for much of the way, when they reached the house he was nowhere to be seen.

Lieutenant Bennett, a pleasant but rather serious young man who had once warned William that their commanding officer would not like Gina living there, was the only one home. As she walked up the garden path he came to the door, startling her for a moment until she realized who it was. She knew he missed his fiancée, and though she declined the glass of wine he proffered, she in turn offered him part of the evening meal she was preparing, and the fair-haired young lieutenant joined her at the kitchen table for the simple meal before she wished him a good night and retired to William's room. What a pity he had not been home early last night also, she thought.

The young man's presence and his pleasant conversation had served to stem her fear of entering the house alone again, but it was with much uneasiness that she finally got into bed. She had a strong feeling this would not be the end of it, for her assailant did not look the kind who would accept defeat, particularly at the hands of a woman.

It was one problem she had not anticipated.

3

"It w-would appear you have a s-secret admirer, Georgie," William remarked after she finished shaving him. "C-can't say I think much of your t-taste, though."

Georgina gave such a start, she was grateful her brother had waited until she no longer had a razor in her hand before making his comment. "If you mean Lieutenant Barker, I doubt that 'admirer' is the right word any longer." She glanced at his face, trying to judge whether or not to tell him the whole. "What did he say to you?"

"Oh, he made some c-crude remark about my k-keeping a hot little b-baggage right under the c-colonel's nose," he replied with a grim smile. "He w-wants to share you."

"Cut me up into little pieces, more like. I was rather less friendly than he had hoped."

"He's threatened to go to our c-cousin. Apparently Lieutenant B-Bennett was right, and our c-cousin is rather strict about this k-kind of thing. What his men d-do in their f-free time he doesn't c-care about too much, but he will not c-countenance any live-in arrangements." William was watching his sister's face, which had taken on a sickly hue. "What did that ape do to you, Georgie?"

She explained briefly what had happened two nights ago, and he berated her soundly for not telling him about it at the time. Despite her fears, Georgina could not help feeling a glow of pride in her brother's increased sense of responsibility toward her.

"He's b-bound to go to Lord Meredith, so you'd best be prepared. Barker d-doesn't know, of course, that you're my sister, b-but our cousin will have to be informed.'' Georgina, silent for once, helped him into his jacket, and brushed a speck of dirt from the shoulder without realizing what she was doing.

Once he and his fellow officers had left, she checked to be sure all doors and windows were locked tightly. She was still very much afraid the lieutenant might try to get physical revenge on her in addition to reporting her brother.

She knew beyond a doubt that her cousin would send her back to England, so she went carefully through William's wardrobe, making sure that everything was clean and pressed, mending his socks and stitching a small tear she found in a jacket.

She was less worried now about William than she would have been a month ago. She knew her proud Gypsy friend would never be anyone's servant, but Isabella would gladly watch out for William, she was sure, and probably knew some local woman who would wash and mend for him.

Despite herself she smiled. At least now she'd get to see again the handsome man who had such an effect on her each time she saw him, but she doubted he would be as kind to her now as he had been during their last two meetings.

When a hammering started on the downstairs door, she thought at first it was the lieutenant, but on opening an upstairs window and leaning out, she found a sergeant standing below. She called down to find out what he wanted.

''Are ye the one as is livin' 'ere?'' the sergeant asked in a loud voice.

When she nodded, he shouted, ''Then ye'd best come along wi' me, sharp like. The colonel wants t' see ye.''

''I'll be down in just a moment,'' she called back. She checked her appearance in the mirror, seeing a face as brown as hazelnuts, and streaks in the chestnut hair where the harsh sun had bestowed some of its own gold color on the short, curling tresses.

Opening the door, she said more jauntily than she felt, ''All right, let's go, Sergeant. Lord Meredith, here I come!''

''Ye'll not be s'chirpy by t'time the colonel's finished wi' ye. Mind yer manners when yer wi' yer betters, or ye'll be an even sorrier sight than y'are now," he grunted, eyeing her Gypsy dress with a look of disgust.

She followed the sergeant up the winding road to the large house that had been taken over as a field headquarters, and was shown into a waiting room.

Fifteen minutes later, William appeared in the doorway.

"I was w-wondering if you'd arrived yet," he said, coming into the room and sitting beside her. "D-did he l-leave you here l-long to c-cool your heels?"

She nodded, almost unconsciously noticing that William was nervous, for his stutter was worse. She sighed heavily. This had all seemed such a huge joke two or three months ago, a way to get back at her grandmother, but now she feared for William that he might be brought up on charges.

A young soldier came to the door. "Will you come this way, please. Colonel Meredith will see you now."

"B-both of us?" William asked.

"So I understand, sir," the soldier replied, and waited for them to follow him.

The room Lord Meredith occupied was spacious, for the house, loaned to the army by a wealthy landowner who had fled south as the two armies approached, was really a small mansion.

Large windows looked out onto a lush garden with a pool and waterfall in the background, and the windows themselves were hung with heavy deep blue brocade curtains. The carved marble fireplace had a huge painting above, and there was a second painting of equal dimensions on the opposite wall.

Bookshelves lined one wall, and in front of them was an enormous ebony desk at which Lord Meredith was seated, apparently perusing some document before appending his signature.

For once, Georgina's boots made not a sound, for they sank into the rich carpet as she and William crossed the room and awaited their cousin's pleasure.

If anything, her usually vivid memory had dimmed somewhat the good looks of their guardian, Georgina thought when she first glanced at him. His glossy black hair curled just enough, and looked so naturally thick and windswept as to have been the envy of half the young bloods in London.

He looked up, and a pair of cold clear blue eyes swept icily over her. She noticed the firmness of his jaw, the compression of the well-shaped, sensuous lips, and the arrogant vitality that seemed to radiate from him, and suddenly felt a thrill of excitement mingled with fear. He showed no sign of ever having seen her before.

"Forsythe, word has reached me that you habitually associate with camp followers and that this particular one lives with you in your quarters."

The penetrating eyes traveled coldly to Georgina and back before he continued. "I had hardly thought it necessary to warn you of the dangers emanating from association with loose women. Nor did I expect you to disobey one of my orders."

Georgina began to seethe. How dare he assume her to be a loose woman! He was not going to get away with that.

Her eyes flashed fire as she said, "Perhaps I should be called a William follower, my lord, for he is the only person I followed. As to my being a loose woman, I—"

"Be silent," he barked. "Your turn will come later. What is your name?"

He looked down at a document on his desk and made a note. William's eye caught Georgina's and she raised her eyebrows in question. He nodded ever so slightly.

"Lady Georgina Forsythe, my lord." Her tone matched her cousin's in arrogance, and she didn't have long to wait for his reaction.

His head swung up sharply. "I'll have no sarcasm here, girl, or I'll send you outside for a good whipping. Now, tell me your given name. Gina what, as I asked you once before?"

She felt a surge of pride as William came to her rescue. "I b-beg your p-pardon, my lord, b-but she is Lady Georgina Forsythe, my sister, and your w-ward."

"My what?" Lord Meredith bellowed.

"There are t-two of us, sir. She's my t-twin, b-born just a c-couple of hours b-before me." William looked desperate.

Georgina couldn't help it. The urge to laugh at the expression of consternation on her cousin's face was irresistible and she let out a deep chuckle that turned into helpless, uproarious laughter.

"Don't try to hold back your hilarity," Lord Meredith drawled ominously. "It may be quite a long time before you find reason to laugh again."

William frowned at her, and finally Georgina took a deep breath and had herself under control, but her eyes still twinkled and her lips quivered.

There was a long pause while Lord Meredith looked closely from one face to the other; then, still frowning thoughtfully, he began, "If my memory serves me correctly, I was advised that I had been appointed guardian to the late Lord Forsythe's son, born thirteen years previously—or could the word have been 'offspring,' I wonder? It had been the intent to appoint my father, who would probably have known how many children there were, as he was a cousin and a good friend of Lord Forsythe's, but I suppose this was not made clear in the document." He looked at William. "I can understand the original confusion there, but I cannot understand why your grandmother mentioned only you."

William cleared his throat and glanced toward Georgina before answering. "Grandmama has always ignored Georgina, I'm afraid, sir. Her one interest w-was in seeing the estates r-restored, and only I, as the heir, c-could p-possibly b-bring that about."

Looking Georgina over, Lord Meredith remarked, "If your grandmother has such a dislike of your sister, there must surely be good cause. Judging by her appearance here, I would imagine she has always been completely ungovernable."

With her almost pure green eyes flashing furiously, Georgina opened her mouth to protest, but her cousin was quicker.

"I warn you, miss. Don't say it or I'll go through with my previous threat," he snapped, and for once Georgina realized she had best obey.

William came to her defense once more. "Grandmama never l-liked our mama, sir, to whom Georgina b-bears a strong resemblance. Most of the t-time, she ignored Georgina, b-but we d-didn't know she'd not m-mentioned her to you. Georgina was usually l-left to her own d-devices, b-but it got worse the l-last six months." It was a lengthy explanation for William, delivered slowly and with much hesitation, but Lord Meredith did not rush him, waiting patiently until he could get the right words out.

"And what happened these last six months to cause her to dislike the young hellion?" Lord Meredith's voice was softly sarcastic, and the half-closed, cynical eyes swept again over the rebellious girl, before returning to her brother.

Ignoring the earlier warning, Georgina answered for herself, speaking in a carefully controlled tone. "I met one of our neighbors in the village, Lady Patrice Charters, and asked Grandmama if she would have her dressmaker make me my first gown, so that I could accept her invitation to visit in something other than faded gingham or breeches."

She finally had her cousin's attention. He raised an eyebrow to her brother, who nodded in confirmation.

"She told me there was no money for gowns for me, and I could wear either William's old breeches and shirts, or faded ginghams. She said it was unnecessary for me to socialize with the local gentry, for no one would ever marry me without a pittance to my name, and especially as I was plain as a pikestaff.

"That's when I first told her she had no authority over me, that Broadacres was not hers, and that I had more right to live there than she had," she continued.

She had no idea how appealing she looked, despite the hint of defiance in her eyes that was not quite concealed by her thick auburn lashes.

"Since then she's hardly spoken to me except when she really had to, and I readily admit I have been most rude in return." As she looked away from those searching blue eyes that had a way of making her feel most uncomfortable, she failed to see her cousin indicate to William that he should leave, nor did she hear the door close behind him.

"Sit down, Georgina," Lord Meredith said quietly, pointing to a seat by the side of the desk.

"What did you do with William?" she asked, looking around.

He firmly repressed a smile as he said sternly, "I sent him away for the time being. I could put him on charges for his part in this prank, you know."

"I beg you not to, my lord," Georgina pleaded. "It was not his fault at all. I talked him into taking me to London as his manservant, and then I was to stay with our old housekeeper, but when I wrote to her, she was just leaving on an extended visit to her daughter, who is increasing. I said I wouldn't live at Broadacres alone with Grandmama, and he knew I meant it, so he had no choice but to take me on the ship."

He suddenly laughed, and to Georgina's bewitched eyes he looked more startlingly handsome than ever.

"If you go a little slower, I think I'll be able to follow. You're supposed to be visiting your old housekeeper, whom I imagine you're very fond of." She nodded emphatically. "And she couldn't have you, as she would be away. So William was forced to take you with him when the orders came so quickly? Am I to understand you started this escapade dressed as a manservant?" She nodded. "That accounts for the shortness of your hair, I suppose.

"You'll not be let off lightly yourself, but William must pay for his part in this also, as I'm sure he'd be the first to agree," he continued grimly.

She had to know! "You wouldn't send your ward to be whipped, I'm sure," she said with a show of bravado. Her pulse was beating rapidly, however, as she remembered with horror a soldier she had seen after he had been flogged.

He smiled then, the corners of his mouth slowly softening and a twinkle just visible through the dark eyelashes. "No, but if that frightened you even a little, I'm glad. I have some duties I must attend to now, but you are to remain here, and when I return I hope to have decided what to do with you."

A long, sun-bronzed finger and thumb tweaked one of her short curls as he brushed past her chair and to the door.

"Now I know why that hair was so familiar," he re-

marked. "When I was eighteen, your mother was the loveliest creature I had ever seen."

She looked around as he stopped speaking, but saw only
the door closing quietly behind him.

At first Georgina was quite relaxed as she sat back in her
chair, but as time passed she became a little nervous, and it
was a relief when he finally returned.

Unsmiling, he walked into the room, quietly closing the
door behind him. He placed more papers on the desk, then
came around and sat on its edge, facing Georgina.

"I've been wondering how Barker realized you were living
with your brother. Did you have some trouble with him?"

She had no idea why he was asking, but there was no need
to dissemble. "Yes, I did. I carelessly left the back door open
one day, and when I returned he was hiding in the kitchen
waiting for me."

"Did he hurt you in any way?" he asked in a matter-of-
fact tone of voice.

"He managed to bruise me a little before I got my knee up
hard. Then, when he bent over, I broke away and ran." She
tried to sound as unconcerned about it as he.

"May I inquire to what part of his anatomy you applied
your knee hard?" he asked mildly, but there was a decided
twitch at one corner of his mouth.

"To his, er . . . between his legs." Lord Meredith sounded
as if he was about to choke. "It was something Isabella
taught me."

Making a quick recovery, he asked, "And who might
Isabella be?"

"She's my friend. A Spanish Gypsy girl I met," she said.
She silently dared him to say something against Isabella, but
he just shook his head.

"Well, neither you nor William need worry further about
Barker," he said lightly. "I dislike that type under my command so I've had him transferred. He's already on his way to
a unit to the south of here, where he'll be given some very
tough duty."

The glint of amusement that had softened his features

faded, and he became very serious again, looking straight at her until she was compelled to return his gaze.

"You love your brother very much, in fact he is your whole life, and yet you deliberately endangered him by persuading him to engage in a foolish prank." He paused to let his quiet words sink in, and she felt as though his eyes were looking into her soul.

"When we arrived in Portugal, I didn't know what we would find here, so you certainly did not. Had there been a battle in progress, instead of obeying orders, William would probably have thought first about his sister, and how he could get her out of the line of fire—stop her getting hurt.

"An officer fighting for his country cannot afford to be distracted for one moment. His entire concentration must be on obeying whatever orders his commander has given, attacking and defending, protecting his men and himself. The second his mind strays is the one when he is most vulnerable, most likely to get hit—he doesn't throw himself on the ground fast enough, or fails to notice an advance on his right flank.

"Not only are you his sister, but you are his twin, which usually makes the relationship much closer. Is that so in your case?" he asked.

She nodded, not quite trusting herself to speak.

"Would it not be usual for him to almost sense when you were in danger, and start to worry about where you might be and what you were doing?"

She swallowed and nodded again, hating herself for the guilt she was feeling.

"Only a very selfish young woman would put her boredom. of staying at home before the life of her only brother. Don't you think it would have been more commendable to have ignored your own problems and let him go on his way to war with a good heart and no worries?

"You have to grow up sometime, Georgina. At twenty you are not a child anymore, you have responsibilities. There is no longer any place for elaborate deceptions and pranks. He'll meet someone soon, get married, and take on the responsibilities of raising a family. You won't be able to live with him then."

"But William isn't . . ." Georgina started to protest. "He needs more help learning . . ." She broke off, unwilling to say anything to William's detriment.

Lord Meredith eyed her steadily as she struggled to explain. "I am fully aware that, since birth, William has been a little slow to grasp things and take the initiative. However, I find he responds very well to orders and has shown considerable improvement in the short time he has been here. His stutter is not as bad as when we first met, except for today, when I can understand his nervousness. He'll do well for himself, I feel. But it's time you faced up to life. Your grandmother wouldn't buy you a gown! What was to stop your writing to me and asking if there were funds available for the two of you that could be used? I may not have known I was your guardian, but you can claim no such ignorance."

If he'd shouted and raged at her she could have stayed defiant, but his calm condemnation was far more effective. She looked away.

He stood up. "Until such time as I can have you escorted safely back to England, I am arranging for you to stay with a friend of mine, Lady Leicester, who resides in Lisbon. While with Lady Leicester, I will expect you to behave like a lady, dress like a lady, and conduct yourself in such a way as not to disgrace your brother and me."

"Am I to travel alone to Lisbon?" she asked.

"No, of course not. For tonight, I'm putting you in the care of the wife of one of my officers, a Mrs. Dover. She will find you some suitable attire for the journey, and I hope to hear you have burned those disreputable garments. You will not go back to your brother's billet. Anything of a personal nature, he will send over to you at Mrs. Dover's."

"Then you'd better tell him to send my horse also. If I have to go, I'm taking Starlight with me. She's mine and I won't leave her to get shot at and likely killed." She set her jaw defiantly. "And I won't go without saying good-bye to William and Isabella, no matter what you do to me."

He came closer to where she sat. Although unsure of his intentions, she forced herself not to move.

As he lifted her chin with his first finger, she had no alternative but to look directly into his compelling silver-blue eyes. "Did I say you couldn't say good-bye to your brother?" he asked softly.

"No." She barely breathed the word.

"Perhaps it would be best, however, if you discontinue your relationship with the Gypsy girl and her friends. She's hardly a suitable companion for a young English lady," he suggested, raising one black eyebrow slightly.

"I won't leave without seeing her. You can't make me," she said stubbornly.

"Don't tempt me to put that to the test, my dear." The quietly spoken words held a decided note of warning. "But if it matters so much to you, then by all means see her. She may not be a suitable companion, but a friend is a friend. As for Starlight, I hadn't realized she was yours. She's too fine a mount to be out here." He paused thoughtfully. "I believe you've just solved one of my problems. I'm taking you to Lisbon myself, but had thought to drive there. Instead, we'll go on horseback and you can ride Starlight. You'd better be a good rider."

"I can ride. You'll not need to make any allowances for me, my lord," Georgina assured him scornfully.

There was a knock on the door, and the orderly announced Mrs. Dover. A pleasant-looking middle-aged lady bustled into the room. She curtsied to Lord Meredith.

"Mrs. Dover, this is Lady Georgina Forsythe, who will accompany me to Lisbon tomorrow. I wonder if you could find some suitable riding habit for her, as we will be on horseback."

The mild, pale blue eyes showed not even a hint of curiosity. "Certainly, my lord. I know just where to get the very thing," she said. "Come along, my dear."

"Thank you, ma'am. I knew you could take care of it." He turned to Georgina. "I'll see you tomorrow. I understand that William is dining with the Dovers tonight."

"Thank you, my lord," she said; then, to her chagrin,

Mrs. Dover curtsied again as she said good-bye. Although Georgina was naturally graceful, she had no idea how to curtsy and dared not try in case she fell on her face.

As she stood waiting for Mrs. Dover, she saw Lord Meredith frown, and knew she was in the suds once more. He obviously thought she was refusing to curtsy to him, but Georgina was too proud to tell him she didn't know how.

4

The young lady who came down to dinner at the home of Captain and Mrs. Dover that evening could never have been recognized as the Gypsy who arrived earlier in the day. In addition to a riding habit, Mrs. Dover had procured a simple, modest gown in a becoming shade of light green, and her young maid had proved to be an expert in arranging hair even as short as Georgina's. Matching green slippers, long white gloves, and a ribbon delicately twisted through her chestnut curls made the transformation complete.

As Lord Meredith did not want Georgina's presence made public, William was the only dinner guest. Captain Robert Dover was one of William's superior officers, for whom he had a deep respect, and after introductions had been performed, the four sat down to a meal of duck roasted with pork sausage and served on rice, over which a spicy sauce had been poured. A sweet of figs and almonds followed, and a jug of refreshing lemon-flavored wine was frequently replenished.

"This is the best meal I've eaten since we left England," Georgina exclaimed as she nibbled a sun-dried fig.

"It was good, but you mustn't think we eat such a dinner every night," Mrs. Dover anxiously explained. "As you two children will be separated for some time, we felt the occasion warranted something rather special."

"I can't get over the w-way you l-look, Georgie," William remarked, letting his glance slide from her stylish curls to where the swell of her breasts could be seen in the high bodice of the dress. "I'd g-give much to see Grandmama's f-face when she sees you."

The glow left Georgina's eyes and she looked quickly down. She would find some way of escaping if Lord Meredith insisted on sending her back home to Broadacres.

After dinner Captain Dover excused himself, explaining it was the only time of the day he was able to devote to his paperwork, and Mrs. Dover tactfully left the twins alone, professing to have a slight headache due to the excitement of the day.

"I m-must say again, Georgie, I've n-never seen you look b-better," William began. "What happened after I l-left? He didn't b-beat you, did he?"

Georgina was indignant. "Of course he didn't. He wouldn't dare!" she said, her eyes flashing.

But William was serious. "Oh yes he would, if he f-felt you d-deserved it," he warned. "Did he g-give you a v-very severe scold?"

Looking at her twin, she shrugged carelessly. "It wasn't exactly pleasant," she told him, preferring not to go into detail. Then, her eyes large and appealing, she explained, "The thing was, he didn't get mad, he just made me feel ashamed of myself for the way I talked you into it."

William had never known her to look repentant. This was the nearest she had ever come to it. He put an arm around her shoulders and gave her a big hug.

"Something g-good may come out of it. You'll get new c-clothes and see something of the city, I d-don't doubt." He grinned sheepishly. "I'm a fine one to t-talk. My turn with him is still to c-come."

His arm was still around her shoulders, and she turned toward him. "It's all my fault, I know," she said contritely. "I was behind the whole thing, and now you're going to be punished for it."

"Don't be silly, Georgie. I c-could have said n-no." He remembered something. "I have orders to b-bring Isabella here t-tomorrow so you can say g-good-bye. How did you g-get him to agree to that?"

"By refusing to go unless he let me see her."

He shook his head. "That didn't d-do anything, I'm sure, except make him m-mad, possibly."

"He indicated that a friend is a friend even if she is a Gypsy and not the kind of company I should keep." Georgina could almost feel Lord Meredith's finger under her chin again as she recalled his words.

"That sounds more l-like it." William got to his feet. "It's t-time I left. Our c-cousin has already t-taken Starlight and stabled her with his own horses for the n-night. I'll be here around t-ten o'clock with Isabella, if that's c-convenient."

She nodded, and he bent to kiss her cheek, then suddenly put his arms around her and held her close for a moment. "It will b-be all right, Georgie, you'll s-see," he promised.

The next morning William brought Isabella to the house as promised, then went to see Captain Dover, leaving the two girls on their own.

Georgina was wearing a deep blue velvet riding habit which Mrs. Dover had obtained from the wife of one of her husband's junior officers, who found herself increasing and gladly exchanged it for a couple of lengths of fabric. A black shako hat had been included for good measure. The outfit suited Georgina every bit as much as had the dinner gown she wore the night before.

Isabella looked her up and down with an impudent grin, then gave her a mock curtsy. "Now you are the lady again," she said. She took the hand Georgina held out, holding it tight and gently patting it. "It will be good for you now—I know."

"I'm going to miss you so much," Georgina said sorrowfully. "You will keep an eye open for William, won't you, and perhaps find someone to do his washing and take care of his clothes?"

Mischief sparkled in the Gypsy girl's eyes. "Both *los ojos* will be open for the *hermoso hermano*," she teased, "but he no *chico* anymore. He no need Gina now." The almost black eyes held a look of understanding.

"I know," Georgina agreed. "He's grown up a lot since he came over here, but I still worry."

She looked away to hide the tears that filled her eyes, and Isabella's strong brown arms were around her in an instant.

"There, I tell truth and make you cry. You worry 'bout Gina now, and let *el primo importante* take care of Gina. You like him, no?"

"I like him, yes," Georgina agreed with a short laugh, "but I don't think he likes me very much." She shook her head and smiled, then said, "I don't know how long I will stay there, but I'm probably being sent to my home, which is Broadacres, near Knaresborough, in Yorkshire. It belongs to William, and if you ever need help, if we can do anything at all for you, please come or send word. Promise me, Isabella."

"I give promise, *pero* not need anything. Your cousin is *un buen hombre, muchacha*. We will meet again. *Vaya con Dios!*"

With a warm hug and a kiss on Georgina's cheek, Isabella was gone, leaving her newfound friend more lonely than she would have believed.

Georgina did not have long to feel downcast, however, as Lord Meredith was announced so quickly that he must have passed Isabella in the hall. Georgina had asked Mrs. Dover to show her how to curtsy, and had been practicing at odd moments ever since, but seeing him so unexpectedly, she forgot for a moment. She quickly recovered, however, and sank low gracefully.

At first he thought she was mocking him, but when he saw her serious face he bowed, brought her hand to his lips, then raised her from the floor.

"To what do I owe this honor, Georgina?" he asked, his eyes gleaming.

"I'm practicing," she confessed, a little breathless and glowing from the touch of his lips on her hand. He hadn't done that to Mrs. Dover, she recalled with satisfaction. "You see, I didn't know how, and I asked Mrs. Dover to teach me."

"She taught you well in so short a time. That was quite lovely, my dear," he said gravely, but an approving half-smile played at the corners of his mouth.

"She has been very good to me, my lord," Georgina

acknowledged. "I have never owned anything as lovely as this and the gown she obtained at such short notice."

She would have been embarrassed had she seen the look in his eyes as she stepped back and turned around, the habit showing her youthful grace and beauty to perfection.

"For a temporary measure she did remarkably well." He nodded approvingly. "The ragamuffin Gypsy I saw yesterday has disappeared completely and—"

"Had you worn the same two sets of clothes for the last month or more, I'm sure you'd have looked as I did, sir," she said tartly, all the more hurt and angry at his criticism because she knew it to be warranted.

"Perhaps." His playful mockery had returned. "But then, I would hardly have put myself into such a ridiculous position in the first place. You must admit it was your choice, my dear," he drawled. "I'd be obliged if you would take a seat so that I may tell you of the plans I have made for our journey to Lisbon."

Making a mental note to find out why she had to sit down first, Georgina flopped into a chair beside the hearth. Frowning slightly, Lord Meredith took the small couch facing her.

"As you have now bade your Gypsy friend farewell, and packing can be no more than a matter of minutes for you, I do not believe there is any reason to delay our journey further. Mrs. Dover has packed some food for us, and we should arrive at our destination late tonight."

He got to his feet and reached for her hand to assist her.

"I'll just have a word with the Dovers, then we'll be off. Do whatever last-minute things you need to do and meet me down here again in no more than five minutes."

"Yes, sir," Georgina said, springing to attention and giving him a smart salute, then hurrying from the room before he could show his disapproval.

Lord Meredith chuckled to himself. She was going to be a handful, he had no doubt, but at least he would not be bored.

It was a half-hour since they'd left the Dovers' house, and Georgina was enjoying herself tremendously. There had just been time to give William a farewell kiss and throw her few belongings into a saddlebag before they were on their way. True to his word, her cousin made no concessions to her because she was a woman, and her only regret was that she had to ride sidesaddle.

"Do you remember your mother and father very well, Georgina?" Lord Meredith asked. "You'd have been about thirteen years old when they died, I suppose."

"Of course I remember them, and so does William," she said with a trace of asperity. "They were so loving and full of fun, and we were so happy—all except Grandmama, of course."

"It was some sort of carriage accident, I seem to recall, actually on your own land." He seemed puzzled.

"They were returning from Knaresborough in the curricle," she told him. "Papa was driving and they were putting a new team of horses through their paces when something startled them and they bolted. Papa died right away, and Mama lived only a day or so.

"In a way, that was why I came out here with William," she continued. "You see, before she died, Mama asked me to promise that I'd take care of William, and I've tried to keep that promise ever since."

"I'm sure you have, my dear, but I hardly think she had in mind the sort of prank you got into out here. Don't you agree?" he asked a little grimly.

"Yes," she conceded. "Not wanting to remain alone with Grandmama played a big part in that." She glanced at him mutinously. "You're not going to read me another lecture today, are you?"

"Not unless you do something equally shatterbrained before we reach Lady Leicester's," he retorted.

They rode in silence for a while until the warm afternoon sun and the feel of Starlight's even stride beneath her lulled Georgina into a mellow goodwill that encompassed even her cousin. She glanced sideways at him under her lashes, secretly admiring the way he looked astride his stallion. He was not wearing his uniform today, but had on a top hat, dark green riding coat, white buckskins, and fine leather boots.

He noticed her stare and his eyebrows rose. "Do I pass muster?" he asked with an amused grin.

She inclined her head graciously. "Certainly, my lord. Your valet must feel proud of your appearance." She pursed her lips and looked down her nose in the way she imagined a haughty young debutante might, then spoiled everything with a giggle she couldn't hold back.

He smiled tolerantly. "My batman, Davis, who serves as valet also, was most unhappy he couldn't accompany us and protect me from any Gypsy spells you might cast on me. Did Isabella or her companions teach you any tricks while you were with them?"

"I learned a lot from them." Her eyes twinkled mischievously as she thought of her expertise with her knives, which were at this moment strapped to each of her legs. "But neither spells nor fortune-telling is among my new accomplishments. Now, if you'd care for me to catch and bake a hedgehog, pluck a bird, or trap and skin a rabbit, then I could really show off my prowess."

"And I had Mrs. Dover prepare a picnic! How wasteful of me!" he exclaimed.

"More wasteful than you probably realize, my lord," Georgina told him, serious now. "The Dovers provided a dinner for me and William last night that must have cost them a month of carefully hoarded treats. He is not a rich officer, and even simple foods are hard to come by when soldiers are not paid for months."

He smiled reassuringly. "They are a little better off than they would have been, for I compensated her well, in supplies and cash, for entertaining you, for the garments she procured, and for the picnic which we may yet use. She accepted the things reluctantly, however, and begged me not to tell the good captain."

Some thirty minutes later, they came to an inn, and since the private parlor was available, they sat down to a simple meal of codfish cakes followed by a dish of pork with sweet red peppers, the whole washed down with a bottle of local wine. A delicious flan and rich black coffee left them quite stuffed.

"It will be dark very soon now," Lord Meredith said, sounding somewhat worried, "and will stay that way for an hour or so until the moon comes up. If riding at night alarms you, my dear, I'll gladly take rooms here for the night, and set out again at first light. How—?"

Before he could finish, Georgina interrupted. "I'd much rather go on to Lisbon, my lord, if you don't mind. Starlight is now quite accustomed to night riding, and I promise I'll be no trouble to you."

"Are you sure that is what you wish?" He was still concerned.

"Quite sure, my lord," she avowed, then couldn't resist teasing. "But I thought you were bound and determined to make no concessions to a female," she said, her brows raised and her eyes twinkling naughtily.

"You are a minx, young lady, to remind me of my firm avowals," he said, pretending to look severe. "But if you're sure you will be all right, I'd much rather push on to Lisbon tonight. If you get tired, we'll stop when the moon comes up and stretch our legs, but this is your last chance to change your mind, as it's the only inn on this road."

They continued in a comfortable silence which was broken only by the sound of the horses' hooves and the cries of birds in the distance. Occasionally her cousin made some remark, more, she felt, to assure himself that she was all right than to start a conversation.

A full moon rose, making it possible for them to see each other quite clearly as they rode, but they made only occasional conversation. Anxious to get her to her destination, he increased their pace a little. Soon they topped a rise and Georgina gasped as she saw the city below her.

'You'll like Lisbon, I believe," he promised softly. Then his voice became sterner. "Before we reach the house, I want a promise from you that you will stay with Lady Leicester until I can complete arrangements for your safe passage, and will make no unnecessary problems for her."

Georgina hated to commit herself to stay an indefinite length of time with some strange lady. Suppose she and Lady Leicester didn't rub along well together? However, there seemed little alternative, for without funds to get herself to England, she would be helpless in Lisbon.

"I'm waiting, Georgina. Don't try my patience too far," he warned, sounding bored and weary of her company.

She glared, angry at him for pushing her to make the commitment. "I give you my word, my lord. I will remain with Lady Leicester and try not to make my company as much of a hardship to her as it has been to you."

He could not see the hurt in her eyes, but heard it in her voice. "You have windmills in your head, Georgina, if you believe this ride has been a hardship to me. I was coming anyway, for I have other business in the area, and your company made a boring ride most pleasant," he said gruffly. "I have every reason to believe that you and Lady Leicester will become bosom bows."

They rode down the hillside and entered the city, and soon turned into an obviously wealthy section. In the light of the flambeaux outside Lady Leicester's residence, Georgina could see decorative tiles on the walls of the house, and beautiful windows latticed with iron. There was a strong smell of the sea, and the cool breezes from the water were refreshing.

While she held both mounts, her cousin rang a huge iron bell. The door was opened by a stiff English butler who bowed low then waited while Lord Meredith ran lightly down the steps and took the horses' reins from her.

"Lady Leicester is already abed, but if you go inside, the butler will send for the housekeeper to take care of your needs and show you to your bedchamber. I'll be back in a few days to see how you're going along."

"Thank you for your escort, my lord," she said primly, and dropped him a curtsy before walking proudly up the steps, past the butler, and into the house. She had not realized he would be leaving so quickly, but would not let him see her disappointment.

She was shown into a luxurious, almost flamboyant drawing room with heavy brocade hangings and massive ebony furniture, and while she waited for the housekeeper she glanced around, intrigued by the intricately worked silver pieces and the Indian artifacts on display.

There was no chance to further inspect the room, as a rather formal middle-aged housekeeper came in then to greet her and quickly swept her up the staircase to a bedchamber already prepared for her use.

Now completely exhausted, Georgina had time only to glance at the comfortable-looking bed before a young maid appeared, and swift, gentle hands undressed her, helped her into the one nightgown she now owned, and tucked her into the gigantic four-poster bed. The tea and cakes the maid had brought remained on a side table, untouched, as Georgina fell asleep almost before her cheek felt the softness of the feather pillow.

When she awoke she had no idea where she was, as her recollection of a bedchamber by candlelight was far different from this lovely room, bathed in sunlight, but she did remember the young maid who was looking in consternation at the one gown Georgina now owned, before hurrying out of the room with the garment over her arm.

Georgina lay quietly enjoying the luxury of the soft bed and remembered her own annoyance when she realized her cousin was leaving her alone at this strange house. She had spent almost eight hours in his company on that long ride, and a stiffness in her bottom told its tale, but she would not have missed any minute of it. She had been angry and pleased, and hurt and soothed, and had felt more alive with him than with anyone else she'd ever met. He had intrigued her the first time she saw him, on the docks in London, and her fascination only increased each time she was in his company.

There was a knock on the door and the young maid returned with a cup of hot chocolate. She wanted to know what Georgina would like for breakfast, and the list of possibilities left Georgina dumbfounded. Finally she selected an omelet with toast and kidneys and tea, and when it came it would have fed four people back at the camp, with some left over. Unaccustomed to such abundance, she merely nibbled on the toast and sipped the fragrant tea.

There was a jug of hot water and a basin, and it was

luxurious to use perfumed soap and thick, absorbent towels. She sat in the too-large underwear Mrs. Dover had provided, and daydreamed as she combed her hair at the massive ebony dressing table. The dark, heavy furniture was a little overpowering, but flower-printed chintz around the bed and at the windows served to soften it.

After a while the maid returned with Georgina's gown and she arranged her short curls attractively. Then, just as Georgina was about to leave her chamber a footman came to the door to let her know that Lady Leicester was ready to receive her in the drawing room. Georgina followed him down the wide staircase and into the room she had seen so briefly last night.

The first person she saw was a tall woman wearing a dark green walking dress, who smiled at her pleasantly; then Georgina turned toward her hostess, an exquisitely gowned and coiffed lady who reminded her of a china doll she'd had years ago, with the same auburn hair, treasured because her mama had given it to her.

Lady Leicester approached with an amused smile and an outstretched hand.

"So you are the young lady who has caused my dear Lord Meredith so much trouble." The brightest of pure green eyes danced merrily. "You must tell me all about it later, but now I want you to meet Mrs. Robinson, who will be companion to you during your stay here, and escort you to your family in England. Mrs. Robinson, this is Lady Georgina Forsythe."

Georgina was a little disconcerted. Unused to being chaperoned, she could envision a loss of her usual freedom and independence.

Lady Leicester led the way into luncheon, and a hungry Georgina particularly enjoyed a chicken soup flavored with lemon and mint.

"It's called *canja,* and is a favorite of mine also," Lady Leicester replied in response to Georgina's question. "I'm glad you like it, for I have become quite fond of some of the Spanish and Portuguese dishes, and my chef, though French, prepares them extremely well."

Georgina could not help commenting on the beauty of the

dining room, particularly the tiles which lined the walls from the floor to about four feet up.

"They are very lovely, aren't they?" Lady Leicester agreed, "and quite old, I believe. I understand they are even older than the house, having come from the ruins of one of the churches after the earthquake. Mrs. Robinson can probably tell you much of the history of the house."

As Georgina glanced at her, Mrs. Robinson smiled and confirmed this with a slight nod.

"Now, my dear," Lady Leicester said, "I have canceled my plans for the afternoon in order to give you my fullest attention. My dressmaker will be arriving shortly, with bolts of fabric, and we will spend an hour or two planning a suitable wardrobe for your stay in Lisbon. It will probably be some weeks before you are able to sail."

She turned a smiling face to Mrs. Robinson. "I will have a footman show you to your bedchamber, Robbie, and let you rest awhile and get settled. I will be dining out tonight, so you two can get to know each other over dinner."

She swept Georgina before her out of the room, up the wide staircase, and into her private suite, waving her to one of a pair of armchairs while she stretched out on a matching daybed opposite.

Although she realized her experience was limited, Georgina thought she had never seen a set of rooms so well-suited to their occupant. The hangings at the windows and the chairs in which they sat were the palest shade of apple-green velvet, framing Lady Leicester's deep auburn hair and making her eyes seem all the more green and sparkling.

A round table near the window, where she no doubt ate breakfast each day, was covered with a blue-and-green chintz, as were the dainty chairs, and through the open door Georgina could see bed hangings of the same material, softening the lines of the heavy ebony four-poster bed.

"From what Lord Meredith told me, in his letter and when I saw him for a moment last night, he intends to keep the details of your stay in this country as quiet as possible, but I am not about to let you out of this room until you have disclosed everything. However, there it must end, and you must not reveal your story even to Robbie. Did his lordship by any chance say you must not tell me?''

"No, my lady, he didn't. But I don't know if . . ." She hesitated, not wishing to offend her hostess, but even more concerned about her guardian's wishes.

"He would have said so in no uncertain terms had he not intended that you tell me, my dear. I suppose he was very intimidating, wasn't he?" The twinkle was back. Lady Leicester appeared to be looking forward to the disclosure with delight.

5

The afternoon proved to be exhausting, both mentally and physically. Lady Leicester was a most thorough inquisitor, and when she finally knew the complete story, her eyes danced with ill-concealed mirth.

Holding a lace kerchief to her mouth to suppress another gurgle, she apologized. "I am sorry, my dear. Please do not think me amused at your discomfiture. You see, I have known your guardian well for a number of years, during which it seems he has become only more handsome, more worldly, and more bored with the social scene as time has passed. To suddenly find himself guardian to a young female would have set him back not a little, but for that same ward to have posed as a manservant and then become part of the rabble who follow an army—well, I should have very much enjoyed seeing his face when you told him who you were!"

"You should have seen his face, I agree, my lady, for I saw it and laughed so much I almost cried. With due respect, you would not have cared to receive the scold that followed," Georgina said.

"No, most assuredly I would not." Lady Leicester then gently added, "But you must know that it was deserved, particularly when you laughed."

Georgina's smile widened as she nodded in agreement.

There was a scratching at the door, and Lady Leicester rose as her abigail came into the room.

"Will you be seeing the dressmaker in here, your ladyship?" she asked.

"Yes, have Carmelita come in, Watkins. I hope she has brought many bolts with her."

"Yes, your ladyship, that she has. It'll take two footmen to carry them all."

As the abigail hurried out of the room, Lady Leicester caught the look of surprise on Georgina's face.

"Don't get too excited, my dear," she admonished. "Although Lord Meredith said you should be outfitted for your stay here, he also specified that you were not to go out socially, so you'll have little chance to show them off, and your wardrobe will lack ball gowns for the present."

More like forever, Georgina thought, for who would pay for ball gowns once she was at Broadacres?

While she stood patiently and listened to discussion of a subject she knew so little about, Georgina's mind wandered back to the encampment she had just left, and she couldn't help but wonder how William had fared with their cousin. It really was unfair for him to be punished at all, as it had been her idea alone, and she who had taken advantage of his slowness of thought, putting him in a position where he was forced to take her with him when the ships left. She ought to have somehow made Lord Meredith realize this, and not let him punish William. To her horror, she felt a tear roll down her cheek and she hurriedly wiped it away with the back of her hand, hoping the others had not noticed.

"I realize you have little interest in the selection of a suitable wardrobe, my love, and to stand so long being pinned and poked is less than enjoyable, but does it hurt so very much?" Lady Leicester, who had glanced up in time to see the surreptitious movement, smiled sympathetically at her charge.

"Oh no, my lady, not at all," a contrite Georgina hastened to assure her. "I was thinking about my brother, William, and wondering what might happen to him."

"I believe Carmelita is in need of some sustenance, so I think we'd best give you a little rest also," Lady Leicester said as she went over to a wardrobe, produced a pale blue wrapper for Georgina, and steered her to a chair. "It's surprising how a pot of tea refreshes one, and by now it will already await us."

* * *

"That's better, isn't it?" Lady Leicester said as they sipped their tea. "I'm afraid that the fitting of gowns is an acquired taste, usually begun when one is still in the schoolroom and soon to learn the excitement of wearing new clothes." She looked with understanding at her charge. "It is most wearisome, but when the gowns are completed, in just a few days, and Carmelita has procured all the gloves, reticules, bonnets, and parasols to match, I look to see a great change in both your attitude and your appearance."

Georgina hadn't considered all the other items, and her eyes opened wide as she thought of the cost.

"Did Lord Meredith say I could have all of these things, my lady? Are you sure he will not be angry when he gets the bills?"

Lady Leicester gave a delighted chuckle. "How very innocent you are, my dear. You mustn't tell him I said so, but when he sets up a new ladybird, he spends a great deal more than is being spent right now on you. He said nothing about jewelry, so I would not go so far, and will lend you suitable pieces as they are needed, but I have it in his own hand that you are to have a complete wardrobe. That bright green velvet over there will be most becoming with those chestnut curls." She nodded to the corner, where additional bolts of fabric stood, not unrolled as yet.

There was a scratch on the door, and the dressmaker returned. Georgina tried hard to show a little more interest, but was grateful when the last item had been chosen and she was allowed to return to her room. After a short rest she joined Mrs. Robinson for dinner.

"I understand you are newly arrived in Lisbon, my lady. It is a most interesting city and I am looking forward to showing some of it to you before we leave for England." Mrs. Robinson smiled pleasantly.

Georgina had not realized she was to be put in the charge of an older woman and felt resentful that Lord Meredith had hired a "watchdog."

She stared at her companion, and applied herself industriously to the bowl of soup a footman had placed before her.

When she looked up and found her companion still awaiting a response, she decided to explain her feelings. "Really, Mrs. Robinson, I have not had a governess for years, but if Lord Meredith has hired you to accompany me to England, I can make no argument. I must tell you, however, that I would much rather travel alone."

The balance of the meal was eaten for the most part in silence, and afterward Mrs. Robinson excused herself without finishing her first cup of tea.

"I wish your ladyship good night," she said quietly, and returned to her room.

There was no reason to stay in the drawing room alone, so Georgina went up to her bedchamber. She had a rather battered copy of one of Mrs. Radcliffe's novels, given her by Mrs. Dover, and she settled down for a cozy read, putting her companion out of her mind as she devoured the lurid romance.

But she was not left in peace for long. Within a half-hour there was a scratching at the door, and Lady Leicester's abigail entered.

"Her ladyship's instructions, ma'am," she said, seeing Georgina's surprise. "You are to have some of this on your hands and face every night until your skin returns to a more ladylike color."

"I'm not going to bed covered in that, Watkins," Georgina declared emphatically.

But this was no ladylike companion, as Georgina was quick to realize.

"That you are, ma'am. I have my instructions, and I'm going to follow them, even if I have to tie you down to do so."

Georgina looked mutinous, but the abigail continued, "Now, just behave yourself and I'll get you ready for bed first. I have some gloves here to cover your hands once the cream is on them."

"I suppose you'll lose your position if I don't let you do it," Georgina said with a resigned sigh.

"I would seriously doubt that, ma'am. But I was her ladyship's nanny before I was her abigail, and you can't throw any worse tantrums than she did."

Georgina knew she'd met her match, so she allowed the

abigail to undress her, brush out her curls, which were growing to a more feminine length, and apply the cream, which
smelled pleasantly of lemon. She had given her word to Lord
Meredith that she would make no problems for Lady Leicester,
and she had strayed far enough from that promise already this
evening.

A troubled conscience invaded her sleep that night, however, and Georgina went down to breakfast the next morning
feeling rather guilty. If her companion was already eating
breakfast, it would be a difficult meal.

She was grateful to find herself alone, and after breakfast,
decided to slip out of the house unobserved for a stroll in the
park she could see from the drawing-room windows. She was
surprised when she was stopped by the butler just as she
reached the front door.

"Lady Leicester has requested that you not leave the
house unescorted, your ladyship," he said, giving her a look
of reproof.

"But I was only going to stroll in the park for a little air,
Darley. I'm sure Lady . . ." she protested with an air of
injured innocence.

He shook his head firmly. "Not outside the door."

With a slight shrug, Georgina turned and went back upstairs.

Lady Leicester was wearing a dainty wrapper and her
abigail was dressing her hair when Georgina entered the suite
in response to her summons.

"Good morning, Georgina," she said brightly. "If you'll
just sit over there, Watkins will be finished with my hair in a
moment and I'll join you."

There was no question in Georgina's mind that Lady
Leicester had received a full report of her attempt to leave the
house alone, and it was also most likely that Mrs. Robinson
had spoken with her. Lord Meredith would be very angry!

The door closed behind the abigail and Lady Leicester took
a seat across from her. Georgina carefully studied the pattern
in the luxurious pale blue carpet.

"Mrs. Robinson has been governess and companion to a
number of young ladies of the best families. She is extremely

well educated for a female, but I chose her to be your companion, not because of that, but because she is a gentlewoman with good breeding, and is also a very nice person." Lady Leicester paused. "Please look at me, Georgina."

Raising her head defiantly, Georgina looked into the lovely green eyes and saw in them an understanding she had not expected.

"I don't want a watchdog. Lord Meredith didn't tell me he was going to send me back to England with a jailer," Georgina protested, but some of the defiance was gone. "I'm accustomed to taking care of myself," she explained a little lamely.

Lady Leicester shook her head regretfully. "As a lady you cannot go abroad in this city, or in most others, without a companion or chaperon. If you refuse her companionship, you will have to have a maid accompany you—or not go out at all."

Lady Leicester rose and held out a hand to Georgina. "I must finish dressing now, but . . ."

Taking the hand that was offered to her, Georgina apologized. "I'm sorry, my lady. I really didn't mean to cause you trouble, and I promised Lord Meredith that I wouldn't. I will try to accept Mrs. Robinson's companionship for the period it is necessary."

Lady Leicester had calls to make after luncheon, and suggested the two ladies might want to go for a walk in the park. Georgina agreed, and when they returned and she was alone once more, she had to admit it had been most enjoyable with a pleasant companion who knew the names of some of the strange trees and flowers and could point out the different landmarks.

6

"Your grandmother should be shot!" Lady Leicester declared emphatically. "The only thing it seems she taught you is excellent table manners."

"That was just because she couldn't permit only William to dine with her, and not me. I missed the end of a great many meals before I became so proficient, I can assure you, my lady. And had she but known that Cook used to send up my sweet course to the nursery, she'd have dismissed her on the spot." Georgina frowned as she recalled the many meals when both she and William had made mistakes at table, but she had been the only one ordered to leave.

"Your curtsy is now very good, thanks to your friend, but you really must practice a more dainty walk, and to sit and rise more slowly. Let me see if I can demonstrate what you're doing."

Lady Leicester moved gracefully to the door, turned around, and then marched across the room with swift, long strides and flopped into the nearest chair. "Now, you do it correctly, Robbie, while Georgina keeps pace with you."

Lady Leicester had taken a liking to the ward that her friend Lord Meredith had unceremoniously foisted upon her. He had made no mention in advance that she was anything but a young English lady stranded in Portugal, and when she saw him again she intended to make him pay dearly for the omission. True, he had not asked her to do anything more than give the chit food and shelter and see that she had suitable clothes, but how could she not try to teach her some of the social graces regarded as *de rigueur* in the society to which she had been born?

The young lady in question was wearing a new gown, one of the garments the dressmaker had caused her seamstresses to work night and day to finish. It was quite simply styled, with a high waist to show off the small breasts Georgina had once been so anxious to conceal, and the soft shade of pale blue looked well with her coppery curls. It was trimmed with lace at the throat, and a large-brimmed blue hat, plus gloves, reticule, and parasol in deep apricot had also been sent.

"Bravo!"

Georgina's last attempt had been perfect enough to draw applause from her hostess, and she heaved a weary sigh. "It is most kind of you to try so hard to turn me into a lady, but I really don't think Grandmama will appreciate it. And these lovely clothes will be wasted in the Yorkshire countryside."

"Nonsense, Georgina! Proper training is never wasted, and I rather think your guardian will now have a great deal more to say about your way of life than he has in the past. The next time you enter the room, I want you to acknowledge me with an inclination of your head, as though you were passing me on the street."

When Georgina had learned to do this both graciously and in a cold enough manner to deliver a deliberate snub to some too-forward admirer, she was allowed to pour tea for her companion and Lady Leicester. A great deal had been accomplished in just a few days, due as much to the inclement weather that had kept them indoors as to Georgina's lack of suitable attire.

Tomorrow, however, Lady Leicester had put her carriage at their disposal and Mrs. Robinson was to take her to Belém to see some of the very fine architecture and sculpture that had been commissioned and built when Portugal was in her glory. It was then that the huge profits from the sale of the first spices from India had made Lisbon the richest and most beautiful city in Europe.

"You're prodigious quiet of a sudden, William." Lord Meredith glanced at his young cousin, riding by his side up

the private road leading to the home of Lady Leicester.
"You'd best not tire now, for it would be gross folly to nod
off on your return journey."

"I'm all right, sir. I was just w-wondering how Georgie
is." William grinned. "No matter how she l-looks, she'll still
be a m-madcap at heart."

"Of that I am certain," his cousin agreed dryly. "I've no
doubt Lady Leicester will still be asleep, but I wish to
converse with the companion she hired, to assure myself of
her suitability, while you and your sibling have some time to
yourselves."

They rode to the stables and Lord Meredith gave instructions concerning their mounts, then strolled around to the
front door.

"We'll no doubt cause some commotion at this unconscio-
nable hour," he said with a chuckle. "When a mistress stays
abed till noon, servants are apt to get lazy also." He gave the
doorbell a resounding clang.

While the two men waited to be admitted, Georgina was
putting the finishing touches to her toilette and looking forward to their outing, for Robbie was everything Lady Leicester
had said of her, and as a guide, she had the gift of making
history come to life. They were to meet in the dining room in
just a few minutes so as to get an early start, and Georgina
was almost ready when there was a scratch on her door and a
maid entered.

"Mr. Darley said to tell you there's two gentlemen below
askin' for you, m'lady. He put them in the drawing room,"
the maid said, trying hard to hide her curiosity as her mistress's face broke into a happy smile.

"Did Darley give you their names?" Georgina asked.

"I think it was Meredy, m'lady." The maid bobbed and left
the room, while Georgina started to race for the stairs, hoping
her brother would be the other man. At the top, she made
herself pause, then saw Robbie just behind her and proceeded
more decorously down to where a footman waited to open the
drawing-room door.

When she saw William, looking somewhat older, leaner,

and even more handsome than he had when they left England, she flew into his arms. He hugged her hard, then pushed her away to take a good look.

"Georgie, it can't be you! You've grown into a beautiful young lady in less than a week. I'll be p-proud to take you for a ride in the park this afternoon, if you're free."

She looked hesitantly at Lord Meredith, who, though engaged in conversation with Mrs. Robinson, was keeping a careful watch on the twins. She held out little hope that he had not observed her highly undignified entrance.

Noting the question in her eyes Lord Meredith allowed a glimmer of a smile to hover around his lips as he quizzed her, "That really depends on what kind of report I receive from Lady Leicester. Have you been behaving yourself?"

With a great show of indignation that he should treat her like a little girl, she turned back to her brother, but Lord Meredith's quiet, lazy drawl held a note of authority she dared not ignore.

"Come here, Georgina. Let me look at you."

With all her newly acquired grace and poise, she walked toward him and curtsied demurely. Before she raised her head, she managed to control a mischievous smile that threatened to spoil everything, but was betrayed by the sparkle in her eyes.

"I have to agree with William: the improvement is quite remarkable in so short a time—but will it last?" he teased.

"Of course it will last, you impossible man!"

All eyes turned to the door, where Lady Leicester had quietly appeared, shocking both servants and guests alike by rising at so early an hour.

"Georgina is gently bred," she continued, "but has been brought up in the most appalling way by that unpleasant grandmother. And if that lady's attitude toward Georgina does not mend, I for one will have much to say about it."

Lord Meredith, who had started forward, held out his arms and asked with playful reproach, "Caroline, my dear, is that any way to welcome an old friend?"

"Matthew, darling," she responded warmly as she tripped daintily across the room and placed both her hands in his.

He raised each in turn to his lips, bowing over them, then twitted her softly, "I am deeply conscious of the honor you do us in receiving us at this hour, my dear, and am indeed most grateful."

"How long can you stay? I will have rooms prepared for you—"

He held up one finger. "I can visit for a few days, but William must depart this evening, I'm afraid. I predicted he would be anxious for his sister, and arranged that he meet me on the outskirts of the city. As I told you the other night, I have duties here which may require as much as a sennight, if you can bear my company for so long. How has my ward been behaving?"

"She is delightful company, quite naive, and refreshing enough to make me regret my years." She glanced across the room to where Georgina and William were in deep conversation. "For twins, they are remarkably unalike. I am aware of her indiscretions. I ferreted it out of her the first day, and much admire her courage."

"So she told you, did she?" he said with a sigh of exasperation. "There am I doing my utmost to preserve her reputation, and she blurts it all out to the first person she meets. I'll give her a piece of my mind later."

Lady Leicester put warning fingers to his lips. "You'd best not, or I won't help you again. She had no wish to tell me anything, but I assured her of your approval so long as it went no further. I swear that she'll reveal it to no one else."

He pressed her fingers against his lips before releasing her hand. "Very well, you can stop threatening me. Come, let me make William known to you and then I think we might safely allow them to escape for the rest of the day. She would protect him with her life, so he needs no chaperon." He grinned down at her boyishly. "I had hoped we might spend a few hours together, my love. Is it possible that you could change your plans?"

"For you, darling, anything is possible," she promised as he slipped an arm around her still-slender waist and escorted her to where William and Georgina were engaged in lively conversation.

That Lady Leicester meant what she said, there was no question. She had known Lord Meredith for a couple of years now, and had at first believed the relationship might develop into something more permanent. However, although he was always very good to her when they were together, something indefinable told her there was little chance he would marry again for some years, and if he decided to do so in order to beget an heir, he would not choose someone as worldly as she.

Nevertheless, knowing she was one of very few women he allowed to be even this close to him, she was happy to take what she could, and be free to enjoy the company of others without jealousy on his part. She was no courtesan, and guarded her reputation most carefully, her objective being to find another wealthy husband.

While listening eagerly to her brother, Georgina had been quietly observing her guardian's behavior toward Lady Leicester. She could not actually hear what they were saying, but did not miss the familiar way he looked at her. She wondered if Lady Leicester was in love with him, though secretly hoping that it might not be so.

His hostess completely charmed William, then guided them all into the dining room, where breakfast awaited them. She explained the plans just discussed.

Georgina was delighted she could have William to herself for the whole day. She had already tried on her new green riding habit, and though she deplored the need to ride side-saddle, she was anxious to show herself to best advantage.

"Do you think we might ride, William?" she asked him. "I haven't exercised Starlight since I arrived here, and I would so much enjoy it."

Lord Meredith appeared about to choke, and William looked at him and gave a helpless shrug.

"What did I say?" Georgina asked. "I know people ride in the park here, for Robbie and I saw them when we took a walk one day."

Her cousin cleared his throat. "It probably didn't occur to you, Georgina, that he has been in the saddle for almost eight hours, has the prospect of another eight hours' ride ahead of him before he gets back to camp, and—''

"It's all right, sir," William interrupted. "I really don't mind, if that's what Georgie would like."

With a weak smile and a shake of her head, Georgina said regretfully, "You're right, my lord, as always. So long as we're together for a while, I don't care what we do. Truly I don't, William." She gave him a sheepish grin and confessed, "It was just that I have acquired my very first all-new riding habit and wanted you to see how splendid I look in it."

"The green velvet?" Lady Leicester asked. "One of those garments of which you were so disdainful?"

"Yes," Georgina admitted with a sigh, "and it's quite gorgeous."

"Then, as you appear to have finished breakfast, I suggest you leave us now and put it on. I'll send Watkins to help you, and then we can all see it before you change into a gown suitable for driving," Lady Leicester proposed indulgently.

As Georgina hurried out of the room, Lady Leicester turned to Lord Meredith. "She seemed totally uninterested when she was forced to stand for hours being fitted for a new wardrobe." She threw up her hands and laughed softly.

William became very serious, however. "If you'd s-seen the only garments she possessed at Broadacres, you w-would understand, my lady. She v-virtually ran around in rags, and I now feel excessively g-guilty for doing n-nothing to improve her situation."

"That's in the past, William, and best forgotten," his guardian said brusquely. "But in a much more serious vein, I must inquire how sizable a wardrobe you have procured, my love. From the length of time it took to fit, it would seem I may be receiving a considerably larger bill than I anticipated."

Lady Leicester pretended to ignore him until he gave a playful tug on one of her auburn curls.

"Ouch! Really, my lord!" The severe set-down she tried to give him was spoiled as he turned away and pretended to admire a figurine on a side table. "The bill will actually be a mere fraction of what it would cost you for the same garments, same materials, and vastly inferior workmanship in London.''

Before he could comment further, Georgina swept into the room, looking enchanting in the emerald-green velvet habit trimmed with black braid, with which she wore a plumed black beaver hat.

''If this is an example, I must admit it to be money well spent,'' Lord Meredith murmured softly to Lady Leicester. ''She'll turn every head in that habit, and I can personally vouch for her exceptionally fine riding ability.''

There was a round of applause and Georgina blushed prettily, then left to change once more into something more suitable for her day with her brother.

''We must be in our cousin's good graces for him to have permitted this visit,'' Georgina remarked as William tooled the small carriage along the quiet streets leading to the park. ''Was he very angry with you?''

''N-not at all.'' William grinned. ''He just l-left orders for me to do five d-days supervising field kitchen and l-latrine workers. According to authorities on the s-subject, and there are m-many, I did an outstanding job. It's l-lucky that Isabella found a good laundress or you'd not want to sit so close.''

''Oh, William, how awful!'' Georgina pulled a face but had to laugh. ''What's the laundress like? Will she continue to work for you?''

''Yes, she's a w-widow with a couple of youngsters, and she needs the m-money.''

''Is she Spanish or Portuguese?'' Georgina was curious.

''English,'' William said grimly. ''Her husband was k-killed six months since and she has n-nowhere to go and no m-money.''

''The poor woman. Won't the army send her back to England?'' She was immediately concerned.

''Now, Georgina, you know they won't, and there'd be n-nothing for her back home if they did.'' He placed his free hand on her knee comfortingly, for she always became upset if she couldn't help people in need.

''I suppose we're the lucky ones, despite Grandmama,

aren't we?'' she asked with a sigh. "If only we could do something for her."

"You c-can't help everyone, Georgina, but I'll see they don't go without food," he assured her, then said, "S-since you left, I've been practicing m-marksmanship in the evenings with some of the other officers. The first n-night I came in twentieth, but last night I came in second."

"That's wonderful, William. You'll be first next time, just you see," she said, then remembered something. "You took your pistols, but you wouldn't let me take mine," she accused.

"I should think n-not. If you had them, you'd probably have d-drawn old Barker's cork, and that would have been a f-fine mess. How do you g-get along with Lady Leicester? She's the most beautiful-looking lady I've ever seen."

Georgina had to smile, for William had actually seen few real ladies as yet. "She's as nice as she's lovely. And she treats me like a slightly younger sister most of the time. I think she's in love with our cousin."

"All the women are smitten with him. No matter what age, they all ogle him, but he p-pays little heed."

"Well, he's certainly paying attention to Lady Leicester," Georgina said tartly. "I wonder what they're doing this afternoon?"

William frowned at her, then changed the subject and they spent the rest of the afternoon talking about Isabella and the other friends they had made.

The five people who met in the drawing room for a glass of sherry before dinner were somewhat subdued. William had a long ride before him, and brother and sister were in low spirits because of the imminent parting.

As they went in to dinner, Georgina was alone with her guardian for a moment and took the opportunity to ask for a private word with him before they retired for the night.

"I was about to make the same request, my dear. I'll see you in the library directly after dinner," he promised.

She could not help feeling a little shiver of apprehension. Lady Leicester must have told him how rude she had been initially about Robbie.

With a sinking feeling she excused herself when tea was brought for the ladies, and made her way to the library, where Lord Meredith was waiting.

"Why such a Friday face?" he asked with eyebrows raised. "I only wanted to emphasize again that I expect your conduct from here on to be above reproach."

Georgina looked at him coldly. "I don't believe I can do any better, my lord. Apart from that first day, Lady Leicester seems most pleased with my behavior."

He chuckled. "You should have kept quiet, my dear. That first day must not have been as bad as you feared, for Lady Leicester said nothing about it, and had only praise for you." He smiled at her and said apologetically, "I was being heavy-handed with you again, I know, but I'm unused to dealing with young wards."

Georgina's mouth twitched and her eyes lit with mischief. "Quite so, my lord," she agreed.

"I know you've tried hard, and I should have commended you for it," he continued amiably. "As soon as passage is available, I will have a carriage waiting at Dover to transport you and Mrs. Robinson to my home near Maidstone. I'm arranging for you to stay with my mother for a few days before undertaking the journey north. Keep up your good behavior when you reach England, and Mother will be enchanted with you."

Georgina was delighted, as she would have been with any arrangement that might delay her return to her grandmother.

"I'll behave like an angel, my lord, I promise," she assured him; then, unconsciously chewing on her top lip, she asked, "How am I to get to Broadacres?"

"By the same carriage, of course. Now, what was it you wanted to talk to me about?"

"I asked to see you, my lord, because I wanted to say how sorry I am for everything. I realize now that what I did was very foolish, and I've thought a lot about what you said to me."

He looked at her big gray-green eyes and earnest face and wanted very much to make her feel a little better.

"That was very well done, Georgina. I was somewhat

harsh with you, but I was trying to make you do just what you did—think it over for yourself.'' He felt a ridiculous impulse to run his fingers through her chestnut curls, and forced himself to resist it. ''I'm sure you'd like to know how proud I am of William. I assigned him to five days of thoroughly distasteful duty, and he took it without the slightest complaint and, I understand, performed admirably. He is becoming an excellent officer.''

Her happiness at such praise for William seemed to light her face from within, showing a glimpse of the real, lasting beauty beneath her youthful prettiness.

''Why don't we make a fresh start—forget the past and the things we both said in anger. I will be your guardian until you reach the age of twenty-five or until you marry with my permission. I'll also be your friend, someone you can turn to for help or advice at any time. Is that understood?'' He held out his hand.

''Yes,'' she breathed, and placed her hand in his. Clasping it firmly, he raised it, and once again she felt the velvety softness of his lips against her skin.

They joined the others in the drawing room, and too soon afterward, William had to depart.

Georgina said all the right things, hugged William and told him to take care, but through it all she felt as though she was in a dream. She had been that way ever since Lord Meredith had taken her hand in his, and thrilling sensations had passed through her arm again and warmed her deep inside as his lips had pressed against her skin. He had said he would be her friend, and since then she had experienced a feeling of security she had never known. Now, someone besides William cared what happened to her. It was wonderful!

7

William's visit had been a huge success. Georgina had been worrying about him ever since she arrived in Lisbon. While living in the house behind the fortifications, he had seemed to change, to grow away from her as he became engrossed, for the first time, in a world she could not enter—a man's world.

Now, however, she was changing also, in part because of her cousin's influence, his stern words having affected her more deeply than she realized, because of both the obvious and the subtle training she was receiving at the hands of Lady Leicester and Robbie. Living with gentlewomen to whom good manners, graciousness, and courtesy were a natural way of life, she had begun not only to behave as young ladies of her age are expected to but also to look more like them. Watkins' nightly ministrations were showing some results in the lightening of her skin color, but it would take considerable time before she was as palely lovely as Lady Leicester.

She was thinking of the events of the day before, and hoping William had arrived back safely as she finished her breakfast and sat sipping the fragrant coffee. When the door opened, she turned to bid Robbie a good morning, and was surprised to see that it was Lord Meredith. Unsure of what was proper, she rose and made her curtsy. He held her hand a little longer than usual, his admiring eyes taking in the attractive sprigged-muslin gown and the way her hair seemed to have grown in just a week. She flushed becomingly, embarrassed at his stare.

"I'm pleased to find Lady Leicester has not convinced you

of the efficacy of staying abed until noon," he remarked. "Unless you have other plans, I'll join you in some breakfast, and perhaps, when you're finished, you might like to change your pretty gown for that green habit you showed us, and we'll take a ride in the park."

From the delighted expression on Georgina's face there could be little doubt as to how she felt about his suggestion. Accustomed as he was to young ladies dropping their affectation of boredom when he appeared, he was unusually pleased to see his young cousin become so excited at the prospect of riding with him, and his own anticipation increased in response.

When she rapidly gulped down the rest of her breakfast and asked to be excused, he gave her a tolerant grin. "Rarely has an invitation of mine caused so much excitement. I am indeed most flattered. Run along, my dear, you're excused, and I'll give you fifteen minutes to change and be back here."

She sprang to her feet, then remembered Lady Leicester's instructions and allowed the footman to move her chair. "I'm very fond of riding, my lord, and I get so little opportunity that I jump at every chance," she told him candidly.

A chuckle rumbled from deep in his chest. "I am chagrined! And I thought it was the prospect of spending time with me that made you so eager!" He held up a warning hand. "Don't say any more or you're bound to worsen the insult and make me wonder what Lady Leicester is teaching you. Hurry, you now have only twelve minutes."

She almost ran from the room, and was pleased to find a maid in her chamber, who assisted her in making a rapid change, and even helped tidy her curls before setting the beaver hat atop them.

When she returned to the dining room, Robbie had joined Lord Meredith and they were making polite conversation.

He rose at once, his eyes showing a warmth and admiration at her quite splendid appearance, and he took her arm as they walked together to the stables where Lady Leicester's coach and cattle were housed.

Starlight was glad to see her and, once mounted, they proceeded at a quiet pace through the city streets until they reached a pleasant park, deserted except for a couple of riders who were just leaving.

Lord Meredith had been watching her out of the corner of his eye. "I don't know who is the more anxious for a gallop, you or Starlight," he remarked. "You see that oak yonder? Off you go, and I'll pass you halfway," he boasted. With a delighted grin, she was away, but he made no attempt to catch up, staying a little behind and never taking his eyes off the picture horse and rider made as they sped as one over the uneven turf.

"I thought you were going to race me, my lord," she said reproachfully as he drew alongside her once more.

He shook his head. "I'm afraid I'm guilty of deliberate deception. I wanted to see you gallop all-out, so I'd know what instructions to give my stables. I believe you're capable of handling all except my stallion, Charger."

He did not miss the mischievous glint in her eyes, and his brows raised warningly, though his smile remained. "You cannot realize what a concession I'm making, young lady, until you see my stables. My nieces are not permitted to ride any number of my horses. If I should, by chance, hear you have cajoled some young stableboy into saddling Charger for you, I can assure you you'll be very sore and very sorry. Do I make myself clear?"

She gave him a scornful glance, with head high, but as he held her rein and continued to eye her with a grim smile, she had no choice but to give in. "Yes, my lord, perfectly clear," she intoned quietly, ashamed of the slight tremor in her voice. "But you didn't need to threaten me. As long as I have Starlight, I don't need any of your precious horses!"

She was about to move on, but he placed a hand over hers, and her breath caught in her throat at his touch.

"I'm not a bully, Georgina, and I would not spoil your enjoyment. I don't want you to get injured, that's all," he told her with gentle understanding. "I have rarely seen a woman ride so well, yet I have a feeling you ride even better astride."

Her cheeks were already flushed from the exertion, else they might have shown how near the mark he was.

"I believe I saw you once, though I thought it was a skinny youth at the time. You wore breeches when we went north to join Wellington, didn't you?" She nodded, and he grinned broadly. "You don't know how close you came to serving in the regiment. Few of my men could ride so well at that time."

She laughed delightedly, her anger forgotten. "I fear you would have known very soon that I was not what I seemed, sir. You also saw me once before that, on the docks in London. I was not long in disguise, for Isabella guessed immediately and persuaded me I would be quickly found out. She was a very good friend to me."

He nodded in agreement. "She still is, as a matter of fact. You were fortunate to fall in with someone like her. She came to see me, you know, to assure me of your virginal innocence. You could very easily have been raped by that brute."

"I know. It was really somewhat of a relief when I was found out, for once I'd got into the pretense, I could see no way out of it," Georgina explained.

"There was a way," he reminded her. "I gave you a good opportunity when I saw you in the Gypsy encampment. I told you to come to me if you needed help, if you recall."

Georgina's cheeks grew pink at the recollection. "I'm afraid Isabella misconstrued that offer. She thought you were interested in me as a woman."

He was silent for a moment. "She might have been right. I don't know now what instinct made me, for the first time out here, suggest you come see me. I know I found you very attractive even in Gypsy garb."

A rush of feeling made Georgina feel shy and then strangely bold. "And then I stopped being attractive when you found I was your ward, and I became a child in your eyes," she challenged.

He reached a hand for her rein once more and drew both horses to a halt. "If you were ever a child in my eyes, my dear, you're certainly not now. I have a responsibility toward you, however, which I take very seriously." There was a strangely gentle expression on his face.

"I am twenty, practically on the shelf by London standards," she said primly.

He laughed, looking instantly younger. "So you are. I'll try to give you the respect your venerable age demands in future, and you have my permission to glare at me whenever I forget. How's that?"

Georgina smiled, and nodded. She really didn't care, so long as he was pleased with her.

"I've been trying to recall our earlier meeting. Were you the clumsy lad who ran into Davis' cart?" Lord Meredith suddenly asked. She nodded once more, trying hard not to laugh. "What a lot of problems I might have saved us both had I only paid you more attention!"

They rode in comfortable silence for some time; then Lord Meredith commented, "You seem very pensive, or are you just enjoying being on horseback again? I assume Mrs. Robinson does not care for riding, but you could always go out with a groom in attendance."

She was enjoying both being on horseback again and riding with him, but could hardly tell him so. But from the nod and grateful smile she gave him, he could have guessed.

They returned to the house, where Robbie was waiting to take Georgina on a small excursion, and she did not see him alone again until the following morning at breakfast, when he was dressed for riding once more.

"I hope you'll join me again, my dear, if only to exercise Starlight," he remarked.

This time it took her less than five minutes to change, as she had left a riding habit out, hoping for a repeat invitation.

They raced to the same spot as his challenge of yesterday, and he won, but only by half a head. "If I'd been astride instead of on this wretched sidesaddle, I'd have beaten you easily," she bragged.

They settled into an easy trot, and Lord Meredith brought up the subject of Broadacres. "I still cannot understand your grandmother's attitude toward you, Georgina, nor why she did not like your lovely mother. Have you any idea from what it stemmed?"

She thought for a moment. "I know I shouldn't have listened to gossip of servants, but I once overheard Mrs. Johnson say that Grandmama expected my father to marry Baron Andover's daughter," she informed him with a slight shrug.

"Who is he?" he asked. "I don't recall anyone by that name."

"He was our neighbor, and Grandmama apparently had in mind acquiring his property, which marches with ours to the east. I believe the family rarely spent time in London." She suddenly remembered the little scene she had witnessed with her grandmother and Smithers. It had completely slipped her mind, with all the excitement of leaving Broadacres, and she had forgotten to mention it to William.

"I'd give much to know your thoughts at this moment. Your expressive face tells me you recall something you should have done." He was still watching her closely. "And now you are wondering whether to tell me or not. If it concerns Broadacres, I am very interested, and am eminently trustworthy with secrets."

The decision to tell him was not a difficult one. "I meant to talk to William about it, and forgot. It's probably nothing, but just before we left, I was looking out of the old nursery window one morning at an hour when Grandmama is rarely out of her bedchamber, when I suddenly saw her going down the kitchen garden toward the potting shed. She looked stealthy and held a white paper in her hand."

"What does an old lady do to look stealthy?" he asked with some amusement.

"She kept looking around to see if anyone were watching her, and stepped behind a bush when one of the gardeners came near," Georgina snapped. "Please forget about it. I shouldn't have told you."

They had slowed to a walk as they talked, but now she made to urge Starlight into a trot. Lord Meredith put out a hand to stop her. "You can't mean to tell me just this much and no more, surely?" he asked with a beguiling smile. "Pray continue."

"I told you there was probably nothing to it," she warned,

secretly pleased that he was interested. "Anyway, she went into the potting shed, then Smithers went in also, and a few minutes later he came out with the paper in his hand, and even so far away, I could tell he was mocking her, making an exaggerated bow toward the door, and smirking. When he'd gone, she came out and crept into the house again."

He frowned, serious now. "Just who is Smithers?"

"He used to be our gamekeeper until five years ago, when he retired and went to live in Knaresborough."

"He's an old man, then?" her cousin asked. "A contemporary of the dowager's?"

"No, not at all." Georgina was surprised he would make that assumption. "He was younger than my papa, for I can recall Papa telling us of fishing excursions he took Smithers on when he was a boy."

Lord Meredith made no comment, but his dark brows were raised in question.

"Let me think. There was something else I noticed, but I can't quite remember." She pondered for a moment, then said, "It was his jacket. I remember thinking how expensively cut it was, very like the ones William gets from Berkeley, the very best tailor in Harrogate. Someone must have left him some money, for his house in Knaresborough is quite large, and he took our parlormaid, Jennie, in as housekeeper when Grandmama put her off."

"Could the paper have been an envelope, do you think?"

Georgina was frank. "I was too far away to see what it was Grandmama was clutching, but it could have been an envelope, of course."

They rode for about an hour in all, then returned the horses to the stables. As they walked back to the house, Lord Meredith returned to the subject of the gamekeeper. "About that little incident—leave it with me. When I'm back in England next, I'll take a look around Broadacres, as I should have done long ago, to protect William's interests. Meantime, I'll have someone check out your Mr. Smithers." He stopped, placing a hand on her arm so that she turned toward him, frowning slightly. "I don't want you to worry about Broadacres," he said softly, smoothing out her frown by stroking his finger across it, and thinking, as he did, how beautifully soft her skin now was. "Things will be very different when you return this time, you'll see."

Lady Leicester was already risen, looking most elegant in a sophisticated morning gown, and she came into the hall to meet them, slipping an arm through Lord Meredith's in a most familiar way.

Georgina went quickly to her bedchamber to change once more into a gown, but did not hasten to join her hostess and guardian. Her head was filled with too many conflicting emotions for her to enjoy seeing the two of them together on such obviously intimate terms. For a moment she had believed what he said about Broadacres, but she knew the conditions there better than he, and could see no way they might change.

"Can I prevail upon you ladies to join me in a drive around the city this afternoon?" an urbane Lord Meredith suggested as they nibbled on marzipan sweets shaped like exotic fruits.

Mrs. Robinson murmured her regrets, as she had a commitment, but Lady Leicester smiled with delight. "What a lovely idea, Matthew. I'll order the carriage right away." She reached for the little bell beside her place.

Taking a sip of the rich coffee, Lord Meredith smiled at Georgina, his eyebrows raised as he saw her shake her head. "Surely you don't mean to disappoint me, my dear?" he murmured, his laughing eyes teasing her out of the refusal she had intended.

"It will be a pleasure indeed, my lord," she said softly, for she had wanted to spend the afternoon in his company, but had felt he might prefer to be alone with Lady Leicester.

There was ample time for the ladies to collect their reticules and parasols before the barouche, with its top down, pulled up in front of the house. The liveried coachman remained in his seat to quiet the fresh horses, while Lord Meredith handed the two ladies into one seat, and he took the one facing them for himself.

"This is the fashionable part of the park, Georgina," Lord Meredith explained as they entered the gate they had used that morning, but proceeded in a different direction. "The path you and I took is used by people who wish to ride, whereas this way the people come to see and be seen, the same as they do in London, but on a much smaller scale, of course."

"We appear to be attracting considerable attention, my lord," Georgina remarked with pleasure as Lady Leicester inclined her lovely head first to one side and then the other, and riders and carriages appeared to be clustered around them like bees around a honey pot.

"I should think so. Lady Leicester has very many acquaintances in Lisbon, and much is made of her when she takes the air," he said as he and that lady exchanged amused glances, "but, for the first time, they are seeing another lovely lady and they are all coming to look at her, hoping we will stop and make introductions, which of course we will not. Henceforth you will be known as the mystery lady."

"How wonderful!" Georgina was enjoying herself. "It's such fun. Can we do it again?"

"Not on this visit, my dear, for I fear I have to leave tomorrow at crack of dawn. And Lady Leicester will be busy receiving calls from half the town. They will, of course, be disappointed to learn that her guest is indisposed." He instructed the coachman to leave the park and return to the house by way of a series of pretty tree-lined streets.

"I have a dinner engagement which may extend far beyond your bedtimes, so I'll say my farewells now. I hope to have some news of a passage for you, Georgina, by the time I see you again."

He handed them out of the carriage, then excused himself, as he had detailed instructions to give regarding a coach and a mount for later. Georgina's spirits were low as she entered the house, but she consoled herself with the thought that at least he'd not told her to behave herself again.

Lady Leicester was also saddened by his departure and the inevitable loss she would feel when Georgina sailed. She had grown very fond of her, for she had become much like a younger sister, and her youth and high spirits had enlivened the whole household.

The fact that the girl's presence enabled her to see Lord Meredith at least once more was an added benefit, and she would later be able to use the excuse of inquiring after Georgina as a means of keeping in touch with him. She had noticed an interesting change in the girl. She no longer spoke of Matthew coldly, and a light would come into her eyes when his name was mentioned. It seemed she had developed a *tendre* for her guardian, and though this could not, of course, be encouraged, it would make his dealings with her a little easier.

8

For once, the three ladies were dining together, Lady Leicester taking a much-needed night of rest at home.

"After Robbie, you are bound to be the most knowledgeable young lady in England as far as the history of Lisbon is concerned, Georgina," Lady Leicester remarked. "Where did you go today?"

"We were in a street that is supposed to be haunted by the ghost of a *fadista* who sang the *fado* as no one else ever has. What did you mean, Robbie, when you said she took her pleasures with *toreiros* and ruffians? What kind of pleasures?"

Georgina's innocent curiosity caused Mrs. Robinson's cheeks to turn quite pink, to Lady Leicester's considerable amusement.

Coming to the rescue, Lady Leicester said, "As I vaguely recall, she was supposedly loved by a nobleman, but he must have been too gentle for her, and she preferred the lovemaking of rougher, more common men."

"Then she was really just a whore," said a disappointed Georgina.

"I wonder if you're too old to have your mouth washed out with soap? That is a word nice young ladies do not know the meaning of, and if you ever use it in front of Lord Meredith, he'll box your ears," her hostess pronounced with mock severity.

At the mention of her guardian's name, it was Georgina's turn to flush. "I wonder when he'll come to see us again," she said. "I'm enjoying it so much here that I don't want him ever to find a suitable passage," she admitted.

Lady Leicester smiled sympathetically. "I had a note from

him this morning, saying he and William will be here within a few days, but he didn't say exactly when. I suppose he'll expect us to change all our plans once again when they arrive without warning.'' She did not miss the glow that lit Georgina's eyes, and hazarded a guess that it was not only in anticipation of seeing her brother.

She was correct in her prediction. Three days later, as they were about to go in to luncheon, there was a loud clanging of the doorbell and the two rather travel-weary soldiers were shown into the drawing room.

Lord Meredith greeted his hostess and then turned toward his ward.

Not since she had left Torres Vedras had Georgina seen him in campaign dress uniform, a scarlet coat, with blue facings and gold lace, light buff breeches, black boots, and a light cavalry saber at his hip. In one white-gloved hand he held the black bicorn hat. She couldn't stop looking, for his handsome sun-bronzed face and the extra trappings of his rank put even William a little in the shade.

He was staring back at her, as if seeing her for the first time, and she suddenly remembered her manners and dropped him a curtsy. He held her hand longer than usual, then slowly raised it to his lips, and once again she felt a tingling sensation deep inside as the warmth of his lips spread through her body. Silently she vowed not to wash her hand for the rest of the day.

''You grow more lovely every time I see you, my dear,'' he murmured, his eyes warm with admiration. ''It was criminal to hide all that beauty in Gypsy clothes.''

''Thank you, my lord,'' was all a suddenly tongue-tied Georgina could say; then Lady Leicester was at her side, with William in tow, and he was swinging her around in a big brotherly hug.

In the meantime, a slightly jealous Lady Leicester slipped her arm through that of Lord Meredith and, smiling charmingly, suggested, ''Why don't we leave the children alone for a few minutes and take a stroll in the garden, darling? We were about to go into luncheon when you arrived, but must now give the chef time to prepare a few extra dishes.''

While William greeted Robbie, Georgina's mind went back to the way her cousin had looked at her and kissed her hand.

She was still smiling to herself when Darley announced that luncheon was served, and they joined the others in the dining room. She looked at Lord Meredith as William seated her, and the smile disappeared from her face at his cool glance.

"I was hoping it would be some time before safe passage was available, Georgina, but his lordship tells me . . ." Lady Leicester turned to give Lord Meredith an apologetic smile and a murmured, "I know you don't mind, darling, do you?" Without waiting for his assent, she addressed Georgina once more. "Lord Meredith tells me that you will sail within a sennight."

There was a startled gasp and Georgina looked at her cousin accusingly. "Thank you for telling me, my lord," she said, then looked down at her plate, trying not to let him see the hurt tears that came to her eyes.

Lord Meredith's mouth set in a grim line, and he frowned briefly at Lady Leicester. "I will discuss the details with you, Georgina, when you and William return from the walk he tells me you have planned."

"Why don't you just tell Lady Leicester, and she can pass it along after you leave," Georgina snapped.

Her cousin's head rose sharply. "Georgina . . ." he angrily began, but she had already seen Lady Leicester's hurt look.

"I'm sorry, my lady," Georgina said quickly. "It's just that I've been so happy here, I didn't want to leave so soon."

Lady Leicester accepted the apology graciously. "I know, my dear. I feel the same way, and was only telling your guardian so just a few minutes ago. It has been like having a little sister staying with me."

Although everyone, with the possible exception of Lord Meredith, seemed to forget her bad temper, Georgina was still relieved when luncheon was over.

Before they excused themselves for the afternoon, he joined the twins for a moment. "I took the opportunity, some time ago, to include a letter to your grandmother with a special courier going to the north of England. I informed her of your whereabouts and said you would be returning very shortly," he told Georgina. "The courier picked up her reply the following day, on his way back, and though I was surprised by it, I am sure you will not be."

"Did she suggest you put me in the line of fire?" she asked sarcastically. "Or perhaps she recommended that you give me to one of the peasants as a present?"

"No, but that was possibly her intent, and there have been times when I might have agreed with her," he replied, his mouth tightening. "What she did say was that I should not bother to send you back, as she is washing her hands of you completely."

Georgina had expected some such response, but William, to her surprise, was furious.

"Now she's g-going too far!" he said angrily. "She's n-never had any normal feelings for Georgina, my lord, and l-little love for me except as a m-means of returning the estate to its f-former glory. She's not g-going to g-get away with this, as it's n-not for her to say whether Georgina l-lives there or not."

"I'm sure she is aware of that, William," his guardian assured him, "and I have no doubt her letter was written in haste and was thought better of after the courier left. However, I have decided it would be to your sister's advantage to avoid the north of England for the time being. I am now arranging for Georgina to stay with my mother indefinitely instead of the few days I had planned."

William and Georgina left the house shortly after that, and following directions Robbie had given them, found a pretty little park with a path along the river.

"You will be careful, William, won't you? I do wish our cousin had given you a Season in London instead of a place in his regiment, but perhaps everything will turn out for the best. I'm going to miss you so much, little brother," she said sadly.

"Little indeed! J-just because you were b-born first does not give you that privilege, Georgie," he growled, pretending to be angry. "J-just you behave yourself when you're w-with our cousin's family, and don't let me down."

"Don't you start threatening me, William. Dear Cousin Matthew will do that soon enough, I'm sure. After what he just said, I don't want to go there, either, but I suppose it will be better than Broadacres." Georgina could not keep the hurt out of her voice, and William took her hand and gave it an understanding squeeze.

They returned to the house in the late afternoon, and while Lady Leicester and Mrs. Robinson served tea to William in the drawing room, Lord Meredith had a tray sent into the study, where he took Georgina to apprise her of the arrangements he had made for her return to England.

"There's a small yacht leaving from Setúbal, a port some thirty miles to the south of here. She will fly the Union Jack and the Portuguese flag," he told her. "I have booked passage for you and Mrs. Robinson. Regrettably, you cannot journey directly there, but must take a coach to the ferry which crosses the Tagus, then another coach will await you on the other side."

"It sounds rather complicated, but I suppose it is the best arrangement you could make." Reluctant to leave at all, Georgina could not like any travel arrangement.

"Your supposition is correct, Georgina. This happens to be the safest crossing I have been able to arrange, and only by bringing to bear considerable influence was it possible at all. However, you ladies will not be alone. My batman, Davis, will escort you from door to door, and there will be two outriders to—"

"Won't it make it very obvious, having a soldier accompany us?" Georgina interrupted, receiving a glare as her reward.

"Davis will be out of uniform, and the outriders will be Portuguese, which should attract little attention," he assured her. "And now, let me go over, once again, what you are to do between here and when you reach Settle House. You will conduct yourself like a lady, as I know you can, and obey Mrs. Robinson implicitly, and she in turn will be guided by Davis. You are in their charge the whole of the way, and I want your promise that you will not give them any cause for worry.''

She could not understand why the teasing and the offer of friendship seemed now to have been forgotten, for she had not been present in the garden when Lady Leicester told him laughingly that she felt his ''little ward'' had developed a strong *tendre* for him, which, with his reputation, it would be most cruel to encourage. Nevertheless, Georgina gravely assured him she would not let him down.

After a subdued dinner, she said a tearful good-bye to William, a chaste farewell to her guardian as he made no offer of his hand this time, and the two men started back for Torres Vedras.

Four days later, with everything packed, Georgina and Robbie awaited the arrival of the batman, Davis. Lady Leicester's coach would take them as far as the ferry, and Georgina thanked her prettily for the loan of it, and also for allowing her to stay these many weeks.

''My dear, it was a delight to have you here, and I hope that we'll see each other again when I finally return to London.'' She pressed a white lace kerchief to her eyes as, to her own surprise, a tear rolled down her cheek. ''I hope that man knows how to take care of you,'' she sniffed daintily. ''It's such a long, worrisome drive before you reach Setúbal.''

Davis arrived and was finally satisfied all was in order, with Starlight tied securely behind the carriage, and they set out for the ferry that would take them across the mouth of the Tagus. As soon as she saw Davis, Georgina realized he was the sergeant who had come to the house to take her to Lord Meredith, but not by a blink of an eyelid did he give any indication this was not their first meeting.

He was an old, seasoned traveler, and with his help it seemed no time at all before the horse, the ladies, and their baggage were on the waiting ferry, which moved sluggishly through the calm waters.

As they approached the opposite shore, Georgina could just make out the outline of a coach, and though it was by no means as grand as that of Lady Leicester, she was glad to see everything going in accordance with Lord Meredith's plan.

The driver and the two outriders, however, though dressed in dark clothing, looked a little rough and spoke only Portuguese, which made Georgina feel somewhat uneasy. Not wishing to alarm Mrs. Robinson, she called Davis to one side and questioned him about the men, but he quickly assured her that they worked for Lord Meredith and were well armed, should they encounter any problems.

"By problems I assume you refer to bandits, Davis?" Georgina asked quietly.

"There's always that chance, yer ladyship," he admitted with some reluctance. "But we're ready for 'em if they try anything."

"I'm sure you are," she said hopefully, and joined Mrs. Robinson in the rather dusty coach.

Blissfully unaware of any possible danger, Robbie put her head back into the corner of the coach and was soon fast asleep. Georgina, however, for the first half-hour kept a close eye on the arid, mountainous country through which they were passing, and became lulled into a false security only when almost an hour had gone by with nothing untoward occurring.

Suddenly, however, she heard shouts and the sound of gunshots as bandits attacked the coach, which came quickly to a halt as the outriders and coachman returned fire. With a little whimper, Mrs. Robinson shrank into her corner, covering her face with her hands.

Peering out of the window on her side, Georgina saw Davis lying on the boulder-strewn sandy ground clutching his leg. They appeared to be in a mountain pass, with sheer rock to their left, the side where Georgina sat, and a high mountain range ahead and to their right, from whence the bandits had apparently come. Georgina moved over to the facing seat so as to better keep an eye on Davis. She would have liked to get out and bring him inside the coach, but knew it would be impossible without help, and the other men were all engaged in trying to fight off the sudden attack.

The shooting seemed to be concentrated on the right side of the coach, but suddenly a big, ugly, bearded man came riding around the front toward where the plucky little disarmed batman lay. From the quality of his attire and the silver and gold embellishments on both his person and his horse, he looked as though he might be the chief bandit. He raised his pistol with the obvious intention of putting a second shot into Davis to finish him off.

A knife had been in Georgina's hand for some time, concealed in the large muff she was carrying, and now she saw her opportunity. Concentrating only on what she must do, she carefully positioned herself at the open window, and with no more excitement than when she had practiced in the woods, sent the knife whistling through the air.

The bandit grabbed for his arm and attempted to remove the knife that had embedded itself in that limb, while his pistol fired harmlessly into the air and dropped to the ground from nerveless fingers. The sudden movement caused his horse to shy, then take off at breakneck speed around the rear of the coach, heading for the mountains from whence they had come, its rider half in and half out of the saddle. Because their leader was obviously injured, the remaining bandits gave up their attempt and followed him at almost as fast a pace, with the outriders in pursuit.

By the time Georgina alighted, Davis had dragged himself along the ground and recovered his own and the bandit's weapons. She thought that her knife was still in the bandit's arm until her eye caught the gleam of the ornate silver handle some ten or more paces away. As she bent to retrieve it, she saw the bright red blood on the blade, and suddenly she felt deathly sick. It was only then that Davis realized it was she who had saved his life.

"Gor blimey, ma'am. Never would've thought to be thankin' a lady for m'life! An' I know where ye learned that little trick!" he gasped.

He held up a hand for the knife, wiped it clean on his kerchief, then returned it to her. She lifted her skirt slightly and slipped it into the strap on her calf while the little man looked on.

"Jus' wait till 'is lorship 'ears this, ma'am. 'E'll never believe it. That 'e won't."

"Hush!" Georgina said as the returning outriders approached.

She stepped to the back of the carriage and found Starlight very nervous, but some of the sugar she had brought with her soon comforted her friend.

They lifted Davis into the carriage and placed him carefully on the seat facing Mrs. Robinson, who had finally taken her hands away from her eyes when she sensed that the danger was past.

The journey through the mountains resumed, and while her companion lay back in her corner of the coach, eyes averted and a vinaigrette in her hand, Georgina examined Davis' leg. Fortunately, the bullet had not touched bone but had passed right through the flesh, so removal would not be necessary. Tearing strips from her petticoat, she bound the wound tightly to stop the bleeding. One of the men had given Davis a stiff drink of brandy, and by the time she tied the last knot, he had fallen asleep.

"Oh, my dear, you're trembling too!" Mrs. Robinson noticed how Georgina could not stop shivering, but it was from shock rather than fear. "I didn't see anything that happened, as I just covered my eyes until the shooting stopped, but apparently poor Mr. Davis was injured."

It was obvious that Robbie knew nothing of her role in the events, for which Georgina was grateful, and decided it was best she not be told. She was glad Davis was sleeping and could not see her trembling, or he would have one more thing to tell his master.

The coach came out of the mountains at last, and descended rapidly to the small port of Setúbal, where the coachman drove directly to the docks. It was fortunate that Davis awoke as they came to a halt, and was able to give Georgina the name of the ship and its captain. He seemed, however, to be a little feverish, so without further ado she alighted and approached the coachman, whom she'd heard speaking English.

"Mr. Davis is going to need some assistance in getting onto the ship. I wonder if perhaps you and I can find the captain and get him aboard as quickly as possible," she suggested, smiling disarmingly at the older man.

"Of course, your ladyship. Yon vessel over there"—he

pointed to where a yacht was being loaded—"seems likely to be the one."

They walked along the dock, sure it was the right vessel, as the small harbor held no other of its size, though there were many fishing boats, bulky, with flat bottoms and gaily painted high prows. Somber groups of women with black shawls covering their heads and shoulders gathered near the sea wall, while on the beach a score or more fishermen in brightly colored shirts called amiably to one another as they mended their nets.

Rough-looking, muscular seamen were carrying boxes aboard the yacht, and as no one paid them any attention, the coachman followed the last of the seamen up a runged wooden gangplank and stepped onto the deck of the ship. He came back quickly, accompanied by a large middle-aged man with a ruddy complexion and a rolling gait, who, to Georgina's relief, gave the appearance of being very capable.

"I am Lady Georgina Forsythe, captain, and I believe passages have been booked aboard your vessel for my companion, our escort, and myself."

He smiled good-humoredly at her. "Captain Bailey at your service, m'lady. Your passages are secure, but a Mr. Davis was supposed to be looking after everything."

She nodded. "Mr. Davis met with an unfortunate accident and is presently lying in the coach unable to walk. If a cabin is ready for him, the outriders could carry him aboard, I am sure, and in the meantime, you could perhaps arrange for our baggage to be put aboard."

The captain nodded, but said, "There are only two cabins available, one for each of the two ladies, ma'am. What—?"

"Then give him the smaller of the cabins and my companion and I will share the other. He must have rest," Georgina said firmly, to the captain's obvious amusement.

She turned to the coachman. "Have the outriders come to the coach to lift Davis out and carry him aboard. Once he is settled, I'll make sure my horse and all our baggage are transferred safely before Mrs. Robinson and I board."

When Captain Bailey saw the condition of Davis, the amused expression left his face and he took charge, making sure that the men carried him as carefully as possible, and personally seeing him settled comfortably on a bunk in the smaller cabin.

Georgina hovered outside until she saw Davis placed securely on the bunk, then turned to go back ashore, but the captain quickly caught up with her.

"What happened, m'lady? Bandits?" he asked grimly.

"Yes, but fortunately their leader was injured and they fled back into the hills," she answered.

"Was anyone else hurt? Where's your companion?"

"She's waiting near the coach, captain. No one else sustained injury," she said a little impatiently, "and if you'll allow me to return to the coach, I will make sure she boards safely also. What time do we sail?"

His grin had returned. "In a couple of hours, ma'am. We're expecting one more passenger at any moment; then, once everything's stowed aboard, we'll be off with the tide."

He accompanied her from the yacht, signaling three of the men helping load cargo to follow him.

"These lads'll take the baggage straight down to your cabin, m'lady," he said to Georgina, then spoke to them in a mixture of Portuguese and Spanish, which they seemed to understand, as two of them unloaded the coach immediately, while the third unfastened Starlight and led her toward the yacht.

A still-nervous Mrs. Robinson had got back inside, presumably for safety, and she gladly accepted the captain's assistance in stepping down.

"Captain Bailey, at your service, ma'am. I'm sorry to hear you ran into a little trouble on the way, but we'll take good care of you from this point on."

"Thank you, captain. I am not usually of such a nervous disposition," Mrs. Robinson hastened to assure him. "But then, I've never been attacked by bandits before. Are you all right, Georgina?"

But Georgina was too busy checking that nothing had been left on the coach to hear her companion's question. The captain, however, answered for her.

"That young lady is just fine, ma'am. She's made sure

Mr. Davis is comfortable in your cabin, and you're to share hers, but that I know you won't mind. Now, if she's certain everything's been unloaded, we'll get you both aboard.''

Georgina had picked up Mrs. Robinson's vinaigrette and returned it to her; then the three of them walked along the dock, the ladies gladly taking the captain's arm to walk up the gangplank.

Mrs. Robinson looked curiously about her. "Are we the only passengers, captain?" she asked, not seeing any other gentlemen or ladies on deck.

"There'll be just one more, ma'am—a Lord Frost will be traveling with us, and he should be along shortly.''

It was not an unpleasant room in which to spend the next day or so—cramped, of course, in comparison to rooms ashore, but the walls were paneled in light oak, and one of them contained bookshelves with an interesting selection of reading material to pass the time. Two bunks were covered to resemble settees, and there were a table and chairs, a commode, and a small armoire in which to hang their clothes.

Mrs. Robinson sank down onto one of the bunks. "What a terrible experience, my dear. I see you have recovered yourself much more quickly than I, but I did notice how you trembled after you bound Davis' leg.''

She still looked very pale, Georgina thought, but, to her relief, was returning slowly to normal. She didn't need two invalids on her hands. She went over to the commode and poured water from a pitcher into a basin, then splashed her hands and face to refresh herself.

"I think I'll go next door to take a look at Davis. His wound needs cleansing properly, and I'd prefer to do it before we sail, if possible," Georgina said thoughtfully.

"Is there no one else who could take care of him, Georgina?" her companion asked with concern. "It's not at all the sort of thing you should be doing, you know.''

"On the contrary, Robbie, it's just the thing I should be doing. That little man was injured trying to protect us, and I think the least I can do is dress his wound,'' she retorted.

"Oh well, if you put it that way, I suppose it's all right.

Do you want me to come with you?'' Mrs. Robinson asked, trying to hide her distaste.

"No. You just stretch out here and rest for a while, Robbie. I won't be very long.'' Georgina felt sorry she'd snapped at her. Robbie was such a gentle person, and the day had been very shocking for her.

She found the captain, who was now busy making ready to sail, but he promised to send clean water and bandages to Davis' cabin, and told her how to get to the area below, where her horse was housed.

Starlight looked quite comfortable, the space clean and airy, and a young sailor who had been assigned to her care was with her.

Davis had a slight fever, but as it didn't seem to have worsened, Georgina felt he would be all right so long as he stayed below and rested. The wound was clean, and the captain had given her a potion for him that he assured her would make Davis sleep throughout the night and most of the next day.

Before she left the little batman, she felt the motion of the ship leaving the dock, and soon a stiff breeze was carrying them swiftly out to sea. Moving carefully until she became accustomed to the rolling motion, she returned to her own cabin to see how Robbie was doing.

"I'm afraid I'm not a very good sailor, my dear.'' Mrs. Robinson's face was turning a shade of pale green and she looked much like William had when they crossed from England.

Georgina quickly handed her a bowl, then poured water from the jug onto some cloths to place on her head.

"Leave me, my dear. I'm afraid I'm going to be very ill, and it can't be pleasant to watch.''

Despite her sympathy, Georgina had to agree, besides which she was longing to be up on deck watching the land recede, which she'd been unable to do on the outward journey. After another glance to be sure Robbie had everything to hand, she gave her a gentle pat on the shoulder.

"I'll just go on deck for a while to get some air, and come back to see how you're doing a little later,'' she said with genuine regret for the poor woman's plight.

Carefully negotiating the companionway, and holding on to anything available, she made her way to the rail, bade a silent farewell to Portugal, then stood facing what she hoped was the direction of England. The wind quickly whipped her bonnet to the back of her neck, and she tied the strings a little tighter to make sure she didn't lose it.

Turning her head toward the wheelhouse, she saw the captain and what seemed to be two members of the crew, and waved a hand to them.

The shrieks of gulls circling above blended with the sound of flapping sails and the murmur of sailors' voices, and she felt more at peace with herself than she had been since her cousin had told her of his plans.

"You seem to have none of the usual female aversions to sailing, ma'am."

The deep voice came from behind her, and Georgina turned, the wind blowing her hair over her eyes for a moment, but she could still make out a tall fair-naired man looking down at her, his pale gray eyes screwed up as they met the glare of the sun on the water.

"Allow me to introduce myself. I am Lord Frost, at your service, ma'am."

9

He was tall, not having quite the inches of Lord Meredith, but much taller than William, and his hair was a gold so light as to be almost silver. His fair complexion bore no signs of exposure to the burning sun she was so accustomed to seeing in this clime.

All at once Georgina felt grateful that her light bombazine carriage dress was of the first stare, if a little creased. Lord Frost's admiring glance took in her dark brown velvet bonnet, which matched the large muff that had hidden her knife not many hours ago and set off her chestnut curls to perfection. She put up a brown-gloved hand to pull it back onto her head—a hopeless task in the sea breeze—and made sure the ribbons would hold it.

She smiled, dimpling prettily. "Lady Georgina Forsythe, my lord," she murmured, and held out a hand, still grasping the rail firmly with the other.

He took her hand in his and raised it to his lips gallantly, and as he did so, Georgina saw something glisten and noticed the unusual gold ring he wore on his right hand, set with a huge diamond.

He was looking at her with a slightly bemused expression on his face.

"I had not thought to have the pleasure of such enchanting company for the crossing, my lady, though I am somewhat surprised to see you traveling alone." He looked favorably impressed, but his sand-colored eyebrows rose very slightly above the silver-gray eyes.

"But I am not alone, sir," she hastened to correct him.

"My traveling companions are somewhat indisposed, and I came on deck only to get a little air. Now, if you will excuse me . . ."

She firmly withdrew the hand he was still holding and turned to grasp some object with which to keep her balance, swaying slightly with the movement of the ship, and he quickly took a firm grasp of her elbow to steady her.

His eyes were full of concern as they gazed earnestly into hers. "Please accept my apologies, my lady. It was not my intention to appear critical, but merely curious. If my presence prevents you from enjoying the fresh breezes, then I will return to the confines of my cabin and not presume on you further."

He had released her arm once she had a steadier footing, and his eyes held a look of wistful sadness as he sketched a bow and immediately lost his own balance, grasping the rail firmly as he seemed about to fall.

Georgina's mischievous sense of humor got the better of her, as a particularly rough wave turned his attempt at gallantry into the antics of a clown. She refrained from laughing out loud, but a naughty grin twitched at the corners of her mouth, and her eyes sparkled with fun.

"Shame on you, my lady, for enjoying a poor fellow's downfall," he murmured, his eyes also twinkling. "For that I think you should pay a forfeit by allowing me a little more of your captivating company."

"Well, for a little longer, my lord, as long as you do not think for one moment that I am being forward, speaking to you like this, completely unchaperoned," she said when her mirth was under control once more.

He turned to wave to the captain in the wheelhouse. "But we are not alone. I am sure the good captain can be considered an adequate chaperon, as he can surely see everything we do from his vantage point," he asserted convincingly. "Now, tell me what providential chance of fortune caused you to be traveling on the same vessel as myself."

Georgina knew instinctively that Lord Meredith would not have approved her striking up such an acquaintanceship, but it was much more fun than sitting watching Robbie be so very ill. Forced to attend William in similar circumstances on the outward journey, she felt it only fair that she had now been offered such a charming companion, and decided to make the most of it. Her guardian need never know!

"I am returning from a visit to Lisbon, where I stayed with my dear friend Lady Leicester," she said, telling only the part of her journey she knew to be acceptable.

"Lucky Lady Leicester! A most charming person, but surely you did not travel all the way to Lisbon, when the country is at war, just to pay her a visit?" he asked, then teasingly suggested, "You have, perhaps, a friend, maybe a fiancé, in Wellington's army?"

He was so good-looking, his speech so cultivated, and his inquiry delivered in such a casual way that Georgina was completely disarmed and could see no reason why she should not tell him about William.

"My twin brother is presently at Torres Vedras, and he was able to visit me at Lady Leicester's home," she confirmed.

"Ah." Lord Frost nodded. "That explains it. A twin brother is very close to a twin sister, isn't he? Does he look at all like you—not your beauty, I'm sure, but your coloring, perhaps?"

"As a matter of fact, we don't look a bit alike," Georgina admitted, "but we are orphans, also, so we have always been very close."

"Will your companions—I believe you said there was more than one—be well enough to escort you to your home when we reach England, my lady? I recall the captain saying that a passenger had been carried aboard with a leg wound. Could it perhaps be . . . ?" He paused, as if hesitant to appear too curious.

Georgina frowned slightly. "The manservant escorting us was injured, my lord, but Lord Mer . . ." She stopped, for some reason reluctant to disclose her cousin's name. "A coach is to meet us at the docks and take us to my cousin's home."

"Then, much as I would have enjoyed extending my travels to escort such a beautiful lady, I see there is little need of my services. Your peregrinations appear to have been well planned.'' Lord Frost looked disappointed. "That is, of course, unless you have a lengthy journey ahead of you.''

"Oh no," Georgina assured him quickly, without thinking. "We have no more than a few hours' drive, for our cousin's estate is in Kent, not far from Maidstone, I believe."

She looked overboard, fascinated by the waves breaking against the bow and melting away in an endless rhythm.

"Your cousin would not by any chance be Lord Meredith, Earl of Settle, would he, my lady?'' His question was asked in a disinterested, casual tone, as if of no consequence.

There was no reason why she should not mention her cousin's name, but Georgina still felt cautious and answered briefly, "Yes, he is our cousin, sir. Are you known to him?''

"We have known each other for years, my dear," he assured her, "but I was unaware he had such a delightfully charming young cousin."

He smiled beguilingly, his admiring eyes so flattering they made her feel quite embarrassed. She flushed as she realized she had been short and discourteous in her impatient answer.

"My brother and I have lived all our lives in Yorkshire, my lord,'' she felt obligated to explain. "Lord Meredith is a distant cousin and our guardian.''

"Ah, yes, the wild moors and bracken. Grouse shooting, I believe, though I am not much for bird shooting myself. So that's where you've been hiding, my dear, and now you are to see the big city. If they plan to enter you in the marriage mart, there'll be an abundance of unhappy mamas this season, for your beauty will surely take London by storm.''

Although flattered, Georgina was uncomfortable, as she was unused to the admiring glances he cast her way and to the nonsense of his compliments, and very shortly thereafter she made an excuse and went below to check on Robbie and the batman. The sea had calmed somewhat, and her companion, though pale, was feeling a little more herself, but looking forward to reaching England and dry land.

After making sure Davis' fever had not worsened, Georgina returned to her own cabin, where Robbie was now asleep, and she had little difficulty in emulating her companion for a few hours.

She awoke as a knock sounded on the cabin door, and was so confused as to her whereabouts that it was Robbie who had to answer the door and step back for a rosy-cheeked cabin boy, closely followed by a neatly dressed steward, to enter with their dinner.

Georgina lifted the lids of the steaming dishes, suddenly very hungry, but at the smell of food, Robbie felt decidedly queasy and settled for a cup of tea and a piece of crusty bread.

After partaking of the simple but delicious meal of fish stew, boiled mutton, and syllabub, Georgina was ready to retire for the night, and as soon as the dishes had been cleared by the cheerful young boy, whose name she discovered was Juan, she settled down for a good night's sleep.

But the seas roughened as they sailed deeper into the Atlantic, and she was awakened by Robbie's moans as great waves tossed the ship about, and for the rest of the night and most of the next day she divided her time between caring for first Robbie and then Davis, who, to Georgina's surprise, was recovering well from his wound but had also succumbed to seasickness.

Georgina saw Lord Frost once more, when she went on deck after supper. Lost in the wonder of the evening as she gazed at the brilliant stars in the sky and listened to the distant sounds of the off-duty sailors, mostly Portuguese, singing songs of love, she was not aware that he had been beside her for some time.

"On such a night, one feels suspended in a timelessness, where there are no England and no France constantly warring with each other, no lands to be reclaimed, no avariciousness, but just the peace and love of a happy, carefree childhood," he said dreamily, his voice so quiet it fit her mood and his presence did not alarm her.

"Your childhood was spent in England, my lord?" Georgina asked softly.

"Yes, but Maman, God rest her soul, was French. She took me, when a little boy of five years, to visit my grandparents, who lived in a magnificent château just outside Paris. They were aristocrats, of course, dear friends of King Louis, and they owned hundreds of acres of farmland and forests. She was their only child, and heir to that vast estate.''

His voice was low-pitched and trembled with the emotions the memories evoked.

''Were they . . . ?'' Georgina hesitated to ask the obvious.

''Of course. Only three months after our return to England, the Bastille was stormed. Friends who hid and were smuggled out told Maman of their bravery when they were taken to the guillotine.'' He held up his hand and the diamond shone in the moonlight. ''I saw you looking at my ring when we first met. It is a treasured heirloom, given to me by my *grand-père* before we returned to England, and worn always around my neck in his memory, until my hand grew large enough for it to fit.''

He looked down at her with unshed tears brimming in his eyes.

Georgina gazed at him in silence, not knowing what to say to ease his sorrow.

He gently stroked her cheek. ''And now I have turned your pleasure into sadness. I am sorry, my dear. Perhaps one day I can make up for it,'' he murmured, and turning quickly, disappeared into the darkness.

''I do hope Davis is able to give us the direction of a reputable inn, for we'll not reach Settle House tonight,'' Robbie remarked nervously. ''I'm sure I don't wish to be on the road after dark, no matter how many outriders accompany Lord Meredith's coach.''

Georgina was in no hurry to get there, and as they approached England she was overcome by a sudden lowness of spirit. She had not mentioned her meetings with Lord Frost to Robbie, for she knew she should not have permitted the conversations without proper introduction and her chaperon in attendance.

When finally the white chalk cliffs came in sight through the cabin window, however, she could scarcely bear to stay below while she completed her toilette and checked for herself that all the baggage was repacked and ready to be transferred.

She was further delayed when she tried to make arrangements for Davis to be carried ashore. The little batman was determined to walk off the boat by himself, and Georgina was emphatic that he must have help. Unable to restrain him herself, she went to the door and quietly asked a passing seaman to request the captain's presence.

"I gave 'is lordship m'word that I'd not let ye out o' m'sight, an' then ye let that cap'n drug me most of the way!" Davis snorted angrily, trying to sit up on the bunk and conveniently forgetting his embarrassing bout of seasickness.

"And rightly so, my man." The voice boomed through the open door as Captain Bailey entered the small cabin, seeming to fill the room with his presence. "While you're aboard, I'm in charge, and you'll be carried off the same way as you were carried on. I'll not be responsible for you bleeding to death on my vessel."

"I know you have much to do, captain, but—" Georgina began, feeling distressed that she had needed to disturb him at such a time, but he would have none of it.

"You did the best thing, my lady, and I'm glad to see you have a head on your shoulders," he said, his eyes once more filled with amusement when he looked at her. "I trust you had a reasonably comfortable voyage. The storm kept me in the wheelhouse more than I would have wished, but my chief steward and young Juan told me you stayed well, though your companions were not so fortunate."

"I was very busy," Georgina said with a weary sigh, "But I must admit I will be glad to set foot on England's shores once more."

With a great many muttered imprecations, Davis was carried ashore and into the waiting coach. Georgina stayed with him to see that he didn't try to get out again, and a much-recovered Robbie was able to take charge of ensuring that all the baggage was safely transferred.

Georgina watched as the young sailor led Starlight toward the carriage, and once she was in the capable hands of Lord Meredith's coachman, she knew she need worry no more about her.

The coach was magnificent, bearing the Settle crest upon the door panel and drawn by a team of four matched grays. The dark blue lacquerwork gleamed, and the interior was unbelievably comfortable, with soft, thick squabs to rest against. The coachman and footmen wore dark blue livery, and two outriders made ready to accompany them as Georgina thanked Captain Bailey once more for his services and they pulled away from the dock.

Davis' eyes closed almost as soon as they were in motion, but Georgina was too tense to sleep. She had not seen Lord Frost again, as she had stayed below until she could accompany the batman ashore. She wondered a little if Robbie had seen him, but did not have long to ponder the matter, as her companion brought up the subject herself.

"I met our fellow passenger when I was busy with the baggage removal, Georgina," she said importantly. "He was a very good-looking man, in his early thirties, I would think."

"Did you have occasion to speak to him, Robbie?" Georgina asked, realizing that her own misconduct must not have been revealed.

"Yes. He had the captain make the introduction, and he offered us assistance, but I assured him we were quite able to manage on our own. He seemed a most charming gentleman, though."

"Do you remember his name?" Georgina asked, wondering if he had, in fact, given her his correct name.

"Frost, I think he said, Lord Frost. I've heard of the family but never met any of them, to the best of my recollection." Robbie sighed heavily. "Oh dear. I do dislike wakening Davis when he needs his sleep so badly, but . . ."

"Not sleepin', ma'am. Jus' restin' m'eyes, that's all." To prove it, Davis' eyes opened wide and he gazed forlornly at the two ladies. "Not sleepin' on the job, not me. Leastwise, not until some cap'n comes 'long an' drugs me."

Robbie looked relieved. "It will be dark very soon, Davis, and I have a distinct aversion to traveling at night. Do you recall an inn on this road where we might stay over?"

Davis appeared reluctant to make an overnight stop, but before he made any comment, Georgina said, "Really, Robbie, if you could just manage to overcome your nervousness, I believe that Davis should see a doctor just as soon as possible, and an overnight stay might cause all kinds of complications."

The tough little batman's reluctance to make a stop promptly disappeared. "Know jus' the place, ma'am," he said with a firm nod at Robbie and a scowl at Georgina. "The Bull's 'Ead, jus' a mile o' two further. Reckon we'd best stop there."

Before Georgina could make any further protest, he signaled to the coachman to stop, then sent one of the outriders ahead to announce their arrival.

The Bull's Head proved to be a first-class coaching inn of a considerably higher standard than the ones Georgina and her brother, with their limited means, had stopped at on their trip south. A suite had been set aside for them as soon as the innkeeper heard they were coming, but a private dining room was not available and the public dining room was crowded and noisy.

Georgina was about to suggest they have something sent to their suite, when a door off the hallway opened and Lord Frost appeared. He glanced at Georgina without showing any sign of recognition and spoke directly to Robbie.

"Pardon the intrusion, Mrs. Robinson, but I couldn't help but hear of your predicament. I would be delighted to share my dining room with you two ladies. In fact, I insist you introduce me to your lovely companion"—his eyes swept over Georgina as though for the first time—"and enliven my lonely repast."

"Lady Georgina, may I present Lord Frost to you . . . Lady Georgina Forsythe, my lord." Robbie did the honors and Georgina curtsied prettily.

"Charmed, I'm sure, Lady Georgina." Lord Frost held her hand a little longer than necessary while he gave it a reassuring squeeze. "Will you keep a lonely traveler company at table, m'lady?"

She looked first at Robbie, who gave an almost imperceptible nod, then told him, "We will be delighted, my lord, if you will first excuse us for a few minutes."

Lord Frost bowed low, and the innkeeper's wife stepped forward to take them to their suite of rooms.

The suite had a sitting room with dark wood paneling, a lovely Tudor fireplace with logs already lit and starting to crackle, large well-upholstered chairs and sofa, and a small breakfast table. Georgina would have preferred to have a glass of wine and a simple supper served in here, but realized her companion was probably quite hungry after being so ill on the voyage.

Her baggage was already in the larger of the two bedrooms, which held a lovely old dressing table and a four-poster bed with faded peach hangings. Resisting the temptation to forgo supper and slip between the lavender-scented sheets, she removed her bonnet, poured some of the warm water from the porcelain jug into the matching bowl, and washed her hands and face.

When Robbie came into the room, Georgina was gazing out of the mullioned window at the courtyard below, where there was much coming and going of carriages and riders.

"Is it not a fortunate coincidence that Lord Frost should be staying at the very same inn as we, after crossing from Portugal on the same ship?" Robbie remarked as they descended the polished wooden stairs.

He rose with a smile as they were shown into the room, and offered them a glass of the fine sherry he had ordered.

This was the first occasion that Robbie felt really needed, however, and she was taking her duties as chaperon very seriously. Smiling graciously at Lord Frost, she shook her head, saying, "Lady Georgina is not yet out, my lord, and not accustomed to drinking before supper. I believe that a glass of wine with the meal will be ample for both of us."

In fact, Georgina had never even tasted wine until after she left Yorkshire, but had enjoyed sampling the bottles of excellent locally produced wines that Isabella had frequently stolen. It was true, however, that at Lady Leicester's she had tasted wine only with dinner, except on the occasions when her brother and Lord Meredith were present.

"I trust that you are quite recovered from your indisposition at sea, Mrs. Robinson?" Lord Frost asked, and Georgina gave him an appealing glance, hoping he would not make reference to their first meeting. "You looked so pale when we first met, that I feared the crossing must have upset you," he continued, and Georgina breathed a sigh of relief.

"I was slightly indisposed, my lord, but completely recovered long before we reached Dover." Robbie seemed to resent any reference to her temporary frailty, and the subject was dropped.

"While sitting here sipping the excellent sherry, I was thinking that fortune must finally have decided to smile on me. To travel on the same vessel as such a beautiful young lady, and hear her charms extolled by the good captain, but never catch a glimpse of her, was most disappointing. To then see you both select the same inn as I is coincidence indeed. Were I a betting man, I would say the odds would be very much against such a thing happening." Lord Frost was feeling the effects of the wine, and his warm glance in Georgina's direction was intercepted by an alert Robbie.

"Very much against it, sir," Robbie agreed. "I said the same thing to Lady Georgina just a short time ago, and I can't tell you how much we appreciate your generosity in sharing this room with us." The meal had been more than adequate, and now both ladies were feeling weary from their travels. Glancing at Georgina, Robbie rose, and obediently her charge followed suit.

On his feet also, Lord Frost asked, "Surely you will remain to take tea with me, ladies? It has been long since I had such charming company, and I am reluctant to let you depart so soon." He addressed both, but his eyes were for Georgina alone.

"I am afraid we are both feeling a little tired, sir. Perhaps we will meet again sometime in London," Georgina said with a gentle smile as she recalled his sadness on deck last evening.

"I've no doubt of that, Lady Georgina. No doubt whatever." There was a playfulness to his smile, as though he knew something she didn't. He bowed low over each extended hand before opening the door, where the innkeeper's wife was waiting to take them back to their rooms.

After the innkeeper's wife left and before the maid arrived, Georgina drew Robbie into her bedchamber. "What do you suppose he meant by that last remark, Robbie? I was only being polite when I said we might meet again."

"I don't know, I'm sure, my dear. His manners were quite charming, but I'm afraid he was imbibing a little too much wine in the presence of ladies." Robbie turned as the door opened and the maid entered. "If you should meet again before we leave, just be sure you're not left alone with him. It would not do at all."

Georgina went quickly into her bedroom before her pink cheeks gave her away. Perhaps it was the wine, as Robbie said, that made him express such a certainty of seeing her again. It had been a most enjoyable evening. His touch did not make her feel the way her cousin's did, but he had a charming manner and no one had ever admired and flattered her, both by looks and words, the way Lord Frost had. It was very exciting.

Once between the fragrant sheets, however, she fell into a deep, dreamless sleep, waking only the next morning when the young maid entered with hot water and her newly cleaned and pressed traveling dress. The sight reminded her so much of when she had performed a similar service for her brother that she felt a momentary pang of loss, and wondered what William was doing at this moment.

After a simple breakfast in their sitting room, there was a knock on the door, and a smart, liveried footman entered to take their baggage to the coach. He looked so stern and proud of his uniform as he left the room with his head held high that Georgina couldn't resist giggling and pulling a face at his back.

"Shame on you, young lady," Robbie pretended to scold, but was unable to keep a severe countenance in the face of Georgina's clowning.

In a happy mood, they descended the stairs, graciously

thanked the innkeeper for his services, and made to enter the coach, where Davis was already half-seated.

"Good morning, Davis," Georgina said, a frown puckering her brow as she saw the injured leg resting on the floor. "This coach is not going to move until you pick up that leg and support it on the seat. Then you can tell Mrs. Robinson and me how you are feeling today."

She remained standing in the doorway, meeting the little man's glare with a sweet smile.

Finally, muttering angrily under his breath, he picked up the offending leg and placed it on the seat. When Georgina still did not move, he settled himself more comfortably in the corner of the seat. "Can we get on wi' it now, yer lady-ship?" he asked belligerently. Then, as Georgina took her own seat and the door was closed, he muttered, "Don't know wot young'uns is comin' to these days."

Once more he closed his eyes, but this time Georgina realized he was not really sleeping, and she and Robbie exchanged knowing smiles as the carriage pulled out of the courtyard and they were on their way once more.

10

The swing of the coach as it turned off the main road suddenly woke Georgina, to find that she had slept the whole journey. They were now traveling along a well-kept private road lined with large oak trees, and she peered out of the window in an attempt to get a glimpse of the house. She knew they must be close when she saw a rolling lawn through the trees, and one more turn brought the mansion into view.

Her first feeling was one of disappointment, as she had not expected the house to be built of red brick. However, as they drew nearer she found herself admiring the uniform elegance of the simple rectangular windows on all three floors, the fanlight over the door, and the black wrought-ironwork which seemed to underscore the overall neatness of appearance.

The staff must have been on the alert for their arrival for the last two days because, the minute the coach came to a halt, liveried footmen came hurrying out. There was a pause when they saw the injured batman, but it seemed no time at all before he had been placed in a light chair and, complaining bitterly, was thus carried up the steps and into the room already prepared for him.

They were ushered into the large hall with a huge staircase, down which a rather small, slightly plump lady with an enviable carriage came unhurriedly to greet them. From a distance her hair looked golden, but as she came nearer a heavy sprinkling of silver could be seen beneath the cream lace cap she was wearing. Fine wrinkles around her sparkling blue eyes only added to their warmth, and gave emphasis to her soft, creamy complexion. Her smile could not have held more welcome.

"My dear Georgina, I am Lady Meredith. Welcome to Settle House. You must be quite exhausted after your journey," she exclaimed, hugging her warmly despite the difference in height. "I have a maid all ready to attend you, but this is to be your home for now, and you must tell me which need comes first. Do you wish to rest for a while, or would you like some refreshment first?"

A stern-looking butler stood discreetly to one side, awaiting instructions from his mistress.

"The very first thing I would like, my lady, is to have a doctor called for Davis. You see, he was injured in Portugal and I . . ." Georgina began.

As she hesistated to acknowledge that she herself had bandaged the wound, a silent exchange took place between the dowager and her butler. In response to her questioning look, Lady Meredith murmured, "It has already been taken care of, my dear. The doctor will be here momentarily."

Georgina looked surprised. "Oh, so quickly?"

Lady Meredith smiled sympathetically. "If Davis suffered injury while looking after you, then the journey must indeed have been a difficult one. However, you need not feel further responsibility for him. He is now in the best of hands, for we are all very fond indeed of my son's batman."

With Davis taken care of, Georgina suddenly realized she was quite hungry, and she turned to Robbie, who had been standing a little to the side after curtsying to Lady Meredith. "Are you as hungry as I am, Robbie?" she asked hopefully.

"Perhaps not quite as much, but I would certainly appreciate some refreshment before anything else," Mrs. Robinson agreed.

"In the drawing room, your ladyship?" The butler was already halfway across the hall in the direction of what must have been the kitchens.

"I think so, Crowther. And please tell Cook to make it very special." Lady Meredith turned back to her guests. "Now, my dears, I am sure you would like to see your rooms and refresh yourselves.'' With a sweep of her arms she was ushering them up the wide staircase as she spoke. ''I'll join you in the drawing room when you're ready.''

An alert footman led them along a corridor, opened a door and bowed Georgina into her room, then disappeared with Robbie.

It was difficult to repress a giggle as Georgina thought about the things she had done for William in Portugal, and the minimal staff her grandmama allowed at Broadacres. Lady Leicester seemed to have adequate staff, but here there appeared to be someone always standing at attention to take care of one's needs. As if to emphasize her thought, there was a rustle of skirts as a maid not much older than Georgina herself stepped out of a dressing room where she had been unpacking and sorting the baggage that had already been brought up.

Curtsying to Georgina, the maid said cheerfully, ''I'm Daisy, your ladyship, and I'm to look after you.'' She took Georgina across the room to a washstand. ''There's hot water waiting, and perhaps you'll be wanting to rest awhile before dinner.''

Georgina gave her a friendly smile. ''Thank you, Daisy, but that can come later. I'm very hungry, and if you'll just help me remove my bonnet and tidy up a little for now . . .''

The girl held a towel as Georgina washed her hands, then with a few deft movements made her hair neat and tidy once more.

''If you'll tell me which gown you'll be wearing tonight, your ladyship, I'll see that it's pressed first.''

Right now it seemed unimportant which gown she wore, but Georgina, aware that she would have to get used to this sort of attention, pointed to a pale green one she'd worn a number of times before, then hurried from the room. As she closed the door behind her she realized she had no idea where the drawing room was, but a footman appeared as if out of nowhere to escort her.

Robbie was not yet there, but Lady Meredith's kind eyes noticed the way her young guest gazed at the crumpets and dainty sandwiches, and suggested they start without her companion.

As she nibbled the delicacies and sipped her tea, Lady Meredith questioned her regarding the voyage.

"I trust you had a comfortable journey, my dear, though I understand from my son that the crossing can be quite rough at this time of year. Did Davis slip on board ship?" she inquired.

Georgina's small laugh held little humor. "Both Robbie and Davis were indisposed for most of the voyage, my lady, but Davis was injured in the mountains south of Lisbon. You see, our coach was attacked by bandits before we reached Setúbal." She saw the little lady's eyes open wide and hastened to reassure her. "It was over in just a few minutes and they fled back into the mountains, but Davis suffered a bullet wound in the leg. I—" She bit her lips as she tried to find the right words. "I did what was necessary to stop the bleeding right away, and changed the dressing once we were aboard ship, which is why I was so anxious for a doctor to be fetched at once."

Lady Meredith regarded her with a worried frown. "My dear, how dreadful for you! And you did this yourself? I should have thought Mrs. Robinson or someone would have looked after him."

Thankful that Lady Meredith knew nothing about her part in routing the bandits, Georgina explained, "Robbie was very frightened by the attack, and then on the ship she was seasick, so I sort of . . . took charge," she explained.

The dowager was made of sterner stuff than had at first appeared. Once recovered from her surprise, she saw Georgina through different eyes, and realized she was not at all the simpering young female one might expect at her age.

"I think it might be best if I do not know where a gently reared young lady learned how to dress bullet wounds. I am sure Davis will give my son a complete report. Does Lord Meredith know all of your talents, Georgina?" she asked, her smile turning to one of genuine amusement.

A devilish light of pure fun shone in Georgina's eyes as she pictured Lord Meredith learning of her prowess with a knife. "Not all of them yet, ma'am," she said dryly, "but I've no doubt he'll find out soon enough."

Robbie came in at this point, a little embarrassed that she had taken so long, but Lady Meredith quickly put her at ease, explaining that they had started because Georgina was so obviously very hungry. She expressed interest in hearing about Lisbon, and drew Robbie out on a subject in which she was at her best, describing the beauty and history of the city.

After meeting Georgina, Lady Meredith had a feeling of quiet satisfaction regarding her son's affairs. Being in charge of what appeared to be a most unusual young lady would be good training for when his own small daughter grew up.

Three-year-old Louise was the only good thing, in Lady Meredith's private opinion, to come out of the marriage arranged many years before between Matthew and Arabella, the daughter of the Marquis of Stanton, whose estate ran next to the Settle estates in Lincolnshire.

It had been disappointing from the start. They had had no love for each other, and Arabella, it seemed, wished only to fulfill her obligation by producing an heir so that she could resume her former relationship with a penniless young count.

At the time, rumor had run rampant among the *ton* as to who was the father of the child Arabella was carrying.

Fortunately, once the tiny baby was born prematurely, after a wild gallop the willful Arabella had insisted upon in Matthew's absence, there had been no question as to who her father might be. She was the image of Matthew, with her black hair and blue eyes, and when her mama developed a fever and severe bleeding a few days after her birth, a wet nurse was found for the little baby.

Matthew had made sure his wife had the best of care, but there was no hope for Arabella, and when she called in her delirium for her lover, Matthew himself brought the count to her.

Following her death, just one week after the birth of Louise, Matthew had arranged for the baby to be attended by his own nanny, then accepted a commission in the army and fought under Sir John Moore, who was defeated and killed in action at Corunna. Matthew had been very lucky to come out of that battle unscathed.

She had not seen him since his regiment left for Portugal toward the end of last year. She felt he had more than done his duty as far as England was concerned, and hoped he would shortly resign his commission, concentrate his energies on his family, and, in particular, marry again and produce an heir.

It would be interesting to see how her son and his ward rubbed along together.

11

The following day the comparative calm of the household was disrupted by the arrival of little Louise, accompanied by her cousin Lady Elizabeth Devon, Lord Meredith's oldest niece.

Georgina had just finished luncheon with Lady Meredith and Robbie, and the three were savoring a particularly fine tea, when she heard through the open window a child's voice calling, "Gwanny, I'm here."

With eyes twinkling, Lady Meredith rose. "You are about to meet the only young lady who has ever been known to bring my son to his knees. If you're finished with tea, let us go and greet my lovely oldest granddaughter, Elizabeth, and my adorable grandchild Louise."

They entered the hall just as the outside door was flung open to admit Lady Elizabeth, a small, dainty, very lovely girl with glossy raven-black hair and large blue eyes framed with thick black lashes. Her creamy complexion rivaled that of her grandmother and seemed never to have been exposed to the hazards of a hot summer sun, and despite her lack of stature, she carried herself with an inborn dignity.

She curtsied to her grandmother, who put her arms around her and held her close, then pushed her away to take a good look at her.

"You grow lovelier every day, child," Lady Meredith said with pride, "and now there is someone very special I want you to meet."

She beckoned Georgina and made the introductions, then left them to get to know each other.

Struggling to free her small hand from the firm grasp of her nanny was an energetic little black-haired bundle who turned an appealing face to her grandmother and called, "Gwanny, please."

"It is quite all right, Nanny. She may come to me now," Lady Meredith said, and the little girl hurtled into her grand-mother's arms.

"I was not aware until quite recently that Uncle Matthew had a female ward," Elizabeth was saying excitedly to Georgina, "but I am so glad that you are staying. It will be much more fun having someone my own age here, and we shall soon become fast friends, I know. Is it true that you were on the Peninsula with Uncle Matthew?"

"Not exactly," Georgina told her, trying hard not to start a new friendship by telling a direct lie. "I was the guest of Lady Leicester in Lisbon. Are you not weary from your journey?"

Elizabeth's laugh was soft and musical. "A journey with Louise *is* wearying," she admitted. "Not because she is naughty, for she's well-behaved on the whole. But she has so very much energy, and I found it necessary to spend some time making sure she understood that her father would not be here when we arrived."

Lady Meredith was trying to bring about some order. "Why don't you take Elizabeth upstairs, Georgina, to tidy up, and Nanny can perhaps persuade Louise to have her nap. You may join me in the drawing room in half an hour, and we'll have some fresh tea and a little something to tide us over until dinner."

As they all started up the stairs, Lady Meredith added, "If you cannot prevail on the little one to nap, she may join us also, Nanny. She's unsettled already, so a change of routine will do no harm, and she'll sleep the better for it tonight."

It would have been impossible for Georgina to do anything other than like Elizabeth. A maid was already busy unpacking her clothes, so they went into Georgina's room and Elizabeth bathed her face and hands in rosewater and smoothed her hair.

"I assume you will stay on with Grandmama, won't you, and accompany us to Bath and to London?" Elizabeth asked.

"I only wish it were possible, but I very much doubt it. It will depend upon how soon my guardian visits, for he'll surely send me packing to Yorkshire when he next sees me," Georgina said regretfully. "But at least let us enjoy ourselves until he gets here."

"I will talk to Grandmama. She will not allow him to send you away, I vow. I am to make my come-out this Season, and she will tell him we need you here," Elizabeth assured her, slipping her arm through Georgina's and drawing her out into the hall. "I trust Cook prepared ample of that 'little something.' I have scarcely eaten a bite since early this morning."

Lady Meredith was already in the drawing room, and her surmise that her little grandchild was too excited to sleep had been correct.

While they had tea and sandwiches, Louise ran from room to room to make sure they were unchanged. Looking so very much like her father, she was such a happy child that it was quite impossible not to share her joy. And her request most frequently repeated, though impossible to grant, was to see her daddy.

She was often to be found playing in the garden with Davis, an old friend, who seemed to be recovering quickly from his wound. Georgina had considered asking him not to tell Lord Meredith of her actions on that day, and only refrained from doing so because she felt sure he would refuse.

Lady Elizabeth seemed, in the more practical ways, to be very much younger than Georgina, and in others to be so much more sophisticated, accepting as her due the arrangements being made for her first London Season.

Although an excited Elizabeth talked of it continuously to Georgina, it was several days before Lady Meredith broached the subject of their forthcoming trip to Bath.

"You will need to acquire some polish before being thrust into the midst of your very first Season, Elizabeth, and it was with this in mind that I rented a house in Bath. We leave within the month. The seamstress will be here tomorrow and we will decide what additional garments you will need." She looked speculatively at Georgina.

"As for you, Georgina, I have decided to bring you out at the same time as Elizabeth. You will be company for each other, and with her dark hair and your lighter chestnut, you will make excellent foils for each other. I am uncertain as to which color will be the more fashionable, for what is to be the rage is frequently decided by some frivolous gesture of the Beau or one of his friends."

Georgina could not believe her ears. Just wait until Lord Meredith heard of this, she thought. There'd be no Season for her once he'd spoken to Davis! But how generous of Lady Meredith to want to include her in their plans!

"My lady, you are most kind, but my grandmother has not the wherewithal to spend on a Season for me. I would indeed be honored if I could just accompany you and make myself of use in any way I can," she said gratefully.

With a magnificent sweep of her hand, Lady Meredith waved away Georgina's protests. "Nonsense, Georgina. My son has ample funds with which to outfit you appropriately for a come-out, and it would cost little more for a ball for the two of you than for just Elizabeth. I will write to him tomorrow, and meanwhile we will get you fitted out with ball gowns for Bath. The other apparel you brought from Lisbon will do very well for Bath, but when we remove to London you will both need outfitting by the best modiste in town. I will not have the Merediths called penny-pinchers!"

When the girls were alone once more, Elizabeth became ecstatic. "This is the best thing yet. I was feeling so moped with Mama increasing again and staying in the country to look after Papa and the little ones. Now we shall go everywhere together and have a famous time." She finally stopped talking long enough to notice Georgina's serious face. "What is the matter? Do you not want a Season, Georgina?"

"Of course I do, and to share it with you above everything, but I dare not hope my guardian will permit it. I am not exactly his favorite ward, you know." She gave a deep sigh. "If only my mama and papa had not met with the accident, I know I would be coming out this year, if not last, for they loved London and went there often.''

Elizabeth looked very knowing. ''My uncle may exert his authority when in Portugal, but he is no match for Grandmama, you can be sure. If Grandmama says you are to have a Season, then it's settled and he has no choice but to accept it.'' Big blue eyes opened wide as a sudden thought occurred to her. ''You are not afraid of Uncle Matthew, are you?''

Georgina squared her shoulders and lifted her head proudly. ''I am not afraid of anyone,'' she declared, ''and particularly not of Colonel Lord Meredith.''

Elizabeth laughed. ''He can be most autocratic at times, but I suppose he got that way from ordering soldiers around. I've never doubted his deep affection, however, for me and all the family.''

There was no answer Georgina could give to that, but a lump seemed to block her throat and she found it hard to swallow. She bent down to attend to the hem of her gown so that Elizabeth would not see the tears she blinked back. She had slowly come to realize that this awful feeling of missing her guardian even more than she missed William, and wanting to see him smile and feel the warmth of his touch, was not about to go away. She'd fallen in love!

On the following day Georgina, despite the doubts she had expressed to Elizabeth, was quite excited as the dressmaker showed bolt after bolt of satins, silks, nets, and laces to Lady Meredith, and she pictured herself floating gracefully around a ballroom floor in the arms of a handsome officer—one particular officer.

Then she remembered. ''Lady Meredith, I'm very much afraid I cannot dance,'' she said.

''Do you mean you cannot dance for some reason, or just that you don't know how, my gal?'' Lady Meredith asked sharply.

''I don't know how. At Lady Leicester's I used to watch the dancing when they had balls in the house across the street, and it looked quite complex and awfully difficult to learn,'' she said doubtfully.

''Nonsense,'' the dowager declared, much amused. ''Unless you've two left legs, you'll learn in no time at all, for you're naturally graceful. Before we leave for Bath, I'll have a dancing master come and show you both how to go along. Mind you, you'll not be able to waltz till you get back to London and are granted permission by one of the patronesses at Almack's.''

There was a tugging at her skirts and she bent down. "Yes, darling, what is it?" she asked her little granddaughter.

"Me too, Gwanny, me too?" Her big round baby eyes were very appealing. "Pwetty dress?"

"But you've got lots of pretty dresses, my pet," her grandmother cooed.

But Louise wasn't to be put off. "Like Gina's—please?" she begged, touching the soft peach-colored muslin embroidered with tiny white flowers.

Lady Meredith gave the necessary instructions to the seamstress.

Georgina was very happy at Settle House. But even surrounded by a kind, loving family, she didn't altogether stop worrying about William, and she wished he could be here for a while and get to know these generous people.

Because of her burgeoning feelings for Lord Meredith, his little daughter was even more dear to her, and after Davis had left, she spent long hours playing with her, fixing her dolls when something came apart, and drinking pretend tea out of miniature cups and saucers.

It was she whom Louise always ran to when she scraped a knee or hurt a finger, to have it kissed better. And the little girl had to have a good-night kiss from Gina every night before she would go to sleep.

Lord Frost lived nearby and was a frequent visitor. Georgina now realized how he had guessed her destination, for there were few estates of the proportions of Settle House in the vicinity of Maidstone.

"Although we've lived close by for years, I've never known Norbert Frost to be so conscientious with his calls," Lady Meredith remarked one day. "It would seem you have an admirer, Georgina."

"Why assume that he is calling on me? Perhaps he comes to see Elizabeth, for he pays us equal attention, as he does you also, ma'am," Georgina added mischievously. "I know his manners are above reproach, but I find myself embarrassed by his constantly flattering remarks."

"There are many who will flatter exceedingly when you are in the midst of your Season, my dear, and I've no doubt you'll learn which are sincere and which are just paying lip service. In a month or two, Lord Frost's flattery will seem commonplace to you." For her part, Lady Meredith enjoyed having him call, for he was no less flattering to her than he was to the girls, and it was very pleasant to be made a fuss of.

As if by some perverse temptation of fate, the butler came in just then to announce that Lord Frost was calling, and Lady Meredith rose to greet him.

"How very good of you to call, Norbert," she said, smiling as he took her hand and pressed it to his lips. "We were just discussing our forthcoming journey to Bath."

"To Bath, my lady?" He seemed somewhat surprised, and his smiling glance showed a hint of playfulness. "Surely such radiant beauty has no need of medicinal waters to further enhance it?"

Lady Meredith gave him an impatient shake of her head. "You naughty boy! You know full well there are far more inviting reasons for a stay in Bath than to partake of the waters," she said with a short little laugh. "As these young ladies will be making their come-out in London next Season, I decided to give them a small taste of what they might expect."

He breathed a sigh of relief. "For a moment I was desolate at the thought of being deprived of such charming company. But as I also intend to be in London for the Season, I will deem it a privilege to escort you to some of the entertainments—in the absence of your son, of course, Lady Meredith. He is still fighting those wretched French ruffians in Portugal, is he not?"

"I never know what my son is doing, Norbert," Lady

Meredith said briskly. "I am assured, however, that if he can come to London to assist us, he will do so."

She had been edging him over to where Georgina and Elizabeth sat with their needlework, and when he started to address them, she murmured quietly to one of the footmen, who hurried from the room. A few minutes later, Mrs. Robinson entered and joined the group.

After allowing a few minutes to make the changeover of chaperonage less obvious, Lady Meredith rose. "I must beg to be excused, Norbert, for I promised my little granddaughter she might see the new ducklings at the pond, and if I don't go very shortly, she will be most unhappy."

"My lady, I cannot tell you how disappointed I am, for it is always such a pleasure to be in your company. However, I will forgive you on this occasion, for I appreciate the depth of your love for the little one." He bowed deeply, then drew his chair closer to Georgina and Elizabeth.

"Lady Georgina, how are you enjoying our soft, balmy weather? So different from the north of England," he remarked with a smile so charming that Georgina could not take insult.

"You most certainly see the sun with more frequency than in the north, my lord," she admitted, "and Starlight enjoys it also, for she was only too eager to return to the stables on a cold, snowy day."

"Ah, yes, you have your own horse with you, I recall. Perhaps you and Lady Elizabeth would do me the honor of riding over to Falcone Priory one day, when you might enjoy seeing the ancient Frost family seat," he suggested.

"Regrettably, Mrs. Robinson does not care for riding," Elizabeth intervened, helping out her friend, "so we needs must stay within the boundaries of my uncle's estates, even though a groom accompany us."

There was no doubt that he was a handsome man, tall and slim, with reasonably good shoulders, and a lithe carriage. He looked to be about the same age as Lord Meredith, Georgina thought.

She had behaved with impropriety by permitting him to speak to her alone on the yacht, but he had done her the kindness of keeping their first meeting to himself, and everyone thought they had met when Robbie made the introductions in the inn.

"Do you think you might enjoy it, Georgina?" Elizabeth's question took her by surprise, and she gave the others a confused glance.

"I regret I was air-dreaming and failed to hear your discussion," she confessed, shamefaced.

Elizabeth's merry laugh rang out, but Lord Frost looked for just a second as though he was annoyed that a young lady had not been hanging on his every word.

He quickly recovered, but his voice held a hint of reproach as he said, "It was my suggestion that, as a stranger to these parts, you might enjoy a trip to Maidstone. It has considerable historic interest, with a hospital founded in 1260 for pilgrims to Canterbury, a fourteenth-century Church of All Saints, and a grammar school dating back to 1549."

"It would seem most interesting, my lord, but I'd much prefer to see Canterbury—if it's not too distant?"

Georgina had not been far from the estate yet, and had little idea where they were in relation to the cities she had read about. She was not prepared to permit Lord Frost's deprecating smile, however, as he shook his head and said, "It is quite obvious that geography is really not your forte, Lady Georgina, but then, it would be foolish to fill such a lovely head with so much learning."

"I readily admit my knowledge of Kent may be somewhat limited, my lord," she said sharply, offended by his remark, "but I'll warrant I know as much about these parts as you know about Yorkshire."

Mrs. Robinson saw the light of battle in Georgina's eyes and quickly intervened. "Now, my dear, I'm sure Lord Frost's remark was meant only to flatter," she murmured. "I must admit I was the one who brought up the subject, for I have been to Canterbury and Tunbridge Wells and Sevenoaks, all most interesting towns, but I have never yet seen Maidstone, and I am given to understand we are no more than ten miles away. Is that not so, Lord Frost?"

"Quite so, Mrs. Robinson, and I must tender my sincere

apologies to Lady Georgina if she misconstrued my remarks. Please show your forgiveness, my lady, by accepting my invitation to spend a day in Maidstone next week. If we can decide the day, I will send a man over to arrange luncheon at a particularly good inn there, where they serve home-brewed ale and Kentish cider with the finest of foods.''

Reluctant to appear churlish, and genuinely sorry for her outburst, Georgina agreed, and the following Tuesday was set for the outing. Lord Frost was to come for them in his carriage at ten in the morning, which would give them time to see something of the town before sitting down to what was described as a sumptuous luncheon.

When Lady Meredith returned with little Louise, she was delighted they had made plans, but declined their invitation to join them, as she did not want to leave the child alone for the day so close to the time when they would be departing for Bath. Besides, as she said, she had seen Maidstone so many times before that there was really no novelty in such an outing for her.

Lord Frost took his leave, having very much overstayed the time usually acceptable for a morning visit, but, as Lady Meredith assured him, there was a great deal more flexibility in such formalities in the country than in the city.

As Georgina had expected, Robbie looked at her reproachfully, then said gently, ''I'm sure you must know that no matter how offended a lady feels, she never makes those feelings known in company.''

''I know, Robbie,'' she said with a heavy sigh, ''but it infuriates me so when men imply that women have empty heads and cannot think for themselves.''

Lady Meredith was listening, and though she said nothing, she raised her eyebrows at Georgina's reply.

''Please don't add your scold, my lady,'' the latter begged. ''I was wrong, I know, and I promise to have better control of my tongue in future.''

''Enough said. I've no intention of belaboring the point,'' her ladyship agreed. ''You'll all enjoy the outing if the weather stays fine, for it's quite a pretty town and the hedgerows and meadows are just coming into bloom. It was most kind of Lord Frost to suggest taking you, and he's always excellent company on such outings.''

Tuesday dawned cloudy and gray, but despite this, Lord Frost arrived punctually at ten in the morning for the three ladies.

Georgina would have liked to ride alongside, but as Lord Frost had given no indication that he intended to do so, she had dressed for driving. When he came on horseback, she felt a little put out, but forgot it quickly enough, and she had to admit that the Kent countryside was very pretty.

When they were a little less than halfway, thunder started to rumble and they stopped while Lord Frost's horse was tied behind and he stepped into the carriage.

''I fear we are in for a downpour, ladies, which might make our sightseeing less than pleasant. However, I had what I think is an excellent idea. We are but a mile beyond my home, Falcone Priory, and it would be my pleasure to show you around the place and provide a luncheon that can surely rival the one I promised you in Maidstone.'' Lord Frost looked directly at Georgina as he spoke, his eyes warm and persuasive, and remembering her rudeness when last they met, she felt herself flush.

''We can always go to Maidstone another time,'' she said, feeling somehow obligated to make amends. ''I, for one, would very much enjoy seeing your home, sir, but would it not be an imposition to provide luncheon at such short notice?''

Just then the storm broke, and the pounding rain made the decision easy. Knocking on the roof, Lord Frost ordered the carriage to turn, and twenty minutes later they drew up in front of a medium-size stone-built house, obviously quite old.

The huge door, surrounded by stained-glass panels, was flung open and footmen hurried out to bring the guests inside before they became soaked. Within minutes they were settled in a large room before a roaring fire. They had moved so swiftly that scarcely a drop of rain had even spotted their gowns.

''May I offer you ladies some mulled wine to keep away a

chill," Lord Frost suggested. "My housekeeper has an excellent old recipe."

"Thank you, my lord," Robbie answered for them, "but I think we might all prefer a hot cup of tea, if it would be no trouble." She waited until he gave instructions to a lackey, then remarked, "I was admiring the plaster chimneypiece. I see it bears a date of 1627."

"Yes, ma'am, it was a later addition, I believe," Lord Frost said proudly. "After we have tea I will take you upstairs to see the upper chambers. The house is small, compared to Settle House, but is vastly superior in historic interest. It is, however, the only property remaining on the Frost side of my family."

Georgina was gazing up at the intricate design of the plaster ceiling. "I wonder how they did that?" she pondered out loud. "One would think it would fall down before it set."

Lord Frost smiled. "I have been told that a generous supply of cow hair was used in the construction, Lady Georgina, but the true art has now died out, regrettably."

After they had finished their tea, Lord Frost gave them a guided tour of the interesting house, pointing out intricately carved newels on the staircase, the lead-glazed windows, and the coats of arms that decorated wood panels in various rooms.

They finally entered the dining room, stone flagged like the rest of the ground floor of the house, and covered with beautiful handmade carpets. The table was already laid for luncheon, and footmen were at hand to seat them.

Georgina was placed at Lord Frost's right hand, and as she had enjoyed seeing the house very much, she hastened to convey her thanks. "I believe I enjoyed this as much as, if not more than, the trip we planned, my lord," she told him with a smile. "You have a home of which you are justifiably proud, and I am honored you showed it to us."

He shrugged deprecatingly. "My father placed considerable value on his family seat, as did Maman on hers. She never gave up the hope that one day, when the peasants were put down, her family estates would be restored to her."

"Surely she felt herself fortunate to have escaped the fate

of her parents, my lord, for her life was of more worth than an estate, no matter how vast,'' Georgina reminded him.

There was a bitterness on Lord Frost's countenance that Georgina had never noticed before. ''She would not have agreed with you, nor do I,'' he said softly. ''Her blood, running in my veins, tells me that it was my heritage they stole and that the vandals have tried to destroy. I have seen what they have done to the château, and one day, when it is mine once more, I will make them pay for every window they broke and every portrait they defiled.'' He was twisting his heavy diamond ring round and round as he spoke.

''You have been back and seen it, my lord?'' Georgina asked.

He glanced at her warily. ''Yes, once,'' he said briefly, then turned to Elizabeth, seated on his left, and was soon engaged in an amusing conversation on the subject of cravats.

Georgina felt sorry for this man, brought up to love something he could never regain, and wondered when he had been in France, for it seemed as though the two countries had been at war forever.

12

Lady Meredith had hoped to see her son before they removed to Bath, and her wish was granted when he arrived unexpectedly, late one afternoon.

As she fondly welcomed him, she was almost pushed off her feet by the small body of Louise that somehow wedged itself between her skirts and his legs and was clamoring loudly for attention.

Releasing his mother, he bent swiftly and picked up his little daughter, who clung to him crying, "Daddy, Daddy," while tears streamed down her upturned face.

"What's all this noise about, sweetheart?" he asked, wiping her tears away with his kerchief. The harsh lines that a long, sleepless journey had etched into his face melted away as he gazed upon his child's tearstained countenance. "If you cry like this, I'll think you don't want me to come home."

"Want, Daddy, want," the little girl sobbed, clinging to him as though she would never let him go.

He carried her over to a large chair, where he sat murmuring softly to her and rocking her gently in his arms until the tears stopped and she lay contentedly with her head on his chest, her eyes closed and the long black lashes forming crescents on her cheeks. She appeared to have fallen asleep with a peaceful smile still on her doll-like face.

Looking up, he seemed surprised to see that Elizabeth and Georgina had entered and were sitting talking to his mother.

Lady Meredith spoke softly to her son, so as not to waken the child. "It is far too long to be away from her, Matthew. I was, of course, aware that she was missing you, but I had no idea to how great an extent.''

Before he could answer, Nanny came into the room, bobbed a curtsy, and said breathlessly, "One minute she was fast asleep in her crib, and the next minute the room was empty. She must have heard you arrive, your lordship, and ran as fast as those little legs would carry her. Would you like me to take her back, sir?''

He looked tenderly at the little girl, then said quietly, "She seems to be in a deep sleep, but I'll bring her up myself in case she wakens. You go ahead, Nanny.''

As he passed the two girls, he smiled at Elizabeth, then said to Georgina, "I want to see you in the study in half an hour.''

There was a definite change in his voice, a sterner tone as he spoke to Georgina, which she did not fail to notice. But she was so happy to see him that she could not concern herself about it now. Lucky Louise, she thought, to be able to run into his arms and stay in their shelter. He'd been in her mind constantly these last weeks, for no matter how many gowns were bought for her, or how comfortable this house felt, she'd gladly have given them up to be near her guardian and her brother.

"I'd best go and comb my hair before I beard the lion in his den,'' she said to Elizabeth with a laugh.

"I think I'll come with you to see what you will wear tonight. I cannot seem to make up my mind,'' the other girl told her, and the two asked to be excused.

Lord Meredith rejoined his mother after putting his daughter into her bed.

"Elizabeth has grown into a very beautiful young lady,'' he remarked to Lady Meredith. "I'd be most surprised if she did not take well her first Season and make a good match right away.''

"She is lovely, isn't she? And her manners are most charming.'' Lady Meredith suddenly decided to take the bull by the horns and get it over with. "The two of them are the best of friends, and look very well together, so I have decided to bring out Georgina at the same time as Elizabeth.''

"You have *what?*'' her son bellowed. "It won't do at all, Mother,'' he said more quietly, "for Georgina's behavior and the family's lack of funds preclude any chance she might have had to make a suitable match. It would be a complete waste of money, and as the money spent would be mine, I forbid it.''

"Then I will be responsible for bringing her out and absorb the extra cost myself,'' she said. "It cannot be so terribly expensive, for both girls will share an abigail, and Devon is paying the cost of the coming-out ball. Georgina's companion, Mrs. Robinson, can look after both girls when I can't be there. The only extra expense will be the cost of Georgina's clothes, and as she already has quite a few excellent day and dinner gowns, it will simply be a matter of buying her a few ball gowns and one for the court presentation.''

Anger blazed in her son's eyes. "I will not permit it, Mother. You know nothing about the chit. She's not at all what you think she is.'' He rose. "Now, if you will excuse me, I will go and perform a distasteful but necessary task.''

When she was alone, Lady Meredith sent for the butler and gave instructions for Cook to prepare some of her son's favorite foods, knowing as she did so that the kitchen was in all likelihood already in an uproar in Cook's haste to comply even before she received the order.

She also sent for Mrs. Robinson, then sat down to write a short note of regret to the hostess whose dinner party she would not be attending. When Robbie entered the room, she asked her to take the girls to the dinner party tonight in her stead.

As she went along the corridor, listening to Elizabeth's chatter, Georgina had a strange sense of foreboding, and as soon as she opened her bedroom door and they stepped into the room, she knew why.

The gown she was to wear to dinner tonight was hanging waiting, but the rest of the room was in a state of dishevelment as Daisy was busily packing the contents of her entire ward-robe into several portmanteaus and other pieces of luggage.

The maid looked startled and unhappy. "It's his lordship's orders, milady. He gave instructions the minute he stepped into the hall. I'm to help you dress, then finish this while you're out to dinner." She pointed to a soft blue carriage dress and a pelisse and bonnet in a slightly darker shade. "Will they suit for the journey, y'ladyship?"

"He can't do this to you, Georgina. Grandmama will not allow him to," Elizabeth cried, appearing at that moment to be the more upset of the two girls.

Georgina dismissed the maid, telling her she would call her back in a few minutes.

"Lady Meredith cannot stop him, as he has already made the decision. He is my guardian, after all," she said as she put her arms around her friend. "I knew all along it was just too good to be true, but Lady Meredith was so insistent." She nodded toward the evening gown hanging outside the armoire. "That was what I intended to wear, but I will not be needing it now."

"You mean you will not come tonight?"

Georgina shook her head. "I couldn't. I have to see your uncle in about twenty minutes, although why he needs must see me after this, I do not know. After tonight you'll not have my company anyway."

"Perhaps something awful happened to your grandmother and you have to return for a brief visit?" Elizabeth suggested hopefully. "Then you'll be back before the London Season."

"Something happened and he did not tell me? You do not really believe that, do you?" As the other girl reluctantly agreed, Georgina pushed her toward the door. "Leave me for now, and take Daisy with you. Come in to see me when you get back, and we'll say good-bye then in case it is too difficult in the morning. And I beg you, do not make a fuss, please, Elizabeth. It will not do any good, and may even make it worse."

When she was alone once more, Georgina packed the remaining garments into the bags. Then she sank into a chair by the side of the fireplace, trying hard to hide her disappointment. The fire had been lit early, as it had turned a little cold, and she sat watching without seeing the flames as they leapt over and around the large log.

Her eyes brimmed with tears, but she angrily brushed them away. I won't cry, she told herself determinedly. I won't give him the satisfaction of seeing he made me cry. He was so fair with everyone else, but he had condemned her again without a hearing.

She'd been excited about the Season, but it was really not very important, and until Lady Meredith mentioned it she had never imagined becoming a part of it all. At least she'd got a lot of new clothes out of it, but most of them would have to remain at Broadacres when she slipped away from there, for he couldn't make her stay unless he locked her in her room forever. And even if he did, she was used to getting out of the window. Grandmama would turn a blind eye anyway, if she got wind of her leaving.

She'd have to cut her hair again and dress as a boy, for now she knew she couldn't travel alone as a young lady. It was a good thing she had brought Starlight back with her.

The half-hour was almost up but she didn't really care whether she kept him waiting or not. Slowly she got up, and without even glancing in the mirror to see what she looked like, she left the bedchamber and walked along the corridor and over to the library. A footman held the door for her and she stepped inside with her head held high.

In the normal way of things, the library was just about Georgina's favorite room in the house. It was lined with the works of every writer she had ever heard of, and a great many she had not, and there were two big wing chairs in the window, where it was comfortable to curl up and read for hours on end without anyone who looked in even seeing you.

It also contained a large mahogany desk, seldom used when Lord Meredith was away, as the ladies all had smaller desks in their bedchambers, where they could write notes to friends or address invitations. In any case, the chair behind the desk was so massive it was impossible for a woman to find a comfortable position in it.

Now, however, Georgina looked enviously at the wing chairs as Lord Meredith pointed to a smaller one conveniently placed in front of the desk, and after he was also seated, she was forced to admit to herself that he fitted the big chair perfectly.

Had she known it, her guardian was already regretting his hasty request to have her things packed and ready to leave in the morning. His orders had been given as the butler was removing his coat, and he had actually intended them to be carried out during the evening while the girls were enjoying whatever entertainment they had planned.

But he had just spent an unpleasant few minutes with his niece, who had stormed into the room just after he entered, saying something about Georgina's clothes having been already packed. When Elizabeth became incoherent, he had unceremoniously thrust her into the drawing room to make her complaints to his mother.

Certainly he had not wished to hurt Georgina by having her enter her room to find her bags being packed without explanation. But if it was already done, there was no way he could undo it now.

She was certainly much improved in appearance from the ragamuffin he had first met—in fact she was fast becoming a very beautiful young lady. He could not fault her manners, even now when she must surely be very hurt and angry with him.

Nevertheless, she had behaved in a most inexcusable manner on the journey from Lisbon to Settle House. She had given her word to be guided through the journey by Davis and Mrs. Robinson, but at the first sign of excitement she had joined in the fight, like an Amazon warrior, brandishing a knife and making a fool of herself instead of leaving the fighting to the men who were paid to protect her.

What if she'd been hit by a stray bullet, or captured by the bandits and abused before being ransomed? She deserved a thrashing for taking such risks.

Then, as if she hadn't done enough, she had made herself known to Norbert Frost on the yacht, probably told him about her part in routing the bandits, too, and before long it would be the talk of the *ton*.

Something had to be done about it, for if word got out while she was still under his roof, Elizabeth's chances of making a good match would be considerably marred by her association with the chit. And what might she not teach his little Louise? He shuddered at the thought.

13

It seemed to Georgina that the man sitting eyeing her with cold distaste could not possibly be the one who had taken her hand in his and told her he would be her friend, someone she could turn to for help or advice at any time.

She hadn't changed, except outwardly, since then. She had just done what she felt she had to at the time. Why, then, had he changed so much?

"I would like you to tell me, in your own words, what happened from the minute you left Lisbon until the time you entered this house," he said coldly. "Take your time, and do not omit anything, no matter how unimportant-seeming."

"Why? Is it not true that you've received a report, made your decision, and have put it into effect? I find it a little late for explanations." She spoke bitterly and her eyes flashed scornfully. "You have tried me, found me guilty, and commenced the execution. Pray do not stop now, but simply tell me the time of departure and who will escort the prisoner. You would not be so cruel as to leave me dangling, sir, surely?"

"Never mind the histrionics," he said in the same icy tone. "I asked for an explanation from you and fully intend to get it."

"And what will you do if I choose not to give you one, sir?" she asked insolently. "You've already done your worst."

"You think so? You will do as I ask, or you'll go home without your horse. Starlight will stay with me until you learn some obedience." The words were uttered softly, but there was an edge of steel to them.

"You wouldn't dare," she said defiantly. "Starlight is mine and if you keep her you'll be no better than a horse thief."

"It's entirely up to you." His drawl was deceptively calm.

"I think I hate you more than anyone I've ever known in my life, including my grandmother." Georgina's voice was pitched low, and every word came out slowly and distinctly.

"Before you left Lisbon, you made a commitment to obey Davis and Mrs. Robinson, but you had not the slightest intention of keeping that promise. You went armed with a knife, and at the first opportunity you burst from the coach like some female warrior brandishing your weapon, instead of allowing the outriders to do the job of protecting you for which they were paid," he thundered. "Did it never once occur to you that you could have got yourself killed?"

Georgina looked shocked. "Is that what you believe happened?"

"It is what I was told. If it is untrue, deny it—if you can," he challenged.

She regarded him in silence for a moment, then said contemptuously, "I did what I thought was right at the time. I did promise to do only what Robbie or Davis told me to, but sometimes things don't go according to plan, my dear doubting lord." She paused to enjoy the anger she was deliberately igniting in him. "Robbie is still unaware I did aught save care for Davis when she was too frightened and too sick. What should I have done, my dear lord? Let that bandit kill your batman?" Her voice rose and she laughed bitterly. "I didn't think of it at the time, but who knows, he might have turned around and shot Robbie and me next."

"He wouldn't have shot you. You'd have been taken prisoner," Lord Meredith remarked, concealing his anger once more behind a facade of indifference, and he saw the shudder she couldn't suppress.

"I cannot think who gave you such damning information against me," Georgina said slowly, gazing at him disdainfully. "Davis was the only one who had the full story, for the outriders were fighting off the attack on the other side of the coach. I know Davis resented me for not allowing him to walk on his wounded leg and start up the bleeding again, but I cannot think he would lie about me. Why should he? I was only trying to help him.''

''It seems you forgot about the coachman,'' Lord Meredith said sarcastically.

Her eyes wide, she gazed in amazement at her guardian. ''He could not possibly have seen what happened. I was seated inside the coach with my back to the horses when I threw the knife through the open window. I stepped out to check on Davis only after the bandit's horse had bolted with him.''

''And would you be willing to swear to that?'' he taunted.

''I don't lie, sir, so I have no need to swear oaths,'' she said with pride.

''Do you also deny that you dined with Lord Frost on the way here from Dover?'' he asked. His voice sounded almost bland, but she knew better.

''That was none of my doing,'' Georgina snapped. She was not going to take the blame for going along with her chaperon's wishes. ''Robbie was afraid to travel at night, so we stopped at an inn. I did not want to stop, but after we did, I would have been content to have something light served in our suite when we found there were no private dining rooms left. While we talked to the innkeeper, Lord Frost came out of a private parlor and offered to share it.''

''How very convenient,'' Lord Meredith said with deep sarcasm. ''He came out and offered to share his parlor with two ladies he'd never met, and Mrs. Robinson agreed?''

''It was not like that,'' she protested, a little weakly. ''Robbie had met him on the yacht while I was attending to Davis, so he offered his parlor to her and was then introduced to me.''

''I see,'' was all he said; then, ''Were there any other passengers on board?''

Georgina closed her eyes for a moment. It would make his decision to return her to Yorkshire an easy one, but she had to tell him, she couldn't lie. When she looked at him again, her face pictured the despair she felt.

''I have to tell you. I'm no good at prevaricating.'' She

looked him straight in the eye as she made her admission. "Robbie did not know that I had already met him. He was the only other passenger on the ship, and he spoke to me on deck when I went up alone for some fresh air. Robbie was too seasick to leave the cabin."

"I see," he said grimly. "And you asked him not to tell anyone, and lied to Mrs. Robinson." He nodded disgustedly, as if it were what he expected.

"I did not ask him anything, and I did not lie—I just didn't tell her I'd spoken to him," she protested heatedly. "It was not arranged. I was looking out to sea when he came up behind me and spoke."

He came around the desk and sat on the front edge of it, quite close to her.

"I believe you, so stop looking so belligerent. I appreciate the fact that although no one else knew of this meeting, you still told me. Did I listen to the wrong people and misjudge you?"

Georgina nodded, then looked down, but strong brown fingers gently raised her chin until she was looking into his eyes. She knew he was going to let her stay before he said the words, and she couldn't quite believe her good fortune.

"I am more sorry about this than you could possibly know. I will personally see to it that your clothes are unpacked during dinner, and I give you my solemn word that if I ever again believe that you deserve to be banished, I'll speak to you before giving any orders. That hurt the most, didn't it?" he asked softly.

She nodded again.

He stood up, helped her to her feet, then offered his arm. "Mother must think that by now I have killed you. Join her and I will return shortly."

He left her at the door to the drawing room, where an anxious Lady Meredith waited.

"I see from your face that all is well at last, child," she said with a sigh of relief. "My son is scrupulously honest and I found it beyond belief that he would be so unjust. But he's had reason enough to distrust women. He doesn't know how very fond of him you are, does he?"

Georgina looked startled. She'd told no one how he made her feel. How could his mother have guessed?

Lady Meredith smiled. "I am likely the only one to notice your face when his name comes up, my dear. But he's not been very kind to women of late. I hope you don't suffer further hurt." She was unable to say more, as her son entered the room and went over to the sherry decanter.

"I think Georgina, in particular, could do with a small glass to steady her nerves after my unwarranted behavior. How about you, Mother, or have you been quietly tippling for the past half-hour?" he asked with a mischievous grin.

Her ladyship pretended to be outraged, though secretly delighted to see him lighthearted once again.

As the second sip of sherry, which she had discovered she liked very much, warmed and relaxed Georgina, she ventured to ask a question she'd been anxious about ever since he arrived, but a sharp knock on the door interrupted and Nanny came in.

"I'm sorry to disturb you, your ladyship, but it's Louise. She never goes to sleep without a good-night kiss from Lady Georgina, and tonight her ladyship forgot about the little one." She looked reproachfully at Georgina. "I thought I could talk her out of it, but she'll have none of it. It has to be her Gina, as she calls her, or she'll keep right on crying until she's sick, I know."

Georgina looked at Lady Meredith, who nodded. "Run along, my dear, then come back and finish your sherry," she said.

She followed Nanny out of the room and up to the nursery, where a pitiful little girl had thrown all her toys on the floor and was crying her heart out. Her Gina hadn't come to kiss her good night! The tears stopped as soon as she heard the soothing, familiar voice.

Georgina's arms enfolded the child she'd grown to love. Soon the kiss and the cuddle did their work and Louise was fast asleep. Taking her kerchief, Georgina wiped away the tears still on the baby face, then kissed her cheek once more.

As she got up to leave, she almost bumped into the tall figure standing quietly behind her. "It seems you have the magic touch," he murmured, placing an arm around her shoulder and leading her out of the nursery wing and into the old schoolroom.

He smiled gently at her upturned, questioning face. "I just wanted you to know that your clothes are being unpacked now, and by morning everything will be newly pressed and back in your bedchamber. Once again, I'm deeply sorry for thinking so badly of you." He grinned. "You're quite a little spitfire."

She suddenly remembered, with mortification, what she'd said to him. "It was untrue, my lord, please believe me—I don't hate you!"

"We both said things we did not mean," he murmured, looking into her eyes that now seemed more green than hazel. He ran a finger lightly down her nose, and as it touched her soft lips, they parted. Without conscious thought he drew her closer and brought his mouth gently down on those parted lips. It was a tentative, tasting kiss, full of sweetness, and for Georgina it was the most wonderful feeling in the world, worth all the heartache that had gone before.

He raised his head, only now realizing that he'd done something he had no right to do. He'd taken advantage of her youth and innocence, and if some other man had done it he would have thrashed him.

"We had best rejoin my mother," he said gruffly, releasing her and steering her into the hall. "Come and finish your sherry, and then we'll have dinner."

As though in a dream, Georgina walked ahead of him into the drawing room, where Lady Meredith still waited.

"I'm glad to see you did not desert me," she said with a happy smile. "You need not change tonight, Georgina, as we are just family."

"Can you tell me how William does, my lord?" Georgina asked, trying not to sound like a mother hen who has lost its chick.

"Very well indeed. I believe the army will be the making of him. His initiative has improved considerably, his natural caution is not a bad thing in an officer, and he is able to take orders much better than a quicker-thinking man." His eyes narrowed as he carefully considered his next statement. "I hate to tell you this, but he probably needed to get away from your influence."

"But, I didn't—" she started to say, perturbed by his remark, but he put up a hand to stop her.

"Let me explain," he said. "You are extremely quick and have an exceptional ability and eagerness to learn. Both in book learning and in physical activities you apparently excel, and it would seem that when William could not compete with you he sat back and allowed you to do things for him. Now that he is forced to do things for himself, he is finding that he actually does quite well many things he never tried before. You'll notice a difference when next you see him."

"You think I made him slow?" Georgina asked, much concerned.

"No, the slowness was there to begin with," he assured her.

He came to sit on the couch next to her and took her hand in his. "You could no more help being quick than he could help being slow. When you see him, take a back seat and watch him, and I think you'll be pleasantly surprised." Her hand felt good in his large one, and her whole arm seemed to be responding to his touch.

"Shall I see him soon?" she asked hopefully.

"I believe so. By the time you're in London, he'll probably be ready for a leave."

As he rose and released her hand, he gave it a friendly pat, and she smiled gratefully up at him. For a moment something warm and tender seemed to pass between them; then he turned away, remembering what Lady Leicester had said, and angry with himself.

After a more intimate dinner than usual, Lord Meredith's port was brought to the drawing room with the ladies' tea, and mother and son spent the evening reminiscing and making Georgina laugh at the foibles and fribbles of a society that put too much emphasis on its own importance in the scheme of things.

They were still there, laughing heartily at an account of one lady's efforts to get an offer from a very high-in-the-instep earl, when Elizabeth and Mrs. Robinson returned from their dinner party.

One look at Georgina's smiling face was all Elizabeth needed to know that all was well, but she refused to let her uncle off scot-free.

"You should be ashamed of yourself, Uncle Matthew, for upsetting us all so," she told him severely. "Had I not seen it for myself, I could not have believed it of you."

He became serious immediately, and for a moment Georgina feared her friend had gone too far in her defense and might have given him cause to be angry once more.

"I am ashamed, little niece, though it was never my intent to cause so much hurt. The packing was to have been done tonight, following my talk with Georgina. As it turns out, there would have been a cancellation of the orders and no harm done. I had forgot how anxious my staff are to do my bidding, and somewhat inclined to be overzealous."

Elizabeth was not yet satisfied, however. "But why were you so angry with her? She had done nothing wrong."

Georgina knew she had to stop Elizabeth from spoiling things by getting him angry again. "You do not know me, Elizabeth. I have been known to behave with shocking impropriety. Your uncle is, in fact, being magnanimous in permitting me to stay, and if you recall, I had no expectation of his allowing me to make my come-out."

"Enough!" Lady Meredith took charge. "I am content that my son and his ward are on good terms once more. The past is done with, so let's not harp on it further. I believe we ladies would all benefit from a good night's sleep—and from the looks of you, Matthew, a little rest would not go amiss with you either."

She ushered the ladies out of the room and, all agreeing with her, they repaired to their respective bedchambers.

Lord Meredith stayed behind, sipping on another glass of the port, which had been left at his elbow.

He had been amazed to find how lovely his ward had become with the right clothes and a little attention to her skin and hair, and he was very sorry indeed to have caused her so much hurt.

He knew of the attack on the carriage, for the outriders were his own men and had informed him of the batman's injury immediately they returned. They had been surprised when, in the midst of the attack, the bandits had turned and headed back to the hills, and assumed that it was Davis who had routed them before being injured, until the coachman gave him a highly dramatized version of what had happened.

When Davis returned to camp, he was reluctant to say much about it other than confirm that Georgina had knifed the bandit. From the coachman's imaginative description of something he had not seen, Lord Meredith had envisioned her entering into battle like some of the women one heard of occasionally, who joined the army in male garb and fought beside their menfolk. Also, Davis had told him about the dinner with Frost, and had got entirely the wrong impression.

Lord Meredith had become strangely fond of his ward on his visits to Lisbon, and when he thought she had deliberately defied him once more, and behaved like a battling Amazon, an unreasoning anger had taken hold of him. With it had also come a fear for her safety, and more anger that she had put herself in danger.

Now he realized that since Mrs. Robinson was actually in the carriage with her and didn't know that Georgina had saved Davis' life, then she must indeed have acted with swiftness and accuracy. He smiled to himself. At some future time, when Georgina felt more like talking about it, he must find out what had really happened.

The fact that Frost was on the yacht returning from Portugal was a piece of information he found most interesting. As soon as he got the chance, he would ask Georgina to try to think of all and anything the man had said, for there was no doubt he would have asked her a lot of questions. He knew for a fact that the inn at which they stayed had many private dining rooms, as it was a very popular stopping place on the road from Dover to London. It was a little hard to believe that although there was a suite available for them, all dining rooms were occupied. There was a very good chance that

Frost wished either to ingratiate himself with the two ladies or to obtain information from them, and had greased the palm of the innkeeper for his own ends.

Yes, he must talk further with Georgina tomorrow. She certainly had a way with Louise, he mused. The child had really been making herself ill with crying, but it had taken just a few minutes of loving from Georgina to quiet her, and she'd fallen asleep contentedly after that.

Ever since Lady Leicester had laughingly told him, in her garden in Lisbon, that the girl had developed a *tendre* for him, he had been gruff with her in an effort to stop her liking him too much and getting hurt. He had no time for women, at least for the ones who were not able to look after themselves, and usually he didn't really care, but he'd not wanted to hurt Georgina in that way. How ironic, he thought, that in the end he'd hurt her even more.

She should take very well this Season. She had looks, and a little something else that was very appealing. His mother would have to keep a close eye on the men who called to see her. He couldn't let her tie herself up to the wrong sort, who would bring her nothing but unhappiness. She needed someone a little older, who would keep her on a loose but secure rein. Someone with a good sense of humor, who would understand when she got herself into a scrape, and love her for it. He had no intention of giving his approval unless the man was absolutely right for her.

Of course, he'd have to talk to his mother tomorrow about a dowry for her. She had the breeding, of that there was no question, and he would come up with enough to satisfy most of the *ton*, but not enough to attract fortune hunters.

He stretched. His mother had been right, as usual: he did need some sleep. With a nod to the waiting footman, he went to his bedchamber.

"How do you like this cream satin, Georgina? It would be just the thing to set off your coloring," Elizabeth pronounced. "White really doesn't suit you so well."

"I know," Georgina said with a chuckle. "After years in the sun, my complexion will never be as lovely as yours. The cream with the apple-green trim would be nice, though frankly, a trim of light coffee would be more sophisticated.''

The dressmaker looked up to see what the young ladies were talking about, and then nodded emphatically, hampered by a mouth full of pins.

A pretty sitting room overlooking gardens at the back of the house had been set aside for the dressmaker's use, and Georgina was standing on the soft green carpet, being poked and pinned once more.

Through the open casement windows she could just catch occasional glimpses of Louise and her father as they played hide-and-seek, and could hear Louise's shrill, happy laughter. What a pain this was. She'd have given much to be able to join in the fun instead of being fitted for even more gowns.

Finally they were finished, and joined Lady Meredith for luncheon.

''Matthew will be along shortly. I hope you'll both forgive him for spending so much of his time with his daughter. For my part, I am only too happy to see the pleasure they derive from each other. It is the exception, in this day, for a parent to see his offspring for longer than an hour a day, but I think Matthew still recalls how much the late Lord Meredith and I loved our children.'' Lady Meredith's smile was a little misty as she recalled those far-off days.

She turned toward Georgina. ''My son and I had a chance this morning to discuss your Season, and despite your misgivings, he is in complete agreement with our plans for both Bath and for the London Season. On the matter of a dowry for you, he is being even more generous than I had hoped. I had considered fifteen thousand pounds a reasonable sum, but my son feels that twenty thousand pounds would be more the thing. So that is settled.''

''You mean he plans to buy a husband for me, my lady?'' Georgina had never heard of such a thing, but then, she had never moved in society before. ''I cannot allow him to. If no one wants me as I am, I would rather stay an old maid!''

''Stop being such a goose, Georgina,'' Elizabeth said, gurgling with laughter. ''Don't you know that every young lady has to have a dowry? Mine is to be thirty thousand pounds, isn't it, Grandmama?''

''Yes, it is, Elizabeth, and I can see that we still have much to teach Georgina about the ways of society . . . and about a ward's ingratitude,'' her ladyship said with some severity.

Lord Meredith entered the dining room and they all took their places. ''It would appear I missed a joke which only you found amusing, Elizabeth,'' he remarked, noting Georgina's downcast eyes. ''Is it a private one, or can you tell me?''

Lady Meredith put up a hand to stop her granddaughter's explanation. ''I was just telling Georgina of the handsome dowry to which you have agreed, and it appears she has never heard of such a thing,'' she told her son.

Georgina shook her head angrily. ''I don't want you to buy a husband for me, even if it is usual. Elizabeth is laughing because I did not know. It is grossly unfair for you to spend your money first on William and now on me.''

Lord Meredith gave her a tolerant smile, then glanced around the table. ''Let me make a suggestion. We'll forget about it until after luncheon; then Georgina and I will take a walk in the garden and discuss it privately. All right, Georgina?''

Although he didn't say so, she got the feeling he had not intended his mother to tell her about it first. ''Very well, my lord,'' she agreed.

A bench was strategically placed in a sheltered spot left in its natural state at the edge of an ornamental lake, and it was here that Lord Meredith took Georgina, made sure she was comfortable, then perched himself on a rock at the edge of the water, from which he could see her face as they talked.

She was very much enjoying the attention he was giving her, and now felt more at ease with him than she had since those morning rides in Lisbon. The water rippled in the background, and she could smell the woodsy scent of blue-bells and primroses that carpeted the ground beneath the tall elms. An excited jay, in his beautiful spring plumage, flew screaming across the lake, as if he resented their intrusion.

Lord Meredith was smiling gently. "I was particularly touched last night, my dear, that you told me, of your own free will, about that first meeting with Lord Frost. I am considerably interested in the questions he asked you, and your replies." He paused meaningfully. "Nothing you tell me will make me angry or displeased with you, I promise. But if you could try to recall, these next few days, the conversations you had, perhaps even write it down when something occurs to you, I would be very much indebted to you."

"I didn't tell him, but he guessed that I was coming here, and he said he knew you well," Georgina remarked. She determined that she would sit down and really try to remember every word that had passed between her and Lord Frost. Above anything else, she wanted to help her cousin in any way she could.

"He has always lived in the vicinity, so we have met more frequently than I would wish," he said, "but as for knowing me well, I can assure you he does not."

Georgina watched a big bumblebee going from flower to flower, then made her decision. "Are you aware that, though he is away at the moment, he is a frequent visitor here, that we've been with Robbie to see Falcone Priory, and that he often takes us out for a drive?"

She had expected him to register surprise, and she was not disappointed, as his usually lazy eyelids lifted and his gentle smile turned to a look of astonishment. "What in the name of . . . ?" he started, then changed it quickly to, "What can my mother be thinking of? I appreciate your telling me, and I will speak to Lady Meredith about it."

"He is always very charming and seems to like your family very much. Has he done something wrong to make you so opposed to him?" Georgina asked.

The former lazy warmth had returned to his eyes. "Nothing I have proof of, but I've been suspicious for some time of the way he is able to travel freely between England and the Continent. You will recall how difficult it was for me to secure a passage for you, yet he goes backward and forward with ease. I'd rather you tell no one about my suspicions, however, for they could be completely unfounded. Just the same, he is hardly the type of man I like you to associate with. But enough of him." His languid smile turned to a broad grin, and his eyes twinkled. "What is all this about not wanting a dowry?"

"Would you like to feel you had been sold like a piece of merchandise?" she asked, drawing herself up with as much dignity as she could muster.

His mouth quirked. "Come down from the boughs, young lady. There are many practices I do not particularly like, but dowering a would-be bride is not one of them. I promise I will not allow anyone I do not feel is worthy to press his suit, and there will be no question of your marrying anyone you do not wish to."

"But I cannot allow you to put money out on my behalf. All these clothes you have bought are bad enough, but . . ." She tried to appeal to his understanding.

"Can you believe how guilty I feel for the years when, had I made the effort, I could have traveled to Yorkshire, found out conditions there, and made your life that much easier? Won't you at least allow me to make up for it a little?" He knew she was being persuaded, and used his last weapon. "And, of course, when you make a very suitable match, it will tremendously enhance your brother's chances in the Marriage Mart."

She pursed her lips, but there was a reluctant acceptance in her eyes. "Very well. I suppose I will have to agree, won't I?" she said; then her lips parted in a smile of thanks and his patience was rewarded.

He reached out, and she took his hand gladly, then walked slowly back with him to the house to tell Lady Meredith that there would be no change in her plans to take both girls to Bath next week and then to London a month or so later.

14

Georgina was meticulous in her effort to remember all the questions Lord Frost had asked in regard to her visit to Portugal and to her connection with Lord Meredith. She wrote them out in her fine hand and gave the piece of paper to him the following day as he was going into the library.

"Come," he said, putting an arm around her and drawing her into the room with him, "stay with me while I read it, in case I have any questions."

This time he took her over to her favorite wing chairs, and when she was seated in one of them, he perched on the arm and started to read.

"I'm afraid it's not much, but I'm sure it's everything he asked," she said quietly.

He gave her a warm smile. "Did you notice him in deep conversation with anyone in the inn or on the ship? The captain, perhaps?"

"No. While we talked, he waved to the captain, but that was all."

"As he told you, his mother was French, and Napoleon has been known to promise restoration of former estates to refugees willing to work for him. Norbert has never forgotten that château and the forests around it. He was always talking of it when we were youngsters, as though it was double the size of his inheritance on his father's side. What did you think of Falcone Priory?"

"To be honest, I loved it. From the large, welcoming front door to the rug-covered stone floors, it was warm and earthy. What kind of a little boy was he?" Georgina was curious.

"Not a very pleasant one, as far as other children were concerned. He was always charming to adults, but my sister and I avoided him whenever we could." He patted her hand with the folded paper. "This is perfect, exactly what I wanted. You've done very well."

She felt she might easily burst with pride at his praise, and her cheeks went a rosy pink.

"Tell me, are you looking forward to your trip to Bath?"

"Very much, my lord," she told him, "but I will miss Louise."

"She is a bundle of joy, isn't she? And you've been quite wonderful with her." He touched her pink cheek lightly. "I depart for London tomorrow, and will not see you until after you return from Bath. Do you think you might start calling me Matthew? If you think of me that way while you're gone, it will come naturally, I'm sure. William has done so for some time now."

She looked at him with wide eyes. "Thank you, my lord," she said, and quickly changed it to "Matthew" as his eyebrows lifted.

He reached for her hand and pulled her out of the chair, then stood looking at her as though memorizing her face. For one joyous moment she thought he might kiss her again, and she was sure she could feel vibrations passing between the two of them, but suddenly he released her hand and moved away.

"Let's see if we can find Louise," he suggested as he opened the door for her and they went off together in the direction of the nursery.

There seemed to be an atmosphere of gloom about the house when he had gone. Louise was too young to be able to keep her promise to him that she would not cry, and she kept waking through the night asking for him, and clung to an also saddened Georgina as though she would never let her go.

After two days of such depression, Lady Meredith could stand it no longer. "Such doldrums are completely absurd, and I, for one, have had enough of them. What you girls need is some useful activity, so I have decided we will journey to

Bath a few days earlier than I planned. Rental of the house on Royal Crescent commenced several days ago, so I will send some of the maids and footmen there today to get the house in order, and we will leave two days hence.''

"But everything has still to be packed, Grandmama,'' Elizabeth protested, "and you were going to send Louise to my mama and papa ahead of time.''

Lady Meredith looked pained. "You girls need something to do, and I propose that you help Daisy with your packing, so it will be done all the quicker.'' She paused, then gave Georgina a searching look. "As for Louise, I have been wondering if we could possibly take her with us. She is so unhappy at parting with her father that I am reluctant to separate her from you also, Georgina. You'll be busy attending balls and going for drives, but if you could just spare her a little of your time, I think she'd be much happier staying with us until we remove to London.''

Georgina's ready smile, which had been noticeably absent these last two days, suddenly reappeared. Seeing Matthew leave had been more painful than she would have believed, but being able to keep Louise with her for a little longer cheered her considerably.

"I'll gladly make time for her, my lady, whatever else there is to do. I was thinking sadly of how much I will miss her, but if she comes along we'll be able to explore Bath together and have such fun.'' She sprang to her feet with renewed energy. "Come along, Elizabeth, let's go find Daisy and get started.''

Settle House became a hive of activity, and only four days later the two coaches, numerous outriders, family, servants, and an enormous quantity of luggage reached the outskirts of Bath.

The only city Georgina had lived in, other than her short stay with William in London, was Lisbon, and though ancient also, Bath was very different. The house Lady Meredith had rented was one of thirty very large residences sweeping magnificently in a semicircle and looking like one gigantic building. Built of a honey-colored stone, and bathed in sunlight when they drove up, it looked to Georgina like a tremendous golden palace, and she knew immediately she was going to enjoy her stay.

"Tomorrow we must put our names in Mr. King's book in order to become subscribers," Lady Meredith announced at dinner. "Mr. King is master of ceremonies, and a very important man in the town, or so he thinks himself."

"Are there balls every night, Grandmama?" Elizabeth asked.

"Not every night. At this time of year they are held in the new Assembly Rooms, and if I recall correctly, there is a dress ball on Mondays when only country dances are permitted, card assemblies on Tuesdays, and a fancy-dress ball on Thursdays. There are concerts every Wednesday evening, and the balls begin at about seven and end promptly at eleven. On other evenings we will either entertain here or dine with some of my acquaintances."

"But we'll be exhausted, Grandmama, and start to look hagged," Elizabeth protested.

"You will stay abed until noon quite frequently, and then pay visits or receive visitors in the afternoons, ride in the park with some of the young men, and so forth." Her ladyship was amused by their surprise. "I cannot imagine that you will not enjoy it once you are accustomed and once you are admired by a few handsome young men."

"Now I understand why we need so many gowns," Georgina remarked, "for we could wear one out very easily, and people would get tired of seeing the same one all the time."

They were all feeling quite weary after their long journey, and as soon as dinner was over, Lady Meredith ordered tea to be served in her bedchamber, and recommended that the others follow suit and sleep late if they wished.

But Georgina was too excited to sleep late, and had never lost the habit of rising early to get William ready for his day. Accordingly, she went in to breakfast and found herself eating alone. She'd scarcely finished, however, when she heard the sound of Louise and Nanny in the hall, and then the front door closing behind them.

Gulping the rest of her tea down quickly, she hastened to the window and saw them crossing to the lawn that ran the entire length of the Crescent and sloped downward toward a park. It took her but a moment to return to her bedchamber for her bonnet, reticule, and pelisse; then, despite the way the butler looked askance at her leaving the house alone, she ran lightly down the steps, across the lawn, and caught up with the pair before they entered the park.

When they drove into the town in the afternoon, Georgina felt somehow comforted by the familiar uniforms, though the reminder of her brother and Matthew made her a little downcast. The Assembly Rooms were not too far away, just beyond a circle of very fine houses built of the same honey-colored stone as the Crescent. Lady Meredith said this was called the Circus, and many of her friends stayed there when in Bath.

When they reached Milsom Street they alighted from the carriage and Lady Meredith gave the coachman instructions as to when and where he should be waiting for them.

While the others were looking at the store windows, Georgina's attention was held by the large number of sedan chairs conveying invalids to the Pump Room for the waters. The chairmen threaded their way fearlessly through the stream of wagons, carriages, and drays, but few of the invalids peered out of the small windows and she supposed them to be too ill to care.

There were more uniforms at the concert that evening, and as they edged through the crowd to find their seats in the rows of gilt chairs, Lady Meredith smiled and nodded to many acquaintances. When the musicians paused, there was a rush to the refreshment room, where lemonade was served, but in the absence of a male to escort them, Lady Meredith preferred to stay in the main room, and soon several young men, dressed in dark coats and buff pantaloons, came to pay her their respects and to seek introductions to Elizabeth and Georgina.

"This is your first visit to Bath, my lady, isn't it?" The question came from a man who appeared slightly older than the others, exquisitely dressed in a deep blue jacket, pantaloons just a few shades lighter, and a most intricately tied cravat. Fine lines wrinkled the corners of his twinkling golden-brown eyes, though his face appeared quite serious.

Georgina knew she had been introduced to him, but she could not recall his name, and realized this was something she must work at if she did not wish to offend. She remembered he was an earl, but the earl of what?

"Oh dear, is it really so obvious that I am a greenhorn, my lord?" she asked him. "I had thought that if I sat here looking slightly bored I might be taken for a longtime resident."

"Tonight that might be possible, my lady, but when I observed you on Milsom Street this afternoon, you were staring at everything as though it was your first day in Bath." More fine wrinkles had appeared now, and a trace of a smile.

"It was, sir. But I shall most likely look the same tomorrow, and the next day, and even the day we leave a month hence, for I find it a quite delightful place and cannot see enough." She didn't want to look bored, like many of the ladies present tonight, and he may as well know it to begin with.

"Perhaps you would allow me the pleasure of showing you a little more of it. May I call on you tomorrow afternoon and take you for a drive?" he asked.

"I think so, but as you're the first person to ask, I'm not sure what I should say." She hadn't expected anyone to invite her out so soon.

"All you say is 'Yes, I would be delighted' or 'No, I'm sorry I have a previous commitment.' Which will it be?" He seemed amused by her honesty.

"Yes, sir. I would be delighted," she murmured.

"Would two o'clock be all right?" he asked with a broad grin.

As she nodded, another young man stepped forward to speak to her, and she was saved embarrassing herself further with her inept handling of an invitation.

In the carriage on the short ride home, Lady Meredith asked both girls how they had gone along. "I'm sure we will have quite a number of callers tomorrow, by the way they flocked around the two of you. Did any of them ask to take you for a drive?"

Taking a deep swallow, Georgina decided it was better to get it over with in the darkness of the carriage than in the lighted drawing room when they reached the house.

"Yes, my lady. And I'm afraid I handled it very badly and accepted the invitation," she confessed.

"There's nothing wrong in accepting an invitation to go for a drive, so long as he does not take you away from town. Who is your admirer?" Lady Meredith asked.

"That's the trouble. I don't know who he is." She sighed heavily. "I know I have to make myself listen carefully to names or I'll get into a fine pickle one of these days."

"I will give you no argument on that score," her ladyship said firmly. "Can you describe him?"

"He was an earl of something, I know. He was wearing a deep blue jacket and slightly lighter pantaloons, and he seemed older than the others, but very nice."

"My goodness, that's the Earl of Barstow." Lady Meredith sounded impressed. "I must say I wondered which one of you had caught his eye when he came over. He's quite a catch, but has been most elusive now for a number of years. I'm surprised, for he's not usually interested in first-year debutantes."

"He seemed to find me amusing, because he said he saw me in Milsom Street this afternoon looking as though it was my first time in Bath, and I told him it was," Georgina volunteered.

"Then he intends to show you some of the town, I'm sure, and is far too experienced to take you anywhere you shouldn't go. His mother has been ill for some time now, but we were always on the best of terms when she was able to get around." Lady Meredith was apparently quite satisfied with the results of their first venture into society.

Elizabeth's disposition was far too sweet for her to be jealous that Georgina had received the first invitation. She gladly helped her select a cream-colored gown in muslin, high-waisted and trimmed with warm beige ribbons, with which she would wear lighter beige gloves and a pretty cream hat.

After the success the night before, Lady Meredith expected to receive some callers, and was not disappointed when, a little before two o'clock, two of the young men they had spoken with the night before stopped by to pay their respects.

Georgina would have liked to see who else might visit, but just then the Earl of Barstow arrived, looking most handsome in a dark green brass-buttoned coat, buckskin breeches, and Hessian boots. His hair was a light sandy color worn *à la titus*, and his golden-brown eyes had a decided twinkle as he bowed low over Georgina's hand.

Lady Meredith had already greeted him, but added an admonition: "You will take good care of our young cousin, I am sure."

"You have my word, my lady," he smilingly replied, then escorted Georgina to where his curricle waited, drawn by two chestnut-colored horses that drew her immediate admiration.

"What beauties, my lord," she said a little enviously as he helped her into the carriage, then sat beside her and took the reins from his tiger.

"Do you, perhaps, drive, Lady Georgina?"

"Oh no!" She was surprised he had asked, as she had not seen any ladies driving themselves as yet. "In fact, this must be the first time I have ridden in such a light carriage."

Georgina felt she should be making conversation, but she was too interested in looking around her.

"If you don't drive, then I'd be willing to wager you enjoy horseback riding, don't you, my lady?" The earl was smiling at her benevolently as she showed her obvious pleasure in everything they passed.

She had no idea how delightful she looked as she smiled up at him. "You'd most certainly win your bet, my lord," she told him. "I love to ride."

She knew she should start to ask the things Robbie and Lady Meredith had instructed her in, to make casual conversation.

"Have you been in Bath long, my lord?" she asked, and had to smile at the trite question.

"Just a couple of weeks," he said with a wide grin. "And I plan to stay for about a month before continuing on to London."

Georgina's eyes opened wide. "What a coincidence," she innocently remarked. "That's how long we'll be here before we go to London."

"I know, that's what helped me arrive at my decision," he said with a deep chuckle.

"And you have, of course, been here many times before?" It was an assumption rather than a question, for he seemed to know his way around extremely well.

"Far too many times, I'm afraid, my dear, and I was beginning to think I would find nothing new here. This time I have been pleasantly surprised," he murmured softly.

She was about to ask him what had surprised him so pleasantly, and turned toward him. There was a warm look in his eyes that caught her unawares, and she blushed with confusion. She felt flattered that he was taking such an interest in her—but he didn't cause her to feel the warmth and excitement that her guardian made her feel without even trying.

They had crossed a bridge and passed a building with a discreet sign reading "Sydney Hotel," and were now coming toward what looked like a park.

"These are the Sydney Gardens," the earl remarked in a pleasantly casual tone of voice. "We'll circle them and then cross the river at a different spot."

He placed a warm hand on her arm as he pointed out a walk, much in use as an afternoon promenade, and she waited for the tingling sensation to start, but it didn't happen. He removed the hand a moment later as they were passing a post chaise, as he needed both hands on the reins. His touch had been pleasant, and she was enjoying herself tremendously, but she was still a little disappointed that the excitement wasn't there.

"Will you be at the Assembly Rooms this evening?" he asked.

"I don't think we will be there, as it's the fancy-dress ball tonight and we've not had time to find anything to wear. Are you going?" she asked, sorry now that she would miss dancing with him.

"No, I don't think so. Fancy dress has never appealed to me, but I was considering making an exception if I could dance with a certain impish young lady with chestnut curls.

Perhaps I will see you there on Friday night?'' Once again it was evident that he found her amusing.

"I'm sure we will be there on Friday," she said, smiling happily. "In fact, I'm looking forward so much to my first ball."

He turned toward her in surprise. "Your first ball? First ever? Now, come, you're funning me. I know they have balls in Yorkshire."

She'd said the wrong thing! Why didn't she think before she spoke? Her smile disappeared as she remembered her grandmother, and the old rags she had worn.

Stiffly she answered, "I'm sure they have, but I never attended any."

His hand lifted hers and his thumb gently caressed the palm. "I had no wish to bring back sad memories, my dear. Don't think back now, but look forward to your first ball, and I'll try my best to make it a very happy one for you."

"Thank you. I'm being silly, and you're very kind, my lord," she said, the more grateful to him for not asking questions.

"Not always, my lady, but with you I want to be kind. Do you understand?" he asked gently.

"Yes, I think so," she replied hesitantly.

They had reached Royal Crescent and he jumped down quickly to help her from the curricle. He held her hand just a little longer than was usual for a first drive, but she was not aware of it.

"Thank you very much, my lord. I thoroughly enjoyed myself," she told him quite honestly.

"It was a pleasure, my dear, that I hope to repeat often."

He bowed, then turned and got back onto the seat as she entered the house. He waited until the door closed behind her, then drove away.

15

Georgina was anxious to find out how Elizabeth had fared with her visitors, and after removing her hat and gloves, she hurried to the drawing room.

From the clink of china and spoons, and the laughter and murmur of several voices, she knew there must still be a number of visitors remaining, but she was not quite prepared to see at least a half-dozen gentlemen, two elderly ladies, and three younger ones about her own age, in addition to Lady Meredith, Mrs. Robinson, and Elizabeth.

"Georgina, my dear," Lady Meredith called to her as she hesitated on entering, "did you have a nice drive? Come here and let me introduce you to our guests."

With a commanding gesture she beckoned Georgina toward her to meet her old friends. Curtsying prettily and smiling at their compliments, she told Lady Meredith she'd had a lovely drive, then Robbie came over to take her to the younger group and make more introductions.

She had been too busy at last night's concert to notice many of the other subscribers, but the three girls had noticed her and Elizabeth and, in fact, had been brought to visit today because their sponsors were old hands and knew just where the more eligible young men would be this afternoon.

Georgina could not help but envy Elizabeth her poise and charm. She looked very lovely, and was making sure that no one, not even a rather frumpy-looking girl called Lady Freda, was left out of the conversation.

When tea was over and everyone had left, however, a very

different Elizabeth came excitedly into her bedchamber as she was deciding what to wear for dinner at home tonight.

"You must tell me all about it, Georgina. Where did you go, and what did he say, and will he call again?" she asked, stopping only to catch her breath. "I was so happy for you, as he is quite the most handsome, eligible man we've met."

Georgina wished her friend could have been the first to be taken for a drive, although, judging by the number of young men who had called, Elizabeth had not been lacking in popularity.

"He's very nice," Georgina agreed, "and despite the fact that I said all the wrong things, he didn't seem to mind. He did seem to like me despite my being a green girl, and he's going to be at the ball on Friday."

"What a pity we're staying home tonight. Did he say he'd be at the fancy-dress ball? Grandmama says we won't need fancy dress, as we will probably dine out or entertain on Thursdays." She sounded a little disappointed.

"He said he doesn't usually go, but he would have if we'd been attending. And he's going up to London about the time we are," Georgina said, and they both giggled like a pair of schoolgirls.

"He's very rich, and not at all old for you, according to Grandmama. He must be about Uncle Matthew's age, as they were at Cambridge together." Elizabeth looked at her friend and saw the telltale pink that had suffused her face. "You do like him, don't you? I know, because you're blushing."

Georgina thought it best for her to believe the blush was for the Earl of Barstow. Perhaps, if he continued to pay her attention, she would feel for him the way she now felt for her guardian.

Lady Meredith was well pleased with the way Georgina seemed to have taken here at Bath, and she hoped she would do as well in London. At Georgina's first ball the earl swept her into the first dance and eased her over her nervousness, and he danced with her before supper so that he could take her in and spend a little more time with her. He did the same at each ball they attended, and she enjoyed being with him more than with any of the several younger men who were also paying her a great deal of attention.

He took her out for a drive once each week they remained in Bath, but he firmly refused to be one of the many callers each afternoon at the house on Royal Crescent.

Despite her many activities, Georgina took time to play with Louise every morning, joining Nanny in the park when the weather was good, or in the nursery when it rained, and she never again failed to kiss her good night.

Finally the day came when all was packed once more, and they set off in three coaches on the return journey to Settle House, where they would spend a week before making the much shorter trip to their town house in London's Grosvenor Square.

Barstow had left the day before, promising Georgina he would call once they were settled, and take her riding in the park, and she was looking forward to this more than anything else in London. She intended to ride early in the morning, as the earl had pointed out to her that they could gallop only at that unfashionable hour.

The journey was tedious, however, and she spent most of her time with an unusually tearful Louise, who knew that the days she and Gina counted each night were getting shorter.

"Much as I love my granddaughter, Georgina, I will not tolerate these tantrums each time you have to leave her for an hour or so. The next time it happens, she will feel her first spanking," Lady Meredith promised, after enduring a half-hour of the child's screams.

"Please don't, my lady," Georgina implored. "I'll keep her with me every minute until we reach Settle House, I promise."

"That is not fair to you, Georgina. She is only a very distant cousin, after all, and should not become an imposition," Lady Meredith said firmly.

But after that Georgina made sure she left Louise only when absolutely essential, and each time, she carefully extracted a promise from her not to cry until she came back.

It was with considerable relief that Georgina glimpsed the familiar landscape, and then Settle House, which seemed by this time to be more like home than Broadacres had ever been to her.

As the carriages came to a halt in front of the house, Georgina stepped down and lifted Louise to the ground, then turned to give an extra hand to Lady Meredith. A cry of "Daddy, Daddy," came from the child, and she was running, so fast she must surely trip, toward the steps a smiling Lord Meredith was descending.

With his daughter riding high on his shoulder, he came to greet them; then, with his mother's hand on his arm for support, and Elizabeth on his other side chattering happily, Georgina watched Matthew climb the steps and enter the house, and she felt lonelier than she had felt in years. They were so complete, so happy as a family. Despite different personalities and petty squabbles, they were always there for each other. She felt so sad for what might have been for her and William if only their loving parents had not died. To hide the tears that suddenly threatened, she stepped back into the carriage, pretending to look for something she had left behind.

Georgina did not see any of them again until she went into the nursery to kiss Louise good night. A maid had come to tell her tea was being served in the drawing room, but she was by then too miserable to join them and they would have noticed she'd been crying, so she sent word that she was very tired and would rest in her bedchamber for a while.

Nanny was just tucking in the blanket covering the little girl when Georgina entered, and as she bent over the bed, Louise reached up and pulled her face toward her, loosening some of the curls she had just tried to arrange.

"Not so rough, you little tyke," she laughed, sitting on the bed and holding the child in her arms.

"Not tyke, Gina. Not tyke," she said, her blue eyes dancing with delight as she gleefully shook her head from side to side. It was a game they played often.

"What are you, then?" Georgina asked.

"Daddy's little girl," she said proudly, to Georgina's complete amazement, as the answer was usually "Louise."

"But of course you are. Did he tell you so today?" she asked, and the little girl nodded emphatically.

She bent to kiss the child; then Louise asked, "How many days?"

"Six days, I think, unless Grandmama has changed her plans," Georgina replied, realizing that Lord Meredith's arrival could change things.

"Six days, six days," Louise chanted, parrot fashion, as her long lashes began to cover her eyes partially. She blinked them open again twice, but the third time they went all the way and she was fast asleep.

Closing the nursery door quietly behind her, Georgina did not at first see her guardian where he stood in the dimly lit corridor waiting for her.

"What auspicious event is six days away?" he asked, mildly curious.

"Our departure for London, and hers to her aunt," Georgina told him.

He looked startled. "Do you think it wise to have her dwell on the separation so much?" he asked with concern.

"I think it preferable to informing her the night before that you will not be here the next day," she retorted with some asperity. "She tried so hard to keep her promise to you, but she just couldn't keep back the tears when you left last time."

"You have a point," he conceded. "She's just too young to understand, of course. Mother tells me that you wore yourself out looking after her on the journey here, to prevent her getting her first spanking. I must thank you, for I do not want her hurt."

"She would have been heartbroken, and I couldn't have made Lady Meredith see it until it was too late," she explained, "but I did not wear myself out. She was really little trouble. I'm glad you, at least, agree with me about Louise."

He nodded. "There's time enough for spankings when she knows what she's done wrong. But as for you, I understood from Mother that you stayed in your chamber because you were tired, and yet you just contradicted that."

They had started to walk along the corridor and he drew

her under a branch of candles and looked at her closely. "Just as I thought," he said, touching the delicate skin under her eyes with a gentle finger. "Why were you crying?"

"I was being very foolish, that's all." She felt even more foolish now. "Seeing all of you together, I could not help but feel how it might have been for us if Mama and Papa had not had the accident. I also felt you should be together for a while as a family, without an outsider always around."

His fingers hurt as they grasped her shoulders hard and pulled her toward him. "Don't you ever do that again!" he said sternly. "You're part of this family now, and I won't allow you to call yourself an outsider and cry alone in your room."

He saw her wince, and his grip loosened. "I'm sorry," he said, "I did not mean to hurt you." Then he changed his mind. "No, dammit, that's not true. I did mean to hurt you and make you understand you're one of us, and we all love you."

He left her at the door to her bedchamber, and she was glad there was no maid waiting to interrupt her thoughts. Her heart sang! She knew he'd used the plural, but he'd said he loved her. It was not the way she wanted him to love her, but it was a start, and she'd gladly take any crumbs she could get.

Georgina hummed softly to herself as she changed into a gown of light sea green that made her eyes turn to green and gold. She threaded ribbons of the same shade through her still-short curls, and smiled at herself in the mirror, then pirouetted and curtsied. "Thank you for the dance, my lord," she whispered.

Elizabeth had picked a gown of palest pink, and as the two girls entered the drawing room, they were like two flowers drifting in.

"It took a while," Lord Meredith said, "but I must admit you were worth waiting for, both of you. If they've looked like this every night, they must have taken Bath by storm."

Lady Meredith beamed proudly. "They did. The drawing room was crowded each afternoon, and their dance cards filled before the first note was played. And they behaved like the lovely ladies they are!''

"That's good news. Is anyone I might know dancing attendance?" he asked.

"Not with Elizabeth yet, although she's very popular and has been constantly surrounded, but an old friend of yours, the Earl of Barstow, has paid Georgina a great deal of attention."

"What? Barstow's far too old for Georgina!" he exclaimed, not exactly pleased at the news.

"He's ten years her senior, which is usually considered a very good difference in ages—the same age as you are, Matthew," his mother pointed out.

"Well, it's certainly better than having Frost around. I trust you've seen nothing of him since I've been gone?" He looked to his mother for reassurance.

"Only because we were in Bath and he was not. I have no doubt at all he will call again, perhaps not here if he knows you are home, for the two of you have never hit it off, but certainly when we reach London. I can't understand what is the matter with you. I find him a charming man," Lady Meredith said rather pettishly.

It was impossible for him to explain why he disapproved of Lord Frost's visits, so he satisfied himself by making a few growling comments on the man having nothing underneath the charm, and how he couldn't understand womenfolk not seeing beneath the surface.

The news of Barstow's interest somewhat affected his growing warmth and tenderness toward his ward, and, sensitive to his every mood, Georgina was quick to notice, but could not fathom the reason. Nor could he, for he was not one to relinquish the field to another, but he had been sure he could not feel again for a woman, and was now uncertain of the depth and duration of his ardor, if indeed it could be called by such a name. Far better, for Georgina's sake, that she be left alone to encourage Barstow, but only if the fellow truly loved her and she him.

He had many duties, long neglected, to perform around the

estate, and he decided to throw himself into these in an effort to avoid seeing much of Georgina for the time being.

He had, however, forgotten her habit of early rising, and when he went down the next morning she was already eating breakfast, dressed for riding. He was going out to a neighboring squire's stable to check a promising foal that was for sale, then planned to see how the spring plantings were coming along.

Georgina started to rise to curtsy when she saw him, but he waved a hand to stop her.

"Don't interrupt your breakfast, my dear. I'm not so formal at this hour," he said, noting with pleasure how lovely she looked in a new riding habit of russet brown. "Do you have plans to meet someone, or are you just going for a ride?"

She would have canceled an appointment with King George himself on the chance of being invited to join him, but she schooled her expression and said brightly, "I was only going out for a little exercise . . . Matthew."

He didn't understand why he felt so pleased with himself all of a sudden. "I'm going over to Bramley Hall to look at a foal. Why don't you join me?" he asked, forgetting his resolves. "I think you'd enjoy it."

They left as soon as he had satisfied his hunger.

"Mother tells me Barstow has been paying you quite a bit of attention. Do you think he's serious?" Meredith asked as they cantered down a narrow country lane.

"I don't know. How can one tell, Matthew?" she inquired, tongue-in-cheek.

He shrugged. "By his attitude, I suppose. If he's very flattering, hangs on your every word—something like that."

She laughed. "If he were to behave like that toward me, I'd quickly send him about his business. Fortunately, he treats me like an intelligent young lady, is interesting to talk to, and I enjoy his company."

Meredith grunted, and Georgina could not understand whether he was pleased or displeased with what he'd learned.

"I've decided to take Louise to my sister's home myself, leaving tomorrow, and I'll stay a day or so to see her settled,'' he volunteered, anxious to change the subject. ''From there I'll join the family in London before I return to Portugal. I hope to be able to spend several days in London, helping Mother to get settled in.'' His mother had made the move many times without help, but he tried to convince himself this was his reason.

''I shall miss Louise more than she'll miss me, for I know she'll be happy with other children to play with,'' Georgina said with a faint smile.

He chuckled. ''Once you're in London, you'll be doing a lot of playing yourself, but it will hardly be with children. Just remember, I'm no longer ordering you, but I trust you not to do anything of which I would disapprove.''

''I wish you would not put it that way,'' she told him with a mischievous grin. ''If you would name specifically what I must not do, it makes it much easier.''

''Easier for what?'' he asked with a smile.

''Easier for me to do the things you forgot to mention, of course,'' she said with a laugh.

''You really are a brat, you know,'' he said, but he did not tell her how fond he was of brats—or of one particular brat, at least.

They arrived at Bramley Hall. Meredith liked the foal and decided to buy it, and after he'd completed the arrangements, they returned home over the fields, giving the horses their heads for short gallops and taking several jumps just for the sheer joy of it. By the time they reached Settle House, Georgina was breathless, but so exhilarated her cheeks glowed. They looked, to Lady Meredith's motherly eyes, like two very contented people as they joined her for luncheon. She had guessed how Georgina felt about her son, but she wondered if Matthew had yet discovered his true feelings for the girl. If he didn't keep running off to the Peninsula, everything would work itself out very nicely, she thought.

The following day there were tearful good-byes, but the tears did not last long, for the little girl still had her much-loved daddy with her. They had made an early start and soon Louise was fast asleep and Meredith passed the sleeping child over to her nanny.

He had much to think about in the few days' respite before he returned to London.

Although still in titular command of his unit, Meredith had resumed his former liaison duties for Wellington, and he now doubted he would ever return to the fighting. The liaison duties provided good cover for another kind of work for the prime minister himself, work to which he was particularly suited—that of tracking down spies in both the ministry and in Wellington's own staff.

He had located two spies in the ministry, but had been unable to find out who their French contact was before someone had got to them and permanently silenced them.

However, the unknown French agent now had to find another source of information if he were to continue his operations. For this reason Meredith was letting himself be seen traveling frequently between London and the Peninsula, and had made it appear that he carried with him secret plans. If he could draw the agent's attention to himself, the chances were good that he might try to hold him up on the highway, or even on the street. He was fully prepared for such a contingency.

Once Louise, her father, and her nanny were gone, it needed little more than a day to complete packing, and only a leisurely half-day's drive before they reached Grosvenor Square.

The house was large, on the south side of the square, with a pleasant garden in the back, and beyond that, in Adams Mews, were a roomy coach house and stables. Georgina found the city to be a much more exciting place than she had thought it when supposedly an officer's manservant.

Matthew was expected at the house in Grosvenor Square daily. Tomorrow night they were to go to their first ball at Almack's; vouchers had been obtained by Lady Meredith, who was hoping her son might be back in time to escort them, as they would be securely in the good graces of the patronesses if he put in an appearance.

Georgina was hoping, also, that he would escort them, but for a quite different reason. She wanted to dance with him and see if it felt like all the others, or if the exciting sensation she had come to expect every time he touched her would still be there.

Georgina's gown was demure, considered by Lady Meredith to be quite appropriate for a first ball in London. It was the palest lemon gauze over a white satin slip, and the tiny puff sleeves and bodice were trimmed with white lace. Jewelry would consist of a simple pearl necklace of Lady Meredith's, and a second, daintier one was to be skillfully entwined in her hair.

By now her skin was almost as pale as Elizabeth's, but the abigail the two girls shared still continued to apply the special cream nightly to make sure the unfashionable hue did not return.

Meredith had arrived late the previous night, after both girls had retired, and readily agreed to provide his services as escort. He looked more elegant than Georgina had ever seen him in the required court dress, and was, she decided, still the most handsome man she had ever met.

Even though the carriage was large, a gentleman and four ladies in ball gowns were a little difficult to accommodate without someone's skirts becoming creased, and at the last minute Robbie begged off, saying the girls had ample escort and she could be more useful on some other occasion. Lady Meredith had to agree, and was glad she had done so when she saw how much space Elizabeth's gown needed.

Georgina's heart skipped a beat, she was sure, when Matthew handed her into the seat opposite Elizabeth, Lady Meredith carefully arranging her skirts on the plush seat before allowing her to sit and admonishing her not to lean back against the squabs, and then they were on their way to King Street. Georgina could not understand how Elizabeth managed to look so wonderfully calm, when she knew that inwardly she was, like herself, bubbling over with excitement.

"Now, don't forget, both of you, no more than two dances with anyone, and you don't accept any partner unless either Matthew or I give our consent." She'd already said it all a dozen times, but didn't want them to get off on the wrong foot with the rigid patronesses. "Your partner must bring you back to me after each dance, and I would doubt very much that you will be given permission to waltz on your first night there.''

''Mother, for goodness' sake! You're almost as nervous as Georgina, who is sitting on that seat as though the upholstery has pins in it.'' He reached over and gave Georgina's hand a reassuring squeeze. ''Don't worry, Sally Jersey and Emily Cowper will be so grateful to you for bringing both me and Barstow, they'll overlook a great deal.''

Georgina found her tongue at last. ''You will dance the first dance with me, won't you, Matthew, just in case I don't get any partners?''

''Georgina, that's just the sort of thing you're not to do. No lady ever asks a gentleman to dance with her,'' Lady Meredith said severely.

Meredith saw Georgina's hurt face as she turned quickly to look out of the window. ''Mother, leave her alone. She wasn't asking 'a gentleman' to dance, she was asking her guardian to give her a little support, and *that* she had a perfect right to ask. If you continue in this manner, she'll be so nervous she won't be able to do anything right.''

Lady Meredith sighed. ''I'm sorry, Georgina, Matthew is quite right, but you must realize how concerned I am for both of you. I was so proud of you in Bath, and I know I will be tonight, but it's just a case of getting over the first hour.'' She smiled at both girls. ''You really do look very lovely. I think those gowns were an ideal choice, and the pearls are just the right touch, Georgina.''

They were all relieved when the carriage turned into St. James Street and they were almost there. Alighting first to help the ladies, Matthew gave Georgina a special smile as he reached for her hand. ''I won't let anything go wrong,'' he promised, making her nervousness take a back seat for a while.

There was a short line to greet the patronesses, and they waited in it quite patiently until their turn came. Lady Meredith introduced the two girls and they curtsied very well, but when they reached Mrs. Drummond-Burrell, that lady looked suspiciously at Lady Meredith.

"Meredith's ward, you say. Who was her father?" she asked haughtily.

"Lord Robert Forsythe," Lady Meredith said quickly. "You may recall he and Lady Forsythe were killed in a carriage accident in Yorkshire many years ago."

"Oh, yes, that Forsythe." She suddenly smiled at Georgina. "I knew your mother, and she was a real beauty. Looks like you're taking after her."

"Thank you, ma'am," Georgina murmured in relief.

Now she had a chance to gaze around her at the ornate square columns and the quite enormous crystal chandeliers, their warm, flattering glow making every girl look like a fairy princess. At first glance the required attire for the men made them seem much alike, until a closer look revealed the intricacies of the various neckcloths, the sometimes ludicrous heights of the starched, pointed collars, and the obvious padding under some of the white hose to make a leg seem shapelier than nature had decreed. Of course, in her eyes, not one of them looked anywhere near as elegant as Matthew.

As things turned out, Meredith did not have the first dance with Georgina, for Barstow was already there and got in before him. Instead, Elizabeth danced with her uncle, and it was the fourth or fifth dance before Georgina was able to test for that tingling sensation she found so strangely delightful. She was not disappointed. None of her partners gave her the thrill that he did, and she wished the dance could go on forever.

"You're certainly very popular. Are you enjoying yourself, Georgina?" he asked.

"I am now," she told him. "I was so disappointed when Barstow came for the first dance."

He looked at her searchingly. "I thought you liked him," he said.

"I do," she told him earnestly, "and he's very good to me."

Meredith let it go at that, and when he saw her later, laughing and obviously enjoying herself with Barstow, he decided she was just being a little flirtatious. He suddenly realized that he had enjoyed the dance more than he cared to admit.

Matthew and Barstow seemed to have a great deal in common, Georgina thought as they stood talking for some time on the edge of the floor. As her light feet carried her through the intricate steps of a quadrille, she was happier than she had ever thought possible.

As had been his habit, Barstow took her in for supper and they made up their own party at one of the tables. Elizabeth, looking charmingly flustered, introduced her to an attractive young sandy-haired man, the Duke of Shreveport, and when he danced with Georgina later in the evening, she found him to be not at all toplofty, and really quite engaging. If he could ruffle the outward calm of her dear friend, perhaps something might develop in that direction.

Lady Meredith had, fortunately, warned the girls to eat a good dinner at home, as the supper at Almack's was quite paltry. The weak lemonade did, however, ease Georgina's parched throat, but she took one look at the stale offerings and agreed with her hostess.

To her delight, though she managed to appear demure, Barstow obtained permission for her to waltz, a dance she and Elizabeth had been practicing for the day when they would be allowed to show off their prowess. She thoroughly enjoyed it and secretly hoped that Lord Meredith might ask her for the next one, but after the one dance with each girl he had been content to watch them enjoy themselves, and seemed more interested in seemingly earnest discussions with some of his contemporaries.

It was late in the evening and Georgina was dancing with a young man who reminded her of William, for he was nervous and inclined to stammer. His toes were as awkward as his tongue, and her feet suffered in consequence, but for William's sake she was enduring it with a gentle smile, when she saw, over his shoulder, that the doors were about to close, permitting no further entry of latecomers. With mild interest she noticed someone had just squeezed through in the nick of time, then realized the tardy gentleman was none other than Lord Frost.

As the dance came to an end and the young man took her back to Lady Meredith, Georgina looked quickly at her card, hoping it was filled, but remembered there was still one empty space that she had kept open, hoping her guardian would ask her to dance again.

It seemed she had hardly reached Lady Meredith's side before Lord Frost was there also, begging permission to dance with Georgina. Lady Meredith gave her smiling consent.

It took little imagination to guess where Lord Frost had been until this hour. He had imbibed a little too much, and there was an amorous look in his eyes.

"How exquisite you look this evening, my dear. What a pity there is no convenient garden where we could slip away, for I'd dearly love to sip on those ripe cherry lips that have invited plunder since the first time we met," he whispered, his lips close to her ear.

Georgina drew as far away from him as the dance would permit.

"I see you have two watchdogs tonight. Has Barstow beaten me to it, you lovely witch, or has that honor gone to your so-called guardian?"

It was pointless protesting, and a relief to Georgina that the dance separated them at this point. However, when they came together once more she held her arms as stiffly as she could, and turned her head away from him, catching a glimpse of her guardian as she did so.

Matthew looked so angry Georgina feared he might interrupt the dance, but when she glanced at him again he gave her an icy stare as though she was at fault.

She thought Matthew might mention Frost on the drive home, but though his manner was cooler than earlier, he said nothing to either Georgina or his mother.

It was somewhat of a relief to find Elizabeth very excited. Her duke had asked if he might take her for a drive the next afternoon, and as she had not shown preference for any of her beaux up until now, it was good to see the change.

The next day Georgina was thankful that Lord Frost did not number among the afternoon callers, nor was he present at the dinner dance they attended for the daughter of one of

Lady Meredith's younger friends. Some of the same young people were present as had been at Almack's, and since many had also been in Bath, Georgina and Elizabeth now had a wide circle of friends of both sexes, but they were still closest to each other, and Georgina knew she was the only person Elizabeth ever confided in. They had become closer than many sisters, and it was a new and cherished relationship for Georgina.

"Do you think you might be up early enough in the morning for a gallop in the park?" Matthew asked Georgina before they went to bed that night.

"Getting up is no problem, Matthew," she said regretfully, "but I'm afraid I have no mount."

He looked amazed. "I know you've been riding since you arrived here. What did you do for a horse?"

"Barstow brought one around for me to ride," she said, "but he didn't offer to lend it to me."

He threw up his hands in disgust. "If I don't take care of things, no one else does. Why didn't you ask Mother to bring mounts for both you and Elizabeth?" he asked impatiently.

She could never have asked, and he should be able to understand that, so she answered rather coldly, "Because it is not my place to ask for special favors."

Now he was angry. "If I ever hear you say anything like that again, Georgina, I'll . . . I'll . . ." A smile twitched at the corner of his mouth. "I don't know what I'll do, but it will be something violent," he ended, his eyes sparkling with fun.

"No you won't," she said impishly.

He chuckled. "You're right, I probably won't, but you'll deserve it. How many times do I have to tell you you're one of the family, and as such, you do have rights?" He ran a hand through her curls, rumpling them affectionately. "If you can be dressed and down here by seven at the latest, I'll have a mount ready for you," he promised, "and I'll send a groom to get Starlight for you tomorrow."

She looked up at him, glowing. "Thank you. I'll be ready by seven." She dropped him a curtsy, said, "Good night, Matthew," and ran out of the room and up the stairs to bed.

A few minutes later, having given the footman on duty some instructions, he followed suit, humming softly to himself as he climbed the stairs.

At first they rode sedately through the quiet streets; then, once they reached the park, they cantered until they came to a suitable stretch. He looked at her with eyebrows raised, and she smiled and nodded; then they raced neck and neck, Matthew, on his own stronger horse, gradually gaining on her until he passed the tree he'd mentally set as the winning post, and slowed his horse to a trot to let her catch up with him.

Their silence was comfortable as they both enjoyed the exhilaration of the ride and the beauty of the early morning.

Matthew finally broke it. "I'm afraid I'll be leaving again shortly, but there's a good chance William will get his first leave soon," he said, "and I'll arrange for him to spend it here in London with you if you'd like that."

Her wide smile and shining eyes told him how much she'd like it, and she was glad she was on horseback or she might have forgotten herself enough to fling her arms around him in appreciation.

"Thank you," she said gratefully. "It will be wonderful to see him, and I'll try to let him take the initiative and not push him into things, I promise."

"I know you will," he assured her. He was thoughtful for a moment, then said, "There's one other thing I must mention to you before I go. I don't at all like you seeing Frost. If he should call, and my mother assures me that he will, I wish you to be as cool to him as possible and not accept any invitations from him," he said firmly. "Apart from being too sophisticated for someone as young as you, he's not everything he appears to be, and in fact, I'm having some extremely confidential investigations made into his activities."

Georgina gasped, remembering their previous conversation. "Don't you think you should talk to Lady Meredith if you don't want me to dance with him, Matthew?" She would not be blamed when it was not her fault. "He'd had too much to drink when he was at Almack's, yet she permitted him to dance with me and he made horrible, suggestive remarks."

Matthew's eyebrows rose. "My mother does not know of my suspicions of him, and I would appreciate your not discussing them with anyone. I am sure, however, she knew nothing of the remarks he made to you. It was your place to tell her, so she could deal with it. You know, you may not dance with anyone she does not approve, but it does not follow that you have to accept everyone she brings forward. You could have said your card was full, or that you were exhausted and wanted to sit down for a moment, or even the old one of having torn your gown and must retire to have it repaired."

"I've been wondering if I could do that," she said, storing the information away for future use. "I'll remember for next time, but as to telling her, I was frightened you might get involved if I revealed what he'd said. You looked so angry when you saw me dancing with him."

"Angry I was, I admit, but I was not about to make a scene at your first Almack's ball, and I imagine Barstow felt the same way." He paused to see if she would make any response to his reference to Barstow, but when she didn't, he continued, "I know it's going to be prodigiously difficult for you to avoid Frost, with your inexperience, but try your best, for I cannot convince Mother to stop him calling, and prefer to let it resolve itself, which it will, if my feelings about him prove to be correct."

To her surprise, he reached out a hand and, with the back of one finger, gently stroked her cheek. "Stay as sweet as you are, Georgina, and don't let anyone make you do anything you feel is wrong," he said softly.

Both cheeks felt on fire, but she met his eyes and whispered, "I'll try hard not to."

16

The weather, which had favored them for many weeks, had finally turned inclement and Georgina had been unable to ride in the park this morning. As a result, she and Elizabeth, who was an accomplished pianist, were sitting at the piano in the music room, leafing through some sheet music. They were trying to find something they both knew well enough for Georgina, who had a pleasant voice, to sing while Elizabeth accompanied her.

They were unused to doing anything of this sort together, but were enjoying the novelty and achieving a fair degree of success, considering it was the first time, when the butler announced that Georgina had a visitor.

She knew immediately who it must be, long before Crowther had intoned the name of Lord Forsythe, and when he appeared she ran across the room and into his arms.

After a moment he held her away from him to get a good look at her.

"I wouldn't have known you, Georgie, if you hadn't b-bounded across the room that way," he told her, giving her another hug before she held his hand and took him over to meet Elizabeth.

"You're both very good-looking, but not a bit alike, are you? I know Georgina told me so, but I still thought there'd be some resemblance, Cousin William. And you look so handsome in your uniform. Uncle Matthew never wears his uniform in England," Elizabeth said a little sadly.

"You'll get tired of seeing me in it, for I'm home for a sennight, and have grown too b-big for most of my own clothes,'' he said rather proudly, as the training had considerably developed his muscles.

"I'm sure if you gave my uncle's name, Weston would be able to make something for you quickly,'' Elizabeth suggested helpfully.

William looked knowingly at his sister, then back to his new cousin. "No doubt he would,'' he agreed, with his gentle smile, "but Weston is a little too r-rich for my pocket.''

Georgina suddenly realized he had probably not even received his pay for some time, and must be very low on funds.

"You will be able to stay here, won't you?'' she asked her brother, but turned a questioning look on Robbie, who had entered behind William.

Before that lady could say anything, however, Elizabeth burst forth with, "Of course he'll stay here. This is his family,'' in what was for her an unusually vehement tone of voice.

William quietly reassured them, "Lord Meredith said I was to stay here, and as it's his home, I'm sure there's no d-doubt.''

Georgina was beginning to realize how much she'd missed him and his loving kindness. She felt so proud of him she might burst.

"It will be prodigious fun to have you here for two whole weeks,'' she said happily. "We'll visit the Tower, and St. Paul's Cathedral, and you can take me riding in the park, and—''

"It will be wonderful, Georgie, but what about your b-beau?'' he asked. "Lord Meredith told me there was someone special. Won't he get a mite jealous if you're out with me all the time?''

Georgina looked puzzled. "There is no one special. I have no idea why our guardian should have told you there was.''

Mrs. Robinson looked at her with surprise. "I hardly think the Earl of Barstow would like to hear you say that, Georgina.''

"He's very nice, Robbie, but he's not special the way William means. I ride in the park with him quite often, I agree, but that's because I do so love to ride. I go driving with a number of different young men, and I never dance more than two dances with Barstow.'' Georgina seemed very anxious to make herself quite clear.

''But if he's there, he always takes you in to supper,'' Elizabeth reminded her.

''Then perhaps I should refuse, if it means our names are linked together, for I think of him only as a very good friend.'' Having made her feelings clear, Georgina changed the subject. ''As it's still raining, I cannot show you the gardens, but I could show you the conservatory if you like, William,'' she suggested.

She did not notice the look of disappointment on Elizabeth's face, and rose eagerly when William accepted her invitation.

When they were quite alone, and comfortably seated on a bench amid the exotic fruit trees and orchids, William took both Georgina's hands in his.

''I've something to tell you,'' he said, ''though from what I just saw, you're probably comfortably settled here. I wrote a very strong letter to Grandmama. I didn't at all like the way she wrote to our guardian. I told her as much, and I also told her she'd b-better not try refusing you admittance, as Broadacres is mine, and she's only living there to k-keep the house in good shape for my return.''

Georgina's peals of laughter might have been heard clear back to the house. In fact, she laughed so much the tears started in her eyes.

When she was recovered somewhat, she asked, ''Does our cousin know that you wrote?''

''Yes,'' William replied. ''In fact, he read my first, rough copy and made a few suggestions. He said he will b-back us to the hilt if she tries to make any trouble.''

She held his face between her hands lovingly. ''It was dear of you to do that on my behalf, and I'm very proud of you. You have changed also, William. You've completely taken to the army life, haven't you?''

''It was the best thing that c-could have happened to me, Georgie,'' he told her earnestly. ''I was never able to keep up with you, and didn't try when you were there to do things for me. Now I have to make d-decisions and I'm starting to enjoy it. Cousin Matthew is a wonderful officer. You and he got off on the wrong foot, but I hope you've grown to know him and to like him.''

"I do," Georgina said quietly, hoping he would continue to talk about Matthew, for she rarely had the opportunity to speak of him.

"He's gone out of his way to help me. He seemed to realize I was slower g-grasping things, and he took me aside and m-made sure I understood. He taught me to think things out and reach my own conclusions. If I'd had a tutor like him, I'd have l-learned a lot quicker, I can tell you.''

"He is an exceptional man," Georgina agreed. "Unfortunately, although he's nice to me about half the time, we seem to be at cross-purposes the other half. He has an adorable little daughter, whom I fell in love with immediately we met, and the feeling was mutual.''

"Well, that should make for a better relationship with her father, shouldn't it?'' he suggested.

She nodded. "It helps. My dealings with little Louise are the reason for the nice half of the time.'' Unknowingly, she gave him a smile that was a little sad.

"It's important to you, isn't it, Georgie?'' He had become much more intuitive.

She had been gazing intently at her left hand, and when she raised her eyes to his, he saw the bleak expression in their depths. She nodded, then said simply, "Yes. Let's not talk about it anymore.''

He put his arm around her shoulders and gave her a brotherly squeeze. "Will you take me inside to meet the dread dowager?''

"Of course," she said with a shaky laugh, "but she's not at all 'dread.' She's really quite a dear. A dear dowager.''

On their way back to the main part of the house, they met the butler, who was coming to let them know that luncheon was about to be served.

"So you're the young cousin who has been helping my son win the war against those Frenchies?'' Lady Meredith gave him a warm smile and allowed him to kiss her cheek. "What's the good of being cousins if you can't be kissed by all the handsome ones?'' she asked, obviously delighted to meet Georgina's twin. ''Unlike your sister, you have the look of the Merediths. Does Crowther know to order a room prepared for you?''

''I don't b-believe so, my lady, although Lord Meredith did say I might stay here.'' William was still somewhat hesitant.

''But of course you'll stay here. Georgina is going to spend every minute she can with you, I know, and it will be much easier for her to do so if you're here with us.'' She had already rung the bell, and when the butler appeared, she gave him the necessary instructions.

''My son rarely tells me what is happening on the Peninsula. I know from reports that Wellington spent most of the winter behind the lines of Torres Vedras, and now Marshal Massena has gone away,'' Lady Meredith continued.

Georgina couldn't help the beginnings of a grin at the brief but accurate description. William gave her a warning glance.

''That was very c-concisely put, ma'am,'' William said dryly. ''We woke one morning to find Massena had ordered a retreat and he's now b-back where he started at Ciudad Rodrigo, with only a third of his m-men left, and with Wellington on his tail.''

Georgina's eyes opened wide with sudden concern. It had not occurred to her that both William and Matthew would now be involved in open warfare against the French, and fear that one or the other might be killed or wounded caused an icy feeling deep inside.

''Don't look alarmed, little sister.'' William read her thoughts. ''Colonel Meredith is on special d-duty for Wellington, and I'm assigned as one of his s-staff officers. We're not in the actual fighting as yet.''

Georgina did not like that ''as yet'' at all.

Though anxious to have William to herself, she knew it would be grossly unfair, and so, when the weather cleared a little in the afternoon, Elizabeth joined them for a drive in the park, drawing many curious glances, and each time they stopped to greet friends, Georgina proudly introduced her handsome twin brother.

The next day was also wet, and William escorted them to the lending library in the carriage. They did not stay out very long, though, as it was still quite damp after the rains, and on their return they found Lady Meredith entertaining several visitors, among them the Earl of Barstow, the Duke of Shreveport, and Lord Frost.

Georgina noticed how Lord Frost immediately attached himself to her brother, and with Matthew's earlier request for information on the man's questions, she vowed to ask William to keep her informed of what Frost talked about.

For her part, she was quite cool with Barstow, as she had decided to keep him somewhat at a distance, not wishing to encourage him, as she apparently had been doing. She regretted, however, having to lose a good friend.

He drew her aside, looking at her intently as she made the usual idle chatter. "I had thought our friendship had progressed beyond this point, my dear, but I feel as though I have done something to offend you. If such is the case, I would wish to know and have the opportunity to make amends."

Her very real unhappiness at the cool manner she had felt the need to adopt showed clearly on her face. As he waited patiently for an answer, she suddenly decided to forget what she had recently been taught and be as frank with him as her honesty bade her be.

"Please do not take offense at what I am about to say, my lord," she begged him. "You see, I have enjoyed our friendship so much that I gave no thought to the fact that it might be interpreted as something more than friendship. Am I making sense?"

She was close to tears, for she liked him very much and had no wish to spoil what had been between them.

He reached over and picked up her hand, looking at it closely. "Such a very lovely, but also very capable hand, on a very lovely and very straightforward young lady, which is what attracted me to you in the first place." His smile was kind and she thought she saw regret in his eyes, but couldn't be sure. "If you're trying to tell me that if I'm interested in more than friendship, your heart is engaged elsewhere, then you *are* making sense. Why don't we stay good friends, unless my frequent presence makes things difficult for you?"

She breathed a sigh of relief. He really had understood, and she needn't lose one of the few true friends she had made in a fickle society. "I'd like that above everything, my lord," she assured him.

"Good. Henceforth our friendship will be a purely platonic one, but there is just one thing that might be a problem. If I continue to pay attention to you, which I mean to do within the bounds of our friendship, it may cause your guardian to ask my intentions. What would you wish me to say to him?"

A telltale flush stained Georgina's cheeks and she looked out of the window for a moment to control her emotions. In doing so she failed to see his expression as he realized where her true feelings lay.

"The truth, I think." She spoke as though there had been no pause in their conversation. "I'd prefer you to tell him that I desire only friendship, if that would not put you in a poor light."

"I think I know how to handle Lord Meredith, should he ask. And I will say this just the once, but the intent will be forever. As your friend, I will always be there for you should you need my help at any time, for whatever reason. Is that clearly understood?" he asked, looking at her very seriously as he awaited her answer.

She nodded. "Yes, my lord," she said softly, "and it is very much appreciated." She felt so pleased that if they had been alone she would have hugged him, but fortunately she restrained herself amid the other guests.

He saw he was still holding her hand, and squeezed it hard before releasing it. "One thing I would like you to do for me, when we are alone, is call me David. I think 'my lord' is too formal between friends, and I shall call you Gina." His raised eyebrows asked for her agreement.

"Of course. 'David' it will be—when we're alone," she readily agreed.

The room was considerably less crowded now, and William excused himself from Frost and came over to meet Georgina's friend.

The two men shook hands and, much to Georgina's delight, seemed to like each other right away. Barstow realized, however, that he had extended the length of his visit as far as he could without causing comment, so after a brief conversation with William, he said his good-byes to the twins and left.

They were to attend a coming-out ball that evening for the grandchild of one of Lady Meredith's old friends, and she had secured another invitation for William. His scarlet uniform stood out against their pastel ball gowns and when they entered the large house on the southwest corner of Berkeley Square, he was, to Georgina's considerable amusement, immediately surrounded by admiring young ladies.

The hostess had attempted to achieve an effect of exotic gardens throughout the ballroom and supper rooms, and the air was heavy with the fragrance of jasmine, gardenias, and orange blossoms. She had borrowed trees and plants from her friends' conservatories in addition to her own, and the seating around the ballroom floor consisted of benches piled with green cushions and surrounded by large potted trees. At intervals trellised bowers were festooned with ivy and hung with flowering orchids, their pots cleverly concealed to give the impression they were growing from the branches. Even the chandeliers were intertwined with leaves that hung several feet beneath them.

Georgina danced first with her brother, then with the hostess's son, a good friend of Lord Meredith's whom she had met before at Settle House. She particularly enjoyed dancing with him, as he talked most of the time of Matthew.

At supper Elizabeth and her duke, Barstow and Georgina, William and the charming Lady Edith, in whose honor the ball was held, were chaperoned by Lady Meredith in a room carpeted in green to resemble a lawn. Every table had its own potted tree beside it, some heavy with peaches, apricots, and oranges, and waiters served champagne to the guests who had already filled their plates from the heavily laden banquet tables on either side of the room.

"Why don't we plan a picnic on the Thames before your brother returns to the Peninsula, Georgina? Richmond might be a pretty spot for it," Barstow suggested.

"I say, that sounds like a splendid idea," William said, having overheard. "Would you care to join us, Lady Edith?"

Georgina was surprised, then smiled at the change in her brother. "Let's see what the best date might be . . . Mrs. Robinson would chaperon us, I'm sure, and perhaps Elizabeth would come also."

When the subject was broached to Shreveport and Elizabeth, they were most enthusiastic and so a date was set for six days hence. Lady Meredith was invited to join them, but she declined gracefully and suggested that Mrs. Robinson would enjoy the trip.

They returned to the ballroom and Georgina suddenly found Lord Frost at her elbow. Without asking, he slipped her card off her wrist and wrote his name in the only space available.

"Your brother is not at all like you, for a twin," he remarked when he came to claim his dance. By now Georgina was very tired of everyone mentioning this fact.

"Not in appearance, my lord, but we are very close," she told him with a false smile. She had begun to feel most uncomfortable in his company, and remembered, too late, her promise to her guardian.

"I find him an excellent young man and would like to join you if you should plan any sightseeing. I am an expert on London museums, and particularly the Tower. And it would, of course, give me an opportunity to enjoy your own charming company. Perhaps Lady Elizabeth would come also?" he suggested.

"We have not made any plans so soon, my lord," Georgina replied smoothly, "but Mrs. Robinson is also an excellent guide, as well as our chaperon."

"I had thought that, under the circumstances, your brother might be chaperon enough," he protested with a strange glint in his eyes that made her even more uneasy.

"I do not believe Lady Meredith would share your views, but I will, of course, ask her." Georgina had at last learned some ways of evading a difficult situation.

She was very glad when the dance was ended and William came to claim the next one.

"Is there no way you can refuse to dance with the likes of Frost?" he asked abruptly.

"Yes, but it's difficult as long as Lady Meredith encourages him and makes him welcome in her home. I had been meaning to ask you why he seeks your company so much, but this is not the place to talk about it," she said, her smile carefully in place. "Stop glaring around the room. You're supposed to be enjoying yourself even when dancing with your sister, so smile."

He did better than smile. He laughed at her as though she had said something funny.

"You don't have to go so far," she said, chuckling also.

"It was more natural than you realized, Georgie. I was just thinking how angry you would have b-been, back at Broadacres, if anyone had expected you to paste a false smile on your face. You're so different—you even sound like a lady now, as well as looking like one."

"I know. It's as if I've been made over from a reckless hoyden into a fashionable city miss. But deep inside I'm still the same. You sound different also, for I seldom hear your stutter, and I've never seen you looking so well, William. I find it very enjoyable to sit back and let you make decisions for a change." She remembered something. "You didn't agree to include Lord Frost in our picnic to Richmond, did you?"

"No, I did not. He knows nothing about it, but he did suggest taking us around the city. Very queer fish, that one, Georgie. Cousin Matthew is right!"

"I don't know. I rather liked him until Lord Meredith made it clear that he didn't. He's half French, you know, and his grandparents were killed in the revolution," Georgina told him.

As she spoke, the dance came to an end, and he returned her to Lady Meredith.

The rest of the evening flew as Georgina danced with Barstow, Elizabeth's duke, and several young men who were frequent visitors to the Merediths' home in the afternoons.

Lady Meredith signaled that it was time to leave, and on the short drive the three younger people discussed plans for the picnic while the more mature ladies dozed quietly in their respective corners. Lady Meredith did, however, express the hope that their own come-out ball might be as successful as this one.

The first week of William's leave had gone far too swiftly for Georgina, and she knew she was going to feel quite forsaken when he had to leave.

Today was their planned outing, and it had been decided not to hire a boat, which was the original idea, but to go on horseback and carriage, the men to ride and the ladies to travel by coach. Georgina, however, refused point-blank to sit in a stuffy coach when she could be on horseback, so Elizabeth, Edith, and Robbie journeyed in the coach, and Georgina rode with the three men.

Situated southwest of London, Richmond was famous for the deer park established there by Charles I, and because Queen Elizabeth had lived there, but these were not the reasons for selecting it for a picnic. It was not too far out of London, the road was good, and the location on the Thames made it an attractive setting.

The duke was the only rider who had felt some misgivings about Georgina's joining them, but once he saw her on horseback he had no further concerns, for clearly she rode as well as she looked in her sea-blue velvet habit and the chocolate-brown shako with sea-blue feathers sitting atop her curls.

They arrived a little before noon, picked out a grassy location on the bank of the river, and all were hungry enough from the fresh air to eat right away. Cook had packed several bottles of champagne with the meats, crusty breads, and fresh fruit, and after they had eaten and drunk their fill, they stretched out against the trunks of trees and more than one of them dozed a little.

Georgina and William walked down to the edge of the water and stood skimming pebbles for a few minutes, then strolled the footpath, keeping the others in sight. There were still several days left before William had to return to the Peninsula, but Georgina was already feeling a little blue at the thought. Now, in the shade of the trees, with the water lapping gently against the bank, seemed a good time to talk.

"Lord Meredith warned me about Frost before I left," William told her. "He does not at all like the attention Frost pays the Meredith family in his absence."

"I know, William, but Lady Meredith has a decided attachment to him, and as I told you, I rather liked him also until our cousin told me I shouldn't."

"He's asked me some deuced odd questions, and seeks me out constantly. Cousin Matthew thought he might, though," William added.

"What kind of questions?" Georgina asked.

"I'd rather not say," William replied, "for I promised not to, but I've made a note of them to give to Lord Meredith."

She would have liked to wheedle the information out of him, as she could easily have done in the old days, but she was far too much impressed with his responsible attitude to even try.

"When you get back, you will tell Lord Meredith that I avoid Lord Frost as much as possible, won't you?" Georgina asked. "I only dance with him occasionally so as not to make it difficult for Lady Meredith."

"Just you see that you're never alone with him, that's all," William warned. "And that includes going riding, for I know you and Barstow c-come out with a groom, but it's usually quite easy to outdistance a groom, who is naturally not mounted anywhere near as well as the people he is escorting."

"I've always refused to ride with him, and I always will," she promised.

"And if things get difficult for any reason, don't forget you can go back to Broadacres for a while. I doubt that Grandmama will welcome you with open arms, but after my letter she will be careful, I'm sure, to do nothing that might send her to the d-dower house." William's smile was a little sad. "I hated to put her in such a threatened position, but there was no help for it after the way she wrote to Cousin Matthew."

"I know," Georgina said. "You've always disliked being harsh with anyone, but sometimes it cannot be avoided."

There remained for Georgina and William a few more rides in the park, an evening at Almack's, when the patronesses made a great fuss of William, dress uniform being even more acceptable to them than court dress, and an evening in the Merediths' box at Covent Garden theater to see and be seen, more than for the enjoyment of the play.

When it came to saying good-bye, her pride in the way William had grown up and at last become a big brother to her made Georgina control her own sadness until after he had left her with a warm squeeze and a kiss on the cheek.

As the door closed behind him, Lady Meredith took one look at Georgina's face and sent her to her bedchamber. "You'd best cry it out of your system, my dear, and then you'll feel much better. With Matthew keeping an eye on him, he couldn't be any safer, but I know now how close you feel, and you were very brave not to let him see your tears."

She even understood when Georgina asked to be excused from their dinner engagement that evening, and agreed to say she had a temporary indisposition.

17

On the morning of their come-out ball, both girls decided to keep out of Lady Meredith's way, for she was much more nervous than when they had gone to Almack's that first night.

Robbie was a great help, bringing a calming influence on Lady Meredith and insisting that she too get some rest in the afternoon. As soon as she had assured herself that her ladyship was, in fact, resting comfortably, she came to Georgina's bedchamber.

"I have a little something to give you to use tonight, which has not been used since my own come-out some years ago," she told Georgina, and handed her a neatly wrapped package.

On opening it, Georgina found the most exquisite white lace fan, and she looked at Robbie in amazement. "It's beautiful, but this is a keepsake, Robbie—you can't give it away."

"It held memories for me, but now they're fading and it's time for it to collect new memories for you. Use it with happiness," she murmured, then shook her head to collect her thoughts and said brusquely, "You have several posies from beaux, and the maid is bringing them for you to choose which one to carry tonight. I'll get along now, for there's much still to do."

"Thank you, Robbie," Georgina said a little breathlessly. "I've never had such lovely gifts."

There were four posies in all, and before reading the cards, she looked at them all, smelling the different fragrances. The one she liked best was a perfect match for her dress, as it was of peach-colored roses and white gypsophila in a ring of white lace, and trailing peach-colored ribbons. She reached for the card, then gasped. It was from Matthew, expressing regret that he could not be there. The others—white gardenias, cream orchids, and palest pink camellias—were from her brother, Barstow, and Frost, respectively.

She thought she'd be too excited to rest properly, but when she put her head on the pillow she fell into a deep sleep from which she was wakened by Lady Meredith's abigail, come to get her ready for the ball.

The gown she was to wear was so delicate that each time she had tried it on for last-minute adjustments she had been fearful of catching the fine lace and tearing it or of spilling something down the front of it. It was pale peach satin, with an overskirt of white lace, and the bodice and short puffed sleeves were also overlaid with the lace. A wide velvet ribbon in the same pastel shade fluttered from the high waist, and dainty rosebuds in various tones of peach were stitched at intervals around the skirt, with smaller ones edging the sleeves and the quite low neckline.

A narrow ribbon had been stitched with small rosebuds, and when she was dressed, the abigail threaded it through her curls, while around her neck she fastened an exquisite cameo, also on ribbon, which was a gift from Lady Meredith.

To Georgina it was like her dreams of fairyland as a child. It seemed as though the house had been turned into a magical garden, with orange trees from the conservatory lining the walls of the entrance hall, and the ballroom itself festooned with garlands of white flowers, roses, chrysanthemums, gardenias, gladioli, and many others she couldn't name. Gilt chairs had been brought out of storage, and the enormous gilt-and-crystal chandeliers at either end shone in the light of hundreds of candles.

Elizabeth would be down in just a moment, and the guests were due to arrive in less than half an hour. After she left the ballroom and returned to the entrance hall, she heard the musicians start to tune up their instruments. She looked at the lovely marble staircase she had descended several times daily ever since their move to London, and was suddenly nervous that when she formally came down those steps she might fall and bring disgrace to herself and her newfound family.

Lady Meredith came bustling in from the direction of the kitchens, looking very elegant in a deep blue satin gown.

"Will I do, my lady?" Georgina asked, whirling around to let her ladyship see the back also.

"You look enchanting, my dear," Lady Meredith pronounced. "How I wish Matthew had been here to see you. I notice you are carrying his posy.

"We've gone over and over what you are to do and not do, and I'm not going to say any more about it. Just behave the way you know how, and enjoy yourself. A girl has her coming-out ball only once in her lifetime, you know." She sounded a little wistful, as though remembering her own.

Georgina kissed her cheek, then allowed herself to be led back up the stairs to wait for Elizabeth and the arrival of the first guests.

The receiving line was short; first, Lady Meredith, then Elizabeth, and finally herself, and she could not help but feel sorry that Elizabeth's father was not here to lead his daughter out for the first dance. Lady Meredith had asked Shreveport and Barstow if they would mind doing the honors, and they had both readily agreed.

Elizabeth and Shreveport stood at the top of the ballroom and Georgina and Barstow at the bottom, and as the string orchestra started up, the two couples whirled around the floor. Georgina deliberately shut out the idea of how she might have felt were Matthew holding her now, for Barstow was too good a friend to treat so. The two men had already discussed what they should do, and at a signal known only to them, they arrived at the top of the room and stood together, waiting for the guests to join in the dancing. Elizabeth and Georgina stood with hands joined, their partners on the outside of them, until everyone was ready; then they joined the others in the first dance of the evening.

Lady Meredith had finally relaxed and was making her round of the room, bringing over young men who were not dancing, to meet the daughters of her friends. Robbie seemed to be everywhere, checking on the caterer to be sure all the food and drink had arrived, looking into the supper room to see if it still looked attractive, and always having a smile of encouragement for "her" two girls as she passed.

Everything was going a little too smoothly, thought Georgina. Her dance card was filled before Lord Frost came over to her, and Barstow was not at all put out when she told him she was carrying the posy her guardian sent. He was to take her in to supper, as he so often did, but that was two dances away, and she was becoming extremely warm, so she slipped away before her next partner came to claim her. She needed just one breath of fresh air and she'd return for the balance of the dance.

As she walked along the hall, her soft dancing slippers making no sound on the polished wood floor, she noticed the library door was slightly open and there was a light inside. Hoping Matthew might have arrived late and not had time to change, she pushed the door wide.

The occupant was not Matthew, however, but Lord Frost, and he was bending over the desk, attempting to open a locked drawer with a paper knife. She had caught him in the act.

"Did you by chance mislay something, my lord?" Georgina asked icily. "I am amazed that one of your substance must needs stoop so low as to burgle the home of a friend."

She knew she should have been frightened, for Lord Frost had the look of a cornered animal, but her anger at the idea of anyone having the audacity to try to rob Matthew made her brave.

She turned to leave the room, but he was beside her in a flash, grasping her arm in a vicious grip and swinging her around to face his cold, calculating eyes. The veneer of charm had finally vanished.

"Not so fast, Georgie." His voice was no louder than a whisper, but nonetheless sinister. He flung her into a chair and quietly closed the door.

"So you were staying with Lady Leicester in Lisbon, were you? Just visiting your brother at a time when no one except the army could get in and out of Portugal?" he asked, his fear of discovery disappearing and his manner increasingly threatening with every word.

Georgina decided the best thing to do was keep quiet and let him talk. If he kept her here too long, surely someone would come looking for her.

"On a recent trip I met an old friend of yours who happens to be still very angry with you. You do remember Lieutenant Barker, don't you?" The voice was silky soft, and he towered over her as she sat bolt upright in the chair into which he had thrown her.

"I wonder how the Earl of Barstow would feel if he were told that the young lady he is paying court to had been a Gypsy camp follower who posed first as an officer's manservant? And I doubt that Mrs. Drummond-Burrell would have any further recollection of your beautiful mother if she were told of your indiscretions."

Ridiculously, some part of Georgina's mind wondered who had told him that, for he hadn't been there at the time. When she showed neither fear nor alarm at his discovery, he changed his tactics.

"And what about Lady Elizabeth? Do you think her duke would continue to call if he learned about your lurid past? Dukes have a way of disappearing the minute they hear a breath of scandal, you know," he went on in the same vein, his expression turning to confidence as he noticed her first show of concern.

"And what about William, your ambitious twin? Do you think any wealthy heiress will look at him after hearing of the scandal surrounding his sister?" He had achieved what he sought, as Georgina was now visibly shaken.

"I see you understand me completely. It will only be your word against mine if you say you have seen me in here, but if you even breathe it to anyone, I assure you I will bring ruin down upon all of you with the greatest of pleasure. Your esteemed Cousin Matthew has been a thorn in my side for a number of years, and one I will delight in removing when the time is right."

As Georgina still sat silently in the chair, he went behind the desk once more to replace the paper knife, which had been clasped in his hand the whole time. Then he walked over to the door.

"I suggest you stay here until you have regained your composure. You will hear from me again, I promise you."

He bowed mockingly, then opened the door and silently disappeared down the hall.

Georgina sat still for a few minutes, then stood and examined her dress, which was only slightly creased by Frost's rough handling. She knew she couldn't stay here, and had no idea how many of her partners had looked for her in vain. She would have to pretend she'd felt faint and gone out for a little air.

The library was too masculine to hold a mirror, so she smoothed her hair with her fingers and hoped it was not too wild, then stepped out into the hall. Before she was halfway along, Elizabeth came hurrying toward her.

"Georgina, where have you been? Grandmama is frantically trying to pretend that you tore your dress and had to have it stitched. Why, you're shaking, Georgina. Are you ill?"

"Hush, Elizabeth, I'm really all right. I became overheated and went out for a little air, that's all. How do I look?" Georgina's voice was trembling a little, now that she had finally found it again, but her calm was returning rapidly and in a moment she was in complete control of herself.

"You look a little pale, that's all. You should have told someone where you were going, you know," Elizabeth scolded, relieved to see Georgina almost recovered.

The two girls entered the ballroom just as supper was about to be served, and were instantly claimed by Barstow and Shreveport.

"Is everything all right, Gina? You don't look well and you were gone for quite some time." Barstow's voice showed his quiet concern.

She smiled and eased the grip she suddenly realized she had taken on his hand.

"Everything is fine now, David," she whispered. She glanced quickly at her card to see whose dances she had missed.

Barstow grinned. "They were none too pleased when they couldn't find you," he remarked.

"I'll apologize to them later, and promise them a dance at Almack's, but I must find Lady Meredith and let her know I'm all right," she said, looking around to see if she could catch a glimpse of her.

"You needn't worry now, but I warrant you're in for a scold later. She was by my side when we saw you and Elizabeth coming through the hall," he murmured. "Smile, you look quite pale—I said a scold, not a beating."

Georgina couldn't see Frost anywhere in the supper room, and sometime later, when Lady Meredith had recovered herself enough to approach her, she found that he had left.

"Poor Lord Frost was helping me discreetly look for you in the garden, and in the darkness he ripped his jacket on a branch. I offered him one of Matthew's coats, but he declined and left. You have much to account for, young lady," she told her.

It was a relief to know that Frost was no longer there, but the enjoyment of her come-out ball was gone, and she smiled and danced mechanically as the night wore on. When Barstow came for his second dance, he remarked on her lack of vivacity, and let her know he was concerned.

"Oh, David, don't you ring a peal over me too, or I think I shall burst into tears. I did nothing wrong, and I couldn't help it, I promise you, but I just can't tell anyone," she said, her eyes pleading her case.

"Would you like me to talk to Lady Meredith and persuade her to postpone her scold until morning?" he suggested. "I know she'll do as I ask."

"Yes, please, David. I don't think I can take any more tonight without making a complete fool of myself. Thank you for being such a good friend." Her false smile had warmed to one of genuine gratitude.

"I only wish I could be more, but if friendship is what you want, then that's what you shall have. If, when you're feeling more the thing, you could confide in me, I might be able to help, you know." He looked at her fondly and, as the dance was over, escorted her back to Lady Meredith, taking that lady on one side and murmuring quietly to her. When Georgina saw her nod, she breathed a sigh of relief. She'd be able to cope better in the morning, she was sure.

It was impossible for her to leave until the last guest was gone, so she put a bright smile on her face and charmed each of her remaining partners, laughing and teasing them as though she was having a wonderful time and hadn't a worry in the world.

When the music stopped for the night, she went toward the door, joining Elizabeth and Lady Meredith in acknowledging the thanks and saying good night as their guests slowly went out into the night, where their carriages awaited them.

By morning Georgina was exhausted. Sleep had eluded her for a long time, and when she finally succumbed, it was only to have vivid nightmares from which she awoke soaking wet and trembling.

But it was not in her nature to evade an issue, so she wearily arose, and by the time the maid came in with tea and a message from Lady Meredith that she was sleeping late and Georgina could do so also if she wished, Georgina was already partially dressed. She had written a note to Barstow to ask if he felt like taking her for an early ride in the park, and gave it to the maid for a footman to deliver and wait for a reply.

The reply was not slow forthcoming, and within a half-hour the earl was there and they set off for Hyde Park with a groom trailing behind.

"I would like to be able to say that you look wonderful, but you look to me as though you slept very little last night, Gina," Barstow began when they had negotiated the early-morning traffic on Park Lane and entered the park.

"Did I wake you, David? I'm sorry, but I had difficulty sleeping, and as Lady Meredith was staying in bed for a while, I felt like a gallop to shake the cobwebs away," she said.

"I believe you are the only person alive I would get dressed in a half-hour for. But your need sounded so urgent that I thought you might even go off on your own if I didn't come right away." He touched her arm and pointed to a tree not too far away. "When we reach that old oak, let's gallop and get the tension out of your system. Then, perhaps, you'll be able to talk."

She went like the wind, feeling her hat fly to the back of her head, and glad her hair was so short that it couldn't get too wild. When they slowed to a canter, she felt much better, but she knew she could not tell David what had occurred. She could not tell anyone!

Meredith returned in the middle of June, just two days before the Prince Regent's grand fete that had all London buzzing. The tradespeople loved it, as it was providing work for many, as more gowns were sewn, furniture was made or reupholstered, painters and carpenters were employed to squeeze every last inch of space out of Carlton House, and cooks and confectioners worked night and day to prepare the finest delicacies imaginable for the delectation of so many guests.

Georgina had reluctantly consented to the purchase of one more gown, and this time the color was pale turquoise trimmed in white, and Lady Meredith had lent her a delicate necklace of aquamarines.

It had taken several days for Lady Meredith to forgive Georgina for her disappearance at the come-out ball. She was not normally one to hold a grievance, but Georgina's refusal to say anything more than that she was overheated and had gone into the garden for some air had disappointed her, and she could not but think the worst.

For the grand fete, Meredith chose not to wear his uniform, which would have been most acceptable, but donned court dress once more. Elizabeth looked her loveliest in a gown of soft rose satin, and Lady Meredith was regally gowned in the deepest purple satin embroidered in gold.

The carriage turned the corner of St. James Street into Pall Mall shortly before eighty-thirty, but the lineup of coaches was so long that they inched slowly forward for a distance they could have walked in two or three minutes, had they wanted to arrive with dirty shoes and hems.

It was a little after nine o'clock when they actually stepped inside Carlton House, shortly before the Prince Regent entered the State Apartments. Georgina and Elizabeth had been presented to him on a previous occasion. They caught just a glimpse of his huge bulk, wearing a scarlet coat trimmed with gold lace, and a brilliant star of the Order of the Garter.

"Do you think he would have noticed had we not attended?" Lady Meredith asked her son. "Whatever we do, we must stay together in this crush." She turned to Georgina. "Did you hear me, Georgina? Just don't go wandering off anywhere this time."

Matthew's eyebrows lifted slightly; then he put a protective arm around his ward and drew her close.

"My goodness," Lady Meredith exclaimed as they wandered through the magnificent palace. "He's turned it into a gigantic dining room! I just heard someone say there are even supper rooms down in the basement, and you can see the ones set up in the garden under all that canvas. What I really want to see are the changes he's made in the ballroom. Do you think we could go there first, for we'll not see a thing if all twenty thousand guests want to dance when the orchestra starts to play at eleven-thirty."

Like a dutiful son, Meredith pushed his way through the crowds, the three ladies linking hands and following in his path, and eventually it thinned out, since few of the guests had the forethought to look at the ballroom before it became full to capacity.

They paused for a moment at the entrance, taking in the vision of rich blue and gold; then they moved to the center of the room.

"I can understand your concern, Mother, but, crowded or not, Georgina is going to dance with me in this ballroom before the night is out," Matthew proclaimed. "Isn't that right, my dear?"

"Oh, yes, please," Georgina said, grateful to him for understanding that it wasn't enough for her just to look at the blue velvet draperies, heavily fringed and tasseled in gold, and the two marble fireplaces, decorated with bronze foliage and figurines, with gold-framed mirrors above.

She wanted to watch herself dancing in those huge gold-framed mirrors, and, if possible, to sit on a sofa in a recess, or on one of the gold chairs.

"But, Matthew, can you imagine how hot this room will be later? With the Prince Regent's abhorrence of drafts, he'll not allow any windows to be opened, you know," Lady Meredith reminded her son.

In the end, they found themselves fortunate to be seated in the gardens for dinner, and not the conservatory, where the Prince presided.

Barstow and Shreveport found them before they finished eating, and the girls had one dance with each of the three men while, at the side of the ballroom, Lady Meredith had the protection of the gentleman not dancing. Her purple gown proved useful for locating her after each dance.

When Georgina took the floor with Matthew, he questioned her regarding his mother's remarks.

"What did you do this time, my love, that put you in such disfavor with my mother?" he asked softly as he guided her around the room.

It was bliss feeling his hand on her waist, and she would have preferred not to converse at all, but knew she must answer.

"I absented myself for too long a time at our come-out ball," she said briefly.

"And what did you find so all-consuming that you forgot the time?" was his mild question, but his hand tightening on hers made her gasp.

"I told her that I became overheated and went into the garden for some air," she murmured, keeping her eyes carefully averted.

"Look at me, Georgina," he commanded, and she obediently raised her eyes. "You didn't tell her the truth?"

"Not completely," Georgina said, still looking into his searching eyes, "but I swear to you I did nothing wrong and nothing I could help."

"But you can't tell me, either?" His eyebrows rose slightly, but he didn't seem angry.

She shook her head.

"Then let's forget about it. I believe you, and I'll try to get you back into Mother's good graces," he promised.

A feeling of relief swept through her and she hadn't realized how nervous she had been about his questions. Her thank-you was barely a whisper, but her face showed her gratitude and he smiled reassuringly at her.

"Did you look as gorgeous as this at your come-out ball?" he asked with a grin.

"Much more beautiful," she replied with a haughty lift of her head, then spoiled it with an irrepressible giggle of relief.

To their surprise, the music had stopped and they made their way through the crowds back to Lady Meredith.

18

Despite the late night, Georgina was awake early, and she quickly dressed and went downstairs.

As she had expected, she ate breakfast alone, and was finished and almost at the door to leave when Matthew entered.

"Don't go, Georgina." He took her by the arm and pulled out a chair by the side of his place. "I dislike eating alone when I'm at Settle House, and I've been meaning to tell you of the trip I took to Broadacres."

Georgina needed no further inducement. She accepted a second cup of tea, and watched Matthew fill his plate with eggs, kidneys and bacon, and the many slices of fresh toast the butler brought, with butter churned from their own herds.

"I deliberately surprised your grandmother and the agent by driving up there without notice. What a churlish woman your grandmother is. Was she always like that?"

"Always, I'm afraid," Georgina told him. "Perhaps she was different before my papa and mama married, but she was so against my mama that she became bitter. William and I can still remember when Papa threatened to accommodate her in the dower house, as she had become so difficult to live with."

"Once she knew who I was, she made an effort to have a bedchamber prepared, but it was dusty at best, and the sheets and blankets quite damp." He saw her pained face. "Now, don't get upset, for it was not your fault.

"The following morning I met with the agent, and a sorry piece of work he proved to be. I demanded to see the accounts, and there were a number of items indicating cash had been sent to your grandmother that obviously had not been spent in the house. I am showing William how to look into these, for I brought away copies of the records just for that purpose." He studied her serious face. "Don't worry. William can do it if he is allowed to work it out at his own pace."

"I know he can," Georgina said, "but I did it, as it always seemed to be so much easier for me."

"Yes, well, William will learn to keep his eye on the accounts, and start to make decisions. The estate is as sorry as its agent, which was to be expected, and there is a great deal of land not being used for anything at all. William needs instruction, but he'll learn how to work up to full crop rotation and production, given time.

"With regard to the other matter, I drove by your ex-gamekeeper's home and it was everything you said. I have given a man I know the job of investigating his source of income, and when I have all the facts, I'll take some action. It certainly looks very suspicious.

"I'm also looking around for a good agent to be of help until William is out of the army."

Georgina tried to express her gratitude, but Matthew wouldn't hear of it.

"It was a duty I neglected, so no thanks are necessary, Georgina," he asserted, and held up a hand to stop any further argument. "Now, shall we see if we can have a ride in the park before the others come down?"

An eager Georgina hurried out to change right away.

For the past month Frost had not visited as frequently as theretofore, but the day after the Regent's fete he called, despite the fact that he must know Matthew was in residence, but as it happened, Matthew was not at home at the time.

"My dear Lady Meredith, how good it is to see you looking so enchanting after the horrors of last night's crush," he gushed, pressing his lips to the back of her hand.

"One wondered if Prinny could have found out if we had not attended," Lady Meredith said brightly, "but I could just imagine a little clerk checking off all the invitations handed in and blacklisting the missing ones.''

"Possible, quite possible, I'm sure." Frost nodded sagely. "I saw you and, of course, could not help but admire how regal you looked in that gorgeous shade of purple. I would have come to your side, dear lady, but saw you were well attended and, quite frankly, was afraid to risk life and limb trying to cross the ballroom floor.''

Lady Meredith drew him toward the two girls and he bent low over first Elizabeth's hand and then that of Georgina, who was far too worried about what a displeased Lord Frost might do to show him how she really felt, so she smiled graciously.

"I was of a mind to visit Somerset Place and take a look at the Royal Academy's exhibition, then thought how much more delightful such a trip would be in the company of such lovely ladies,'' he told them, and Georgina tried to make her brain work to find some excuse for not accepting his invitation. "Now the fete is over, many of the *ton* are busy packing for the country, so it would be possible to see the exhibit under less crowded conditions. Lady Elizabeth, would you perhaps be free tomorrow afternoon?''

"I would have liked nothing better, my lord," Elizabeth said, "and I truly appreciate the invitation, but I have another commitment tomorrow afternoon. Perhaps Georgina and Mrs. Robinson are available, for I'm sure they would enjoy themselves tremendously.''

Robbie leaned forward. "You did say the Earl of Barstow would be out of town tomorrow, did you not, Georgina? I know how much you enjoy seeing the paintings, and I am also available tomorrow afternoon, so I believe we can accept Lord Frost's kind invitation.''

It was quite impossible for Georgina to refuse without making her dislike obvious, so she bowed to the inevitable and smiled her acceptance. He arranged to call for them at two in the afternoon and arrived promptly, to find Georgina and Robbie ready and waiting.

He handed Robbie into the carriage first; then, as he bowed over Georgina's hand, he murmured, "I'm glad you had sense enough to accept. It would have been very foolish of you to refuse me, my dear.''

He was once again the perfect host, pointing out particularly handsome portraits, and he even introduced them to one of the artists whose paintings was on display.

On their return to Grosvenor Square, just as Robbie started up the steps, he caught Georgina's arm and pulled her on one side.

''I will pay another call on Lady Meredith tomorrow afternoon. Be there if you know what's good for you,'' he threatened.

She hurried to catch up with Robbie, and as they entered the hall, she saw Matthew standing in the open doorway of the library. ''As soon as you have removed your bonnet and gloves, I would like to see you, Georgina,'' he said quietly, then went inside, closing the door behind him.

No more than five minutes later, the footman opened the library door and closed it firmly behind her. Matthew pointed to the seat in front of his desk, the same one that Frost had flung her into, and she took it and sat gingerly on the extreme edge.

''I had thought by this time, Georgina, we were on the kind of terms that would preclude your going against my wishes, but this does not seem to be the case,'' he said sternly. ''Elizabeth had the good sense to make an excuse, but I understand you jumped at the idea of an afternoon in Frost's company, and begged Mrs. Robinson to join you.''

It was so very unfair. She looked up at him angrily, and his expression became even more severe.

''Are you never going to grow up and behave with the kind of consideration and restraint a young lady of your age should? I had thought these months in the company of the ladies of this house would have wrought a considerable improvement in your behavior, but instead I find you are just as much the hoyden, caring only for your own pleasures and disregarding the advice of your elders.'' He had started out by being coldly sarcastic, but now he was angry, and at the sound of it in his voice, Georgina's own temper flared up.

''Why does being ten years older than I make you always

the one who is right?'' she asked, her eyes flashing a green warning. ''You're away ninety percent of the time, and when you come back you are the supreme judge of everything I do and of everything anyone tells you I did in your absence. Well, I'm not one of your soldiers and I won't be shouted at and scolded all the time!''

He got up and walked around the desk, then stood towering over her, his brows drawn in a straight, angry line. ''If you were ten years older than I am, young lady, you would still obey me as head of this house, and right now you'd better take heed when I tell you to mind your manners, for I'll not suffer much more of your insolence.''

Georgina had worked herself up into such a state that she really didn't know what she was saying, and she shouted, ''You're threatening me again, as you've threatened me since the first time I ever set eyes on you. I've tried to do what you want, but whatever I do, you're always furious with me, and I hate you, I hate you!''

She got up to try to run out of the room, but he grabbed her shoulders and shook her.

''Go to your bedchamber and stay there until you can behave like some semblance of a lady,'' he ordered as he released her, and she ran out of the room, just succeeding in holding back her sobs until she reached her chamber, where she threw herself onto the bed and cried as if her heart were broken.

She must have cried herself to sleep, for she awoke to see Lady Meredith carrying a candle with which she lit the other candles in the room. She sat down on the bed next to Georgina, who was now sitting up, blinking.

''What's all this about, my dear, quarreling with Matthew and making him storm out of the house in a fury?'' she asked, her gentle smile belying her words. ''You should know by now that he is jealous of Lord Frost. And I happen to know he was planning on taking you out himself this afternoon.''

''Oh, no,'' Georgina moaned, ready to start weeping again because of what she had missed.

''The people we care for are always the ones who make us

most angry, you know. That's because it really doesn't matter to us what the others say or do.'' She got up slowly, showing her years for once. "You've missed supper, so one of the maids will be bringing you something to eat in a few moments. Wouldn't you like to wash your face? I'm sure you'll feel a lot better.''

Lady Meredith stayed with her until she'd made herself a little more presentable and had eaten most of her supper.

"I think I heard my son returning," she said. "It's always the woman who has to make up, you know. Why don't you come downstairs, apologize to him, and see what happens next. You did say some rather naughty things to him.''

"You heard?'' Georgina was surprised.

"The whole house heard, Georgina. You have a very good pair of lungs.'' She held out her hand. "Will you come with me?''

Matthew was in the drawing room with Elizabeth and Robbie, standing by the side of the fireplace sipping a brandy when they went in, and Georgina went straight up to him before her courage failed her.

"I'm sorry, Matthew. Please forgive me,'' she said, her misery showing in her face and her decidedly puffy eyes.

"We both said things we didn't mean, my dear. Shall we try to forget it happened?'' he asked softly, not taking his eyes away from hers.

Mrs. Robinson had already left the room, and Lady Meredith signaled a reluctant Elizabeth to come out also, leaving Georgina alone with Matthew.

When the door closed, he drew her into his arms and held her comfortingly close, stroking her hair soothingly; then he took her face in his hands and she knew without a shadow of a doubt that he was going to kiss her—a real kiss this time. His lips were tender and warm at first; then, as his passion mounted, they became demanding and she found herself very willingly responding. His hands caressed her shoulders and back, molding her to him, and her skin began to tingle as she relaxed and let her own passion sweep through. She could taste the brandy on his lips as her mouth opened to his kiss, and the misery of the last few hours disappeared as her body came alive with a new, strange sort of urgency.

He finally came to his senses and lifted his head, looking down into her eyes, half-drugged with passion. "I had no right to do that, my love, but I'm not going to apologize, for I'm not sorry," he said, running a finger over her slightly swollen lips.

"I'm so glad you did. It was beautiful. Won't you do it again?" she asked, softly appealing.

He shook his head sadly. "I'm not the sort of man who should be kissing young debutantes, any more than Frost is, and I don't believe you have allowed him to do so."

"No, I haven't. I know I wouldn't like it with him. Does it always feel like that?" she asked, still in a state of wonder.

"Very, very rarely, Georgina," he said, looking worried. He had remembered Barstow, and from what his mother had told him, it seemed as though he might be asked shortly for Georgina's hand in marriage.

"Was this to make up for shaking me?" Georgina asked, some of her natural mischief returning.

He chuckled. "Not at all," he said. "You provoked me to violence, and you deserved it." He became serious. "I didn't really hurt you, did I?"

She shook her head. "No. It was the fact that you did it that hurt."

He drew her head close to his chest again, and his hands stroked her back until she felt she might melt completely into him.

"I have to leave tomorrow to visit Louise." She looked up and he saw the question in her eyes, and shook his head. "No, I will be on horseback to save time, and though I know you're an excellent rider, it really wouldn't do for us to ride all that way alone. I will be back in a few days, and if all goes well, will return to the Peninsula shortly after that."

She turned her face away to hide the disappointment in her eyes.

"Will you promise not to see Frost while I'm gone?" he asked, not demanding but asking her.

"I'll promise not to go out with him, but if he calls here

when there are visitors, I cannot help but see him," she said, deliberately stalling, for a walk in the garden would not really be going out.

He nodded. "You're right. As Mother allows him to visit, you cannot be rude. I'll be gone by dawn tomorrow, so I'd better have an early night, but I'll see you on my return." He bent and kissed the tip of her nose, then murmured softly, "You get some rest too," and left the room.

The following afternoon they received a number of visitors, not least among them being Lord Frost.

When Frost murmured to Georgina that he wanted to see her alone, she suggested a walk in the garden, as that would not in any way interfere with her promise to Matthew.

Unlike the garden at Settle House, the one in Grosvenor Square was a patch no larger than the ground floor of the house itself, but it was prettily laid out, with shade trees and benches on which to relax with a book on sunny afternoons.

It was to one of these benches Frost led her, and when she was comfortably seated, he put his arm along the back of the bench, close to her but not quite touching, and leaned toward her.

"It seems you took my advice and told no one you had found me in the library," he said. "Since you've shown how well you can take direction, I have a small assignment for you."

She turned sharply toward him, almost banging her head into his face. "What on earth do you mean? I'm not going to do anything for you, whatever it might be!" she declared, her lovely mouth setting in an angry line.

"Oh yes you are, my dear, if you don't want all those interesting facts about your past revealed," he said with a sneer. "You don't need time to think about the consequences, I'm sure."

The color left her cheeks as she realized the position she was in. "What is it you want?" she snapped as bravely as she could.

"Just a simple matter of an exchange. I am going to give you a sealed envelope, and you are to exchange it for another sealed envelope which will appear to be identical, but the contents will be a little different, that's all.''

He withdrew from inside his jacket an envelope of a size that might be used for documents. "Examine it carefully, for I want you to understand you can play no tricks with me. The word 'Governments' appears on this envelope, but on the one you are to bring back too me it will show only 'Government,' without the S. In case you should try, let me assure you that there is no way the S can be removed on this envelope, and if you have tried, I will notice right away.''

She shook her head. "I don't understand what this is all about,'' she said.

"You're not intended to understand,'' he snapped. "It would be too complicated for your woman's mind, in any event. When Meredith returns from the country, he will go into the city and bring back the envelope with the S missing. You will watch for his return, and see where he puts it. Then when no one is around, you will make the exchange.''

"And I'm to give it to you with your cup of tea when next you call?'' she asked sarcastically.

"Oh no. You are to bring it to me at this address.'' He gave her a slip of paper with some writing on it. "I will know when Meredith leaves for Dover, and you will be at that address at eight o'clock in the evening of the same day with the other envelope.''

She breathed an unconscious sigh of relief. She would tell Matthew the whole, and he would know how to deal with it.

"Don't even think of it,'' Frost snarled, cleverly reading her. "Should you warn Meredith, or tell anyone else, not only will you and your relatives be scorned by the *beau monde*, but you will also be without a guardian, for my agents, who are watching him constantly, will receive word to effectively silence him—forever. Do you understand me?''

As she looked at the cold, hard eyes of the man, stripped of the veneer he showed to Lady Meredith and the rest of society, she realized he meant every word, and she was very frightened.

"I see you do,'' he said in icy tones that almost made her shiver. "Let there be no mistakes, or you will be the loser.''

He stood. "I will leave you here to think on it, and you'd best conceal that envelope in your skirts. Don't come back indoors until you look less like a frightened rabbit," he sneered.

After he left, Georgina went up to her bedchamber and examined the envelope. There was a good possibility she could ease up the seal and glue it down again. She would borrow a knife with a very thin blade from the kitchen, and she was sure there was a pot of glue in the old nursery.

The difficult part would be finding the other envelope and keeping it long enough to open it and exchange the contents, then reseal and return it. She remembered that Matthew always went into the library when he came back from White-hall, and assumed that he would do so again and put the envelope away somewhere. For now she would prepare Frost's envelope, then wait.

She pinched her cheeks to bring back some color to them, tidied her hair, and joined the others in the drawing room. Lord Frost had already left, and she was able to slip in unnoticed while everyone was talking and strike up a conversation with the person nearest the door.

The three days before Matthew returned felt more like three years to Georgina as she impatiently waited. But he finally came back, early in the morning, as Georgina was returning from a ride with Barstow.

The sight of Barstow served to remind Matthew of the guilt he had been feeling ever since he last saw Georgina. As her guardian he had no right to touch her, let alone kiss her passionately. Until he knew Barstow's intentions, he would, he decided, keep a safe distance between himself and his lovely ward.

When she came in to breakfast, he was sitting at the table reading the morning paper.

"Good morning, Matthew," she said softly.

He peered around his paper. "Good morning, Georgina," he said rather gruffly.

"How was Louise?"

Once more he looked around his newspaper. "Very well. Enjoying being with a lot of youngsters."

She stared at the newspaper for a few minutes, then came to a decision.

"What did I do wrong this time, sir?" she asked clearly.

"Georgina, can't you see I'm catching up on the news?" He sounded impatient now.

She looked at the plate of kidneys, bacon, and eggs before her, for which she'd just lost her appetite. At this hour the footmen were otherwise engaged, so she pushed back her chair and rose.

"I'm sorry, my lord. Please excuse me," she said, and walked quickly toward the door.

"Stop being so silly, Georgina. Come back and eat your breakfast at once," he ordered, throwing down the newspaper, but Georgina was halfway across the room and she made no attempt to obey him.

Her hand was on the doorknob as he grasped her shoulder and swung her around. "What on earth is the matter with you, you silly girl?" he snapped, knowing full well that he was being very rude to read a newspaper with another diner at the table.

"Let me go," she demanded, trying to push away the hand that held her shoulder in its grasp.

Instead of doing as she asked, he turned her gently around and led her back to the table, seating her before the breakfast she'd just abandoned. He drew another chair close to hers and sat down also.

"Now, eat your breakfast, and then tell me what this is all about."

He sounded as though he were humoring a little girl, and suddenly Georgina was glad he was going away the next day, if Lord Frost was to be believed. When she had seen him at the table, she had thought for a foolish moment that she could tell him everything and let him deal with it. It was a good thing he had been so unreceptive.

"I am sorry I disturbed your reading, but I am no longer hungry and would like to return to my chamber. Would you please excuse me?" she asked politely.

"Not yet, Georgina. I thought we were friends."

He was close, but not touching her, so it was easier to tell him what was on her mind. "A long time ago, at Lady Leicester's house, you offered me friendship," she said softly, "but it was withdrawn the very next time we met, and since then I've never known from one meeting to the next how I stood with you. If that is your idea of friendship, Matthew, I cannot accept it. You've been a good friend to William, but I don't think you're able to be friends with a woman any longer." There was a catch in her voice; then she asked, "Now, may I go?"

She never knew how her head became pressed against his chest, but his arms were around her, so he must have put it there, and what she had thought made such sense was suddenly idiotic. As long as he made her feel like this, she would accept friendship or anything else he had to offer.

"I'm sorry, my love. In trying not to hurt you I just succeeded in making it worse, didn't I?" he murmured, his lips so close to her cheek that she could feel his breath on her face. "This is the worst possible time, for I have to leave shortly and will be out most of the day and evening. Then sometime tomorrow I'll be off to the Peninsula again.

"But I'm going to resign my commission very soon now, and when I do, I promise that things will be very different. Can you bear with me for a little longer, do you think?" he asked, turning her face toward him.

She nodded, and was about to say more when they both heard Robbie greeting one of the footmen outside the door.

They immediately sprang apart, and as the door opened to admit her, Meredith rose to his feet.

"Good morning, Mrs. Robinson," he said; then, "I'll see you before I leave, Georgina," and he walked quickly out of the room.

"I hope you won't be insulted, Robbie, but I thought I was hungry and now find I'm not at all. Would you excuse me? I think I'll go lie down for a while."

Robbie's voice was full of concern. "Of course, my dear. I hope you're not coming down with something."

"Oh no, it's just a headache," Georgina assured her. "Lord Meredith left his newspaper, if you want to read it."

Robbie reached for the newspaper as Georgina hurried upstairs. On the pretext that she still had a headache, she declined an invitation to go for a drive in the afternoon, and was pretending to rest in her room when Matthew's carriage stopped at the front door and he alighted and entered the house. It was what she had been waiting for.

As the butler greeted him, she ran quickly down the back stairs, out of the house, and around to the library windows, the curtains to which had not yet been drawn. As she waited but saw no sign of Matthew entering the room, she thought she had been mistaken and he would probably keep the document in his bedchamber, but as she started to leave, she heard a sound and he entered the room, closely followed by his mother.

He was carrying a small bag, and he dropped it into the bottom drawer of his desk, then, without bothering to lock it, steered his mother out again.

It couldn't have been better! Earlier in the day Georgina had left the window at which she was standing unlocked, and now she opened it and climbed in and dropped quickly to the floor. With bated breath lest he should return, she opened the drawer, pulled out the bag, and looked into it. The envelope was there! She picked it out, dropping it onto the floor in her nervousness, then replaced the bag in the drawer and, closing it carefully, went back out of the window with the envelope in her pocket.

Returning the back way, she had reached her floor when she heard Lady Meredith still talking to her son in the hall.

"It was no more than a headache, I'm sure. If you feel so strongly about it, Matthew, why don't you seek out Barstow and ask him what his intentions are?" she heard Lady Meredith suggest, and she waited to hear Matthew's answer.

"I think I'll do that. I'm dining at White's tonight, and if he's not there I'll stop at Brooks's and see if I can get a word with him."

Georgina heard the two doors close, and not a minute too

soon, as she realized a maid was just starting to come up the back stairs behind her.

Once in the hall, however, she was safe, and she walked calmly to her bedchamber as if she had never been out of the house. Hiding the second envelope, she hurriedly dressed and dined with Lady Meredith, Elizabeth, and Robbie as though she had not a care in the world, secretly congratulating herself that she could go on the stage after this performance.

When the ladies retired to the drawing room for their tea, however, she pretended her headache had returned and begged to be excused.

Once in her room, she turned the key in the lock, then set to work opening the second envelope as carefully as she had opened the first. It was delicate work, but finally she succeeded, and after exchanging the contents, resealed both envelopes. The one for Lord Frost, which contained his original documents, she returned to her dresser drawer, and now came the problem of getting the other back into her guardian's desk.

She undressed and slipped into a night gown and wrapper, then suddenly realized how easy it was. All she had to do was go quite openly to the library to borrow a book, and replace the envelope at the same time. Why hadn't she thought of it before?

As she left the library with a copy of Shelley's works, Lady Meredith was coming out of the drawing room. "Georgina, if you can't sleep, I'd better have a potion mixed for you. It's not like you to be so indisposed, my dear," she said with some concern.

Georgina assured her she would be all right in the morning, but if not, would let Lady Meredith know for certain, and she reached the safety of her bedchamber without further incident.

Now she had to go over, once again, the rest of her scheme to beat Lord Frost at his own game.

Meredith left shortly after a late breakfast, and she could only assume he did not meet with Barstow, or he would have known what their relationship really was, and surely said something to her. She wondered why he wanted to push Barstow, but she dared not speculate any further.

The day dragged abominably, with no callers at all, and she wondered where Barstow had got to, for he had not called the previous day either.

Lady Meredith had made plans to dine with an elderly friend this particular evening, and Robbie and Elizabeth had become engrossed in a game of chess they had started some days before. There were just the three of them for dinner, and Georgina retired immediately afterward, saying she was feeling exhausted and was anxious to get an early night.

"Are you sure you're not sickening for something, Georgina?" Elizabeth asked. "You were out of sorts last night also."

"I don't think so," Georgina lied, "but I feel so tired that bed seems the best thing. Don't bother to check on me, though, as I'm a light sleeper at the best of times, and I'd hate to be wakened when I've just dropped off."

Once in her chamber, she reached into a drawer and carefully withdrew the knives Isabella had given her, automatically checking the blades for sharpness, as the Gypsy had taught her. When they were secured to the calf of each leg, she pulled a dark cloak out of the press and threw it around her shoulders.

Feeling dreadful because of all the lies she had told, she once again crept out of the back door, but this time she went down the garden and into the mews, coming out into Upper Grosvenor Street, where she was sure to find a hackney.

She had pulled the cloak over her head to hide her hair and most of her face, but even so the driver looked at her strangely when she told him to take her to Hertford Street. As she paid him the money he asked, however, he took no further notice and within ten minutes they were there. She was a little surprised, as she had expected to be sent to a house in some seedy neighborhood, but though the house was small and the street poorly lit, it appeared quite respectable.

Lord Frost opened the door himself, and took her into the front parlor. "How very prompt of you, my dear," he said with a contemptuous smile, and held out his hand.

She placed the envelope in his hand and turned to leave, but he caught her arm and swung her around. "Not so fast, my dear," he murmured. "Won't you have a glass of wine while I take a look at what you've brought me?"

"No, I must return right away or I will be missed. Elizabeth will wonder where I've gone," she started to say, but stopped as he withdrew the pages from the envelope.

Once again she tried to reach the door, but she couldn't pull her arm free of his grasp. Dropping the papers on the floor, he jerked her toward him and hit her across the face with the back of his hand, sending her flying across the room. As her head caught the leg of a chair, everything went black.

19

Consciousness returned slowly, and Georgina's first sensation was one of nausea as she found that her mouth had been stuffed with a foul-tasting gag, there was a sharp pain in her head, and her right cheek hurt. Before opening her eyes, she tried to reach up and touch the source of pain, but found she couldn't move her arms—they felt as though they were tied at the wrists to each side of the chair on which she was sitting. There was no help for it, she would have to face that awful man, for she now remembered trying to run and him striking her down.

"So you decided to open your eyes finally," Frost sneered. He was sitting facing her, stretched out in an easy chair sipping a glass of brandy. She had been placed on a hard wood chair against the wall. "I'm sorry you are not more comfortable, but you brought it upon yourself, you know. What a lot of trouble you must have gone to, prying open those envelopes, and all for naught.

"I'm sure you must be wondering what we're waiting for, and why you're gagged. I could say, of course, that you've been gagged to stop your chatter, which has bored me for the longest time, but that was only a small consideration. You see, I can't allow you to shout and warn Elizabeth when she comes."

Oh no, she thought, he must have tricked Elizabeth so that she too would fall into his trap. And she could do nothing to stop him.

"You're fond of the chit, aren't you? And she's fond of you, or so I hope. I sent her a note telling her you were being held for ransom. I see you're surprised. It was a bit of luck that Lady Meredith told me one day that Elizabeth has a key to her safe. I've told her she'd better bring the Settle diamond necklace and earrings, and the emerald ones too, if she wants to see you alive again.''

With Lady Meredith out for the evening, Elizabeth would panic and do exactly as he told her, Georgina was sure. She wondered how long she had been unconscious.

As if reading her mind, Frost said, ''She should be along very shortly, and then I will tie her and the coachman up also, set fire to those naphtha-soaked rags, and you'll never be found. Why should anyone associate the disappearance of two young ladies with a house burned to the ground? It is rented for a few days only, by a Mr. Farthingale, so nothing will lead back to me.''

Georgina wished her head did not ache so much. It was stopping her thinking clearly. She saw several piles of dirty-looking cloths around the room, and realized that the odd smell she'd noticed must be the naphtha. Surreptitiously she moved a leg, which was not bound, and rubbed it against the leg of the chair to feel if her knife was still there.

''I have a few things to do in the other room, so you must excuse me for a while, but I would not attempt anything if I were you. I did not need to bind your legs, for if you move, you will take the chair with you and I will hear the crash. Then you'll be very sorry, I assure you!'' he threatened with a malicious smile, as though he was looking forward to her attempt and how he would deal with it.

As soon as he left the room, she slid her right leg backward, straining hard to make it reach her hand. She was glad he had placed her on a plain wood chair without arms, or it would have been impossible, and even so, it took three attempts before she had the knife out of the garter on her leg and securely in her hand. Manipulating it slowly, so as not to drop it, she got it in position to saw at the bonds around her right wrist, and after what seemed an age, the last thread was cut and she swiftly freed her left hand.

She would have liked to take the gag out, but decided it was better to pretend that she was still tied, and she could then take him by surprise. She still didn't know whether or not he had an accomplice in the house.

As she heard his footsteps coming back, she carefully placed her arms in the uncomfortable position in which they had been. Her knife rested securely in her right hand.

"Excellent timing," he murmured, giving her an evil grin, then peering through the curtains. "She's stepping down now, and she has a most interesting-looking package in her hands."

As a knock sounded on the door, Frost turned his back to Georgina and started to cross the room. In a fleeting moment the fact that there must be no one else in the house registered, as she took careful aim and sent the knife whistling through the air toward its target. It entered his back with a sickening thud, and he fell forward on his face.

He made no further movement, and she automatically noted from the visible side of his face that his eyes were closed and there was blood coming from the corner of his mouth and also seeping through his jacket. Not stopping to find out if he was still alive, Georgina pulled the gag from her mouth and ran from the room.

She opened the outer door to a surprised and delighted Elizabeth, then closed it quickly behind her so that her friend would not see Frost's body. The carriage was only a short distance away, and she grabbed Elizabeth's hand and pulled her, stumbling and running, toward it. As she pushed Elizabeth inside, she called to the driver to get away as fast as he could, and flung herself down beside her friend. Once they reached the end of the street and turned into Park Lane, she sank against the cushions, too relieved to think for a moment.

"What happened, Georgina?" Elizabeth asked. "I was so frightened when I got the note telling me to bring the jewels. Grandmama was out, as you know, and—"

"What did the note say?" Georgina interrupted.

"That you had been kidnapped, and if I wanted to see you alive again, I was to bring the jewels to that address and not tell anyone. That was all," Elizabeth answered. "How did the kidnapper manage to capture you when you were in bed?"

"I stupidly went into the garden for some air, and the mews gate must have been left open. I was bound and gagged . . . and blindfolded," she added, "so I never saw him, but he said you were coming with the jewels. When he went into the other room, I managed to unfasten my hands and escape him."

"It must have been horrible for you," Elizabeth murmured sympathetically, and reached to hold her friend's hand.

"So horrible that I don't want to talk about it anymore tonight. Do you think you could put the jewels back where you got them from and not tell your grandmama? All I want is to get into bed—my head aches terribly, for he knocked me out and I was unconscious for a long time."

"But shouldn't someone be told?" Elizabeth asked nervously.

"There's nothing I can tell anyone, for I never saw my kidnapper, and he's sure to be long gone from that house. It would just upset and frighten Lady Meredith, I know." She tried to smile, but her face refused to form more than a faint movement of her lips. "Let's leave it until morning at least, and see how we both feel after we've had a good night's sleep."

The coach driver was by now an old friend, and it had taken little to persuade him to say nothing of where they had been.

Elizabeth went in the front door while Georgina stayed in the carriage and entered through the back of the house so that Crowther would not see her disheveled state.

When she reached her bedchamber, Elizabeth was waiting and gave a little cry. "Your face is bleeding, Georgina."

A glance in the mirror showed a nasty cut on Georgina's right cheekbone. She remembered the gleam of something when Frost knocked her to the ground. It must have been his diamond ring that cut her.

"It's nothing to worry about, Elizabeth. I'll put a little salve on it before I go to bed," she told her convincingly.

Once Elizabeth had left, however, Georgina started to shake all over and the tears would not stop. She bathed her face, and her cheek throbbed. The cut was quite deep and might possibly leave a scar, but she could not worry about that now.

She tried to get a grip on herself, to shut out the memories of what had happened in that front parlor, but the picture of those piles of cloths as they would have blazed, had she not succeeded, was so vivid she could almost smell the smoke and feel the heat, and her limbs shook all the more. When she closed her eyes, she saw the more real image of Lord Frost falling forward with the knife sticking out of his back.

She slept little, and by morning looked every bit as bad as she felt, so she sent word to Lady Meredith that she was indisposed once more.

"Whatever happened to your face, Georgina?" Lady Meredith asked with concern.

"I got up in the night for a little water and tripped, I suppose, for I hit my face on the corner of the writing table. I put some salve on it and it feels much better," Georgina offered.

"You must stay in bed today, my dear, and I'll send up a potion to make you sleep. I want to leave for Settle House in a few days, and you must be well enough to travel. I'll look in on you later."

It was a relief to Georgina when the potion was brought by Elizabeth. She needed to convince her skeptical friend of the virtue of silence, for if Frost was dead, she had killed him and might even be arrested and charged with murder. The fewer people who knew of her night's work, the less likelihood there was of a dreadful scandal. When she refused to drink the potion until she had secured Elizabeth's promise, her friend finally assented.

But the mild sedative in the potion was unable to combat Georgina's overactive mind, and she had to pretend sleep when Lady Meredith returned.

As she tried to relax against the pillows, she remembered the knife she had left behind, unable to even try to remove it from Frost's back. What if he wasn't dead, she suddenly thought, and still able to blacken her name? They were all going to Settle House in two days' time, and he could start the rumors spreading around Kent, perhaps even to Brighton, where the Prince Regent would probably be staying with many of the *haut ton*.

Her mind went around and around the problem and always came back to one solution, which she was trying not to accept. She must go back to Yorkshire, to Broadacres and her grandmother. The old lady would not be able to refuse her admittance, after the letter William had written, and she couldn't be more unpleasant to her than she had been previously, for it was an impossibility.

That night, when everyone else was asleep, she packed a half-dozen of her plainer gowns. The decision was made.

"I know I look a mess, but I feel fine now, Lady Meredith, and this would be a splendid opportunity for me to take the stage north and check on Broadacres as I told William I would. I can return directly from there to Settle House in a few weeks," Georgina told Lady Meredith.

"You're not going alone by stagecoach, young lady. Matthew would have my head if I permitted such a thing. We have some last-minute shopping to do now, but when we return I'll arrange for you and Robbie to take one of the coaches tomorrow."

As soon as they left, Georgina wrote a brief note to Lady Meredith and ordered a reluctant Crowther to get her a hackney. She'd never traveled on the stage, but knew where it left from, and was lucky to get there just before one pulled out. She had money saved from the generous allowance Matthew had insisted on giving her, and this was ample to pay for an inside seat and meals on the way.

Despite her youth, Georgina found the long journey very tiring, and when she arrived at Broadacres her grandmother at first looked amazed at the fashionable young lady she had become.

"So you're back. They finally found out what a liar and a cheat you are, didn't they?" The old lady's face twisted spitefully. "Don't think I'm going to put up with airs and graces from you now that you think you've been in society. You're no better than your mother, a tramp, that's all."

227

Georgina had intended to just let her grandmother talk herself out, and ignore her, but when she maligned her mother, she saw red.

"Listen to me, you old harridan, and listen carefully." Her voice was hardly more than a whisper, but cold as icicles. "If you ever say a word against my mother in this house again, I'll personally pack your things and take you to the dower house, if I have to drag you there myself." Her eyes flashed a bright green.

"Your brother's the heir here, and not you, missy," the old lady snorted. "He's the only one can put me out of this house."

"Don't pretend you didn't get his letter, for I know you did. As soon as he comes back, you'll be out of here, for he won't live in the house with you—he told me as much," Georgina lied calmly. "For myself, I don't care whether you're here or not, but I've heard you malign my mother in this, her home, for the last time. That's a warning."

"You're hoity-toity in your fine clothes, all of a sudden," her grandmother sneered. "What did you have to do for his fine lordship to have him put good money on your back? By the look of your face, he knocked you about and sent you packing. He came here, you know, snooping around, but he found out nothing."

The old lady's words were sharp, but she had gone slightly pink, and there was a whine in her voice that Georgina had never heard before.

"I'll also be snooping around, as you call it, trying to see what can be salvaged for William," Georgina told her, "whether you like it or you don't."

After that one unpleasant confrontation, the dowager went out of her way to avoid Georgina, and when they met at the dinner table it was in the old silence.

Georgina was unhappy that her own horse, Starlight, was now presumably in Matthew's stable at Settle House, but she rode an old hack each day, checking on some of the tenant farmers and making notations to pass along to William.

The evenings were the worst time of day, though, when

she couldn't occupy her mind with the work at hand, and thoughts of Matthew haunted her. She had sent a letter to Lady Meredith as soon as she reached Broadacres, augmenting the brief note she had left.

She found herself, one afternoon, riding disconsolately around the estate, thinking of the past few weeks and of the bleak future that seemed to lie ahead for her.

As the miserable nag crept along, unwilling or unable to move at more than a snail's pace, she tried to think of a way to get Starlight back. Perhaps if William got a leave he might ride her up north, she thought; then she looked and saw in the distance a horse and rider coming from the direction of the house. When they drew closer she thought her imagination was playing tricks, for why would Matthew be here in Yorkshire?

He looked her up and down, taking in the light tan that had returned to her skin, the cut on her cheek that was now healed, and the decrepit mount she was astride.

"I'm pleased to see you are not at death's door, as my mother intimated," he remarked casually enough, though she thought she detected a slight twitch at the corners of his mouth.

"Is she very angry with me?" she asked hesitantly.

"Not at all, but she might very well be if she knew what I know about you." He reached into a pocket. "According to Davis, this is yours," he said, deceptively casual as he handed her the knife she had last seen in Frost's back.

She gasped. "Where did you find it?"

"Where you left it, I believe," he said dryly. "Very careless of you to leave things like that around! Let's make as much speed back to the house as that creature is capable of, and we'll find a spot where your gorgon of a grandmother can't hear us. We have much to discuss."

"How is Elizabeth?" Georgina asked, avoiding the topic she knew was inevitable.

"She is about as close to heaven as a young engaged lady may come," he said, as Georgina let out a cry of delight. "I think that she and the Duke of Shreveport will make an

229

excellent match, as he is a charming young man, and she, given a few years, will no doubt make a formidable duchess.''

"I'm so glad," she said, then added as she tried to nudge her mount into a faster walk, "That was one of my worries."

He was becoming impatient at the slow pace. "Don't you have a decent horse to ride, Georgina? I know you are an excellent horsewoman, but on this nag—''

"Starlight is, I hope, in your stable at Settle House, my lord. I could hardly bring her with me when I boarded the—'' she started to tell him.

"Of course," he exclaimed. "I never thought to check on her. Don't worry, she'll be well cared for and happy to see you soon."

She glanced quickly at him, feeling a glimmer of hope, but could read nothing in his impassive countenance.

"Did my grandmother behave very nastily to you?" she asked, remembering his description of the old lady.

"She did not dare. But she still shows insufficient interest in you to care where you are and when you will be back. Don't you tell her when you leave?"

"Why should I? We have spoken only when necessary these past three weeks." She was surprised he would trouble himself about something so unimportant.

They reached the stable and handed their horses to the elderly retainer and his lordship's groom, who eyed the old man with suspicion.

As they entered the house, the dowager came hurrying toward them. "You found your hoydenish ward, I see, my lord. I've had a bedchamber prepared for you, and tomorrow I'll have the man of business show you the estate," she hurried to tell him.

"I thank you for the accommodation, my lady," he said with ill-concealed dislike, "but tomorrow Georgina will show me the estate. I would doubt that much has changed since I was here."

Georgina gave him a grateful look and he said no more for now, so she ran upstairs to check on his room and make sure everything was in order, then returned to the hall, where Matthew was still conversing with the now obsequious dowager.

"I'll show you to your room, my lord, when you are ready," Georgina said quietly.

His glance was sharp, and when they were out of earshot, he asked, "Why are you performing servants' tasks, Georgina?"

"There's a mere handful, my . . . Matthew," she replied, and brought a smile to his face.

"Thank goodness for that." He heaved a sigh of relief. "I thought you were reverting to 'my lord' again. Is there no housekeeper?"

"There was, but I have as yet been unable to find out why she isn't here. Grandmama ignores my questions, and the servants are too scared of her to tell me. But I will get to the bottom of it eventually."

Molly was standing at the top of the stairs, waiting for instructions, and he told the girl to show him his room, and asked Georgina to meet him in whatever served as a study in ten minutes. She almost skipped as she hurried to the book room to make sure it was presentable for him.

As she put books away and cleared the desk, the dowager appeared in the doorway. "So that's the way the land lies, is it? No Friday face for his lordship, eh? Just wait till I tell him all about you, missy, just wait," her grandmother grunted, then disappeared down the hall.

Georgina was dusting off the shabby wing chair behind the desk when Matthew came into the room.

"Here, stop that," he said, taking the duster from her hand.

For a moment she was trapped between him and the chair; then he pulled her toward him, cradling her face in his hands.

"You shouldn't have run off like that. Settle House is much more your home than this sorry mess," he said softly, a finger slowly tracing the outline of her damaged cheek, and a look in his eyes that made her heart leap. "Mother was beside herself until she received your note from here."

He released her face with obvious reluctance, and taking her arm, eased her gently into the wing chair, while he perched on the edge of the desk, their legs almost touching.

"Let me tell you, first of all, what I found out about the gamekeeper. William now knows the whole story also.

"As you surmised, your grandmother wanted your father to marry the Andover girl and increase the estate. It didn't happen, and he married your mother, and then the Andover heiress lost her husband.

"It's difficult to prove your grandmother's intentions, but she told Smithers to shoot rabbits just at the time your mother would be returning from town. Your father apparently decided to ride out and meet your mother at the last minute, the gunshots scared the horses, and your parents were killed.

"Even if she had planned it, the odds of their being in that spot at the right time would be very poor. But it did happen, and the gamekeeper's been collecting on the flimsy evidence ever since."

Matthew took Georgina's hand and held it tightly in his. "I had a long talk with Smithers, and he'll not be back, for when I finished telling him what the penalty is in this country for scum like him, he signed over the deed to that house in Knaresborough, and rumor has it that he went abroad. My agent is arranging for the sale of the house, and the proceeds will help William make a start on this place when he returns from the Peninsula."

"What about Grandmama?" Georgina asked.

"William has been persuaded to forgive her, but insists that she will remove to the dower house when he returns." He looked at her very seriously for a moment; then an almost tender smile softened his face.

"After tomorrow, you won't be living here anymore, but I feel strongly that your grandmother should be told that you and William know everything."

Georgina nodded. "Whatever you think best, Matthew. But I'm afraid you won't want me in Kent once you know all about me," she said unhappily.

He reached for her other hand and pulled her roughly out of the chair and into his arms. "For a most intelligent young lady, you sometimes say some very foolish things. I want you for myself, whether it's in Kent, in London, or even here," he told her, and his lips captured hers in a tender kiss which stopped any further protest.

She closed her eyes and savored the feeling of his lips on

hers again, then slipped her arms around his neck. She could feel the strong muscles of his legs as they pressed against her. Just as her head started to swim and she felt a strange urgency inside, he released her. "Why didn't you come to me when you started to have problems with Frost, my love?" he asked gruffly. "Was I such an ogre that you couldn't tell me?"

"He said he had men watching you and he'd have you killed if I said anything. I tried to tell you that morning when you insisted on reading a newspaper at breakfast, but when you were so grouchy, I changed my mind. I couldn't let him kill you," she said earnestly.

He bent his head and the gentle touch of his lips on hers felt like soft butterflies, but even that light touch set them on fire again. He led her to the shabby sofa under the window.

"Is Frost dead?" Georgina had to know if she had actually killed him.

"Of course, you wouldn't know, would you? Another half-inch and he would have been. Even though my men went in right after you left, he lost a lot of blood, but he'll live to hang as a traitor," he said grimly.

"You mean there were some of your men outside the house all the time?" Georgina asked.

"Yes. I was having him watched by a couple of government agents, for I strongly suspected he was the spy we were looking for, but he was very clever and we had no proof until he showed his hand." He gave her a fierce look. "They saw you go into the house, but thought you were just a lady friend come to spend the night with him," he growled.

Starting from the beginning, she told him how she had caught Frost trying to break into his desk, and how later, he had wanted her to exchange the documents. As she explained how she changed the envelopes but not the contents, he looked at her in amazement.

"You're sure the envelopes were identical except for the one letter he mentioned? There was some handwriting in the bottom-right corner, I believe," he said.

"They were identical except for that one deliberate error," she assured him.

"Then there's another leak that can be stopped right away. I must say, you had a very busy evening. I gather he opened the envelope before you could get away?"

She nodded and swallowed hard. "When he discovered what I'd done, he knocked me to the ground and I hit my head, I suppose, for when I came to I was gagged and bound to a chair."

"Is that when Frost did this?" he asked, touching her cheek.

She nodded. "It must have been the famous heirloom ring."

"It may leave a slight scar, you know. How I wish I could get my hands on him for just five minutes," he growled.

"It doesn't matter. If it does leave a scar, I'll wear it with pride, for when I think what might have happened . . ." She shook her head slowly. "It still seems unreal. I was tied up, and he planned to tie both Elizabeth and the coachman up and set fire to those naphtha-soaked cloths. Elizabeth must never know what a close call she had."

He shuddered. "My men said he must have planned a fire, for there were naphtha-soaked rags around, but they didn't realize his full intent." He shook his head. "If I ever hear again of your going off alone in a hackney at night, I'll put you over my knee, and this time I do mean it," he promised. "How did you manage to untie yourself with Frost there all the time?"

She explained how she had maneuvered her legs until she finally reached her knife, then pretended to be still tied when he returned.

"What would have happened if you'd dropped the knife, or you couldn't reach it?" he asked.

"I'd have reached the one fastened to my left leg, of course," she told him with a touch of her old insolence.

He laughed uproariously. "Georgina, you are completely impossible. One thing you must do, when we have the time, is teach me to throw knives. I have never tried my hand at it, but it obviously can be extremely useful."

"Certainly, my lord. When would you like your first lesson?" Her eyes were dancing with mischief.

"Minx," he said lovingly. "By the way, I finally got to see Barstow."

"What happened to him? I couldn't believe that he didn't let me know he was planning to leave town." She was curious, that was all.

"He had to go home in a hurry, as his mother was seriously ill. But he did send you a letter. It was found on the hall table after you left. Someone had forgotten to give it to you." He eyed her a little suspiciously. "You should be ashamed of yourself as far as that gentleman is concerned, you know. He is very much in love with you, has been for ages, but in your inimitable way, you managed to let him know you wanted him only as a friend, and yet were able to keep him with you to ward off other would-be suitors. Don't you think that was unfair to him?"

"I did tell him," she said in excuse.

"That you loved me?" he asked softly.

Color suffused her face, and she turned her head away. "No, I think he guessed that for himself," she muttered.

As he tried to pull her into his arms, she at first resisted, but he was too strong for her. "Don't be a little idiot," he scolded. "Surely you know that I don't go around kissing young ladies unless I love them and mean to marry them?"

"How many have you loved?" she asked impishly.

"Just Louise and you," he said, his voice muffled as his lips brushed the skin below her ear. "How will you like being Louise's new mother?"

"I've always felt as though I was," she said honestly. "Can we have more children?"

"As many as you like, my love," he promised, and sealed it with kisses that left Georgina breathless. Expertly he positioned her so that she could still breathe while his tongue plundered her mouth, and as wonderful sensations passed through her, she wantonly pressed herself closer to him.

Reluctantly she left him, for she had to check on preparations for dinner and to change into the prettiest of the gowns she had brought with her.

For the first time in her recollection, there was conversation at dinner, although it was mostly between her and Matthew, but she arranged with him to give her a few minutes with her grandmother over the tea tray before he joined them with his port.

Georgina poured, and as she handed a cup to the old lady, she remarked casually, "I understand that Smithers has left his house in Knaresborough and gone abroad. I wondered if you knew why, as the two of you have been so close ever since Mama and Papa died."

The old dowager went white as a ghost, and her hand shook so much she had to place her cup back on the table.

"Don't know what you're talking about," she snorted. "The man was just a gamekeeper here once, that's all."

Georgina's eyes were cold and they never left her grandmother's face, though her voice sounded quite casual. "Wasn't it nice of him to give the large house he bought to William? It makes you wonder a little if he had a guilty conscience, doesn't it?"

Lady Forsythe rose shakily, looked at Georgina under half-closed lids, then walked to the door, holding on to furniture as though very tired.

At the door she almost bumped into Matthew. "Leaving so early, ma'am? Have a good night's sleep," he advised.

When the door had closed behind her and they were alone, he asked, "Did you tell her what you know?"

"I didn't have to," Georgina said. "I just mentioned Smithers and his house, and her conscience did the rest."

She was sitting on the small couch, and he joined her there, pulling her into his arms. His hands caressed her shoulders while his lips traced patterns along her chin and neck until she thought she would go crazy. As he took her chin gently in his hand, his warm mouth touched hers and instinctively her lips parted. Their kiss was long and deep, and left her trembling with love for him. Matthew looked quite shaken also, but not enough to stop his trying again to see if the feeling could be duplicated.

It was sometime later that he remarked gruffly, "I forgot to give you a message from the Peninsula."

"From William?" she asked, her lips slightly swollen and her eyes still glazed with passion.

"No, I have a letter for you from him. The message is from Isabella. She said to tell you she'll dance at our wedding," he said with a grin.

"You told her before you even asked me?"

"No. Don't you know that Gypsies have a way of knowing these things? But it may be some time before she gets here. The last time I saw her, she was very busy teaching Wellington how to throw knives."

About the Author

A native of Yorkshire, England, Irene Saunders spent a number of years exploring London while working for the U.S. Air Force there. A love of travel brought her to New York City, where she met her husband, Ray, then settled in Miami, Florida. She now lives in Port St. Lucie, Florida, dividing her time between writing, bookkeeping, gardening, needlepoint, and travel.